me to read *Unscripted*. I was in tears. What a great story of redemption in so many ways."

"Bravo! *Unscripted* runs the full gamut of emotions. Bunn's fascinating characters reveal an amazing introduction to Hollywood, something we audiences catch only glimpses of on-screen. Bunn's knowledge of the film world and what making movies entails is truly remarkable. This story deserves great success and hopefully someday will become a movie itself."

"*Unscripted* is a thrilling emotional journey. The story has both heart and purpose and swiftly engages the reader through wonderful characters and intriguing complications. Bunn's work is entertaining from page one and carries the drama smoothly to a powerful ending. I have already started rereading. This story is simply too enjoyable to experience only once."

"I read *Unscripted* in a single sitting. Part of my job as a director of photography was reading scripts, and as a result I have become somewhat jaded when it comes to emotions displayed on a page. Today I was amazed to find my eyes damp twice and my throat constricted on a third occasion. I stand in awe of Bunn's talent. I truly love this work. It is, quite simply, outstanding."

"Davis Bunn has absolutely done it. *Unscripted* kept me hooked to the end. What a suspenseful roller-coaster ride! The industry insights and the mystery surrounding this project were excellent. And what an ending!"

Janette Oke, bestselling author of *When Calls the Heart*

"Wow. What an incredible story of hope, challenge, and redemption. The characters and their journey remain vividly alive in my mind. The settings and the drama both hold such energy and life. I was there with them and was in tears at the end. *Unscripted* is a triumph."

Jeff Arresty, president, Internet Bar Association

"This is Davis Bunn at his storytelling best. I couldn't turn the pages fast enough, caught up in this intriguing tale of Hollywood. The story is filled with insider information entwined in a tale of love, loss, and redemption. Bravo, Davis. You deserve a standing ovation."

Debbie Macomber, #1 *New York Times* bestselling author

"Bunn brings his story of the LA film world to vivid life with just the right level of grit and raw emotion. The negotiations, filming, and talent issues were incredibly realistic. As a film producer, I felt a genuine sense of very real stress over the deal in play. Thankfully the story developed into a project well done and an ultimate success. I for one would love to read a sequel!"

William Campbell, president, Apex Films

"Bunn's characters remain firmly in my mind. The settings came to such vivid life. The industry and its characters, especially the lawyers and the movie moguls, are heartfelt. This book meant a lot to me—so many emotions stirred up as the characters struggled to move ahead, confronted demons, persevered with courage, and thrived in the end. What a treat for

UNSCRIPTED

Books by Davis Bunn

Outbreak
The Domino Effect
Unscripted

UNSCRIPTED

DAVIS
BUNN

Revell

a division of Baker Publishing Group
Grand Rapids, Michigan

© 2019 by T. Davis Bunn

Published by Revell
a division of Baker Publishing Group
PO Box 6287, Grand Rapids, MI 49516-6287
www.revellbooks.com

Printed in the United States of America

Library of Congress Cataloging-in-Publication Data
Names: Bunn, T. Davis, 1952- author.
Title: Unscripted / T. Davis Bunn.
Description: Grand Rapids : Revell, [2019] | Summary: "A Hollywood producer reeling from his best friend's betrayal and an LA lawyer who has sacrificed everything for her career are drawn together to untangle a web of lies and deceit that threatens their future"—Provided by publisher.
Identifiers: LCCN 2019017713 | ISBN 9780800727871 (paperback) | ISBN 9780800736767 (cloth)
Subjects: LCSH: Domestic fiction.
Classification: LCC PS3552.U4718 U555 2019 | DDC 813/.54—dc23
LC record available at https://lccn.loc.gov/2019017713

19 20 21 22 23 24 25   7 6 5 4 3 2 1

This book is dedicated
to the friends
who introduced me
to the world
behind the camera:

Ken Wales

Susan Wales

Chad Gundersen

Paul Wheeler

1

THE ENTIRE BEVERLY HILLS JAIL was nonsmoking and air-conditioned. Four inmates to a cell. No overcrowding. Decent food for a prison. Three hours each day in the central pen rather than the customary one. Showers with hot water. And most importantly, the inmates were safe. All violent offenders were sent to Men's Central Jail, which was a totally different story. The threat of being reclassed and shipped out kept the Beverly Hills inmates meek as kittens.

Not that Daniel Byrd had much experience with prisons. Just one stint in juvie, convicted when he was twelve and released three days before his fourteenth birthday. For robbing a bank.

This time was different. For one thing, he was innocent. Totally.

Of course, he was guilty of a whole host of other offenses. The difference was, the things he had gotten so terribly wrong were not actually against the law.

Trusting the wrong partner. That was a lifetime felony, for sure. This being the same person Danny had called his best friend since childhood. But that was before John Rexford had cleared out their accounts and skipped town with a would-be actress. Leaving Danny to take the fall.

It was probably just as well that Danny had no idea where the louse was, since the vengeance he spent so many imprisoned hours imagining was definitely on the wrong side of legal.

Which was exactly how Danny was spending the morning when his world shifted on its axis.

The first notice he had of pending change was when his cell door opened and the guard said, "Let's go, Byrd. Gather your belongings. You're being moved."

Danny protested, "I'm not due in court for another three weeks."

The guard was a pro at ignoring anything a prisoner might cast his way. "Don't keep me waiting, Byrd."

His three cellmates were an Israeli smuggler arrested with half a pound of conflict diamonds, a Rodeo Drive salesclerk who tried to play hide-the-turnip with an emerald pendant, and a professional cat burglar from Freeport, Bahamas, dark as the nights he loved. The smuggler shifted on his bunk, turning his back to the world. The salesclerk offered Danny a grimace. The thief said, "You just remember what I told you."

"Take a chill pill," Danny replied. "Keep my eyes on the next step. See nothing, say less."

The thief offered Danny a palm. "You stay cool now."

The guard pointed to the invisible line in the corridor. Danny's month and a half in jail had taught him to keep his mouth shut and wait. The officer locked the door and started down the long hall. Danny fell into step behind him. His gut was one solid block of dirty grey ice.

Beyond three more steel doors loomed the shadow world of California's general prison population. Gangs. Drugs. Brutality. Danny knew with every shred of his being that he would probably not survive.

The guard's name was Escobar. Danny suspected he was the only prisoner who knew that. Most inmates in the Beverly Hills Jail were just passing through, held here for a few months or less. Once their convictions were set, they were processed into the California penal system. There was no need to bother with such trivialities as learning guards' names. But Danny had been memorizing people's names for so long the habit was ingrained. He knew the identity of every guard in their wing.

Escobar led him through four of the five steel doors separating Danny from daylight. They entered the octagonal booking chamber, and Escobar pointed him onto a side bench. "Sit."

Danny took one look at the others occupying his perch and felt his last shred of hope drain away.

When he didn't move fast enough, Escobar gripped his right shoulder and guided him over. "I said sit." He examined Danny's face. "You gonna be sick?"

"No."

"You better not get my floor dirty, you hear?"

Danny swallowed hard. "I'm good."

Escobar nodded, clearly satisfied his words had the desired effect, and turned away.

There were fourteen others lined up along the bench. They were cuffed and linked together by waist chains. Their ankles were bound by a flexible link just long enough for them to take little half-steps. They all wore orange prison-transfer jumpsuits with the dreaded MCJ lettering across the back.

Men's Central Jail was a bunker-like structure between Chinatown and the Los Angeles River. It looked like a windowless, high-security warehouse with an electrified fence and guard towers. MCJ held five thousand inmates in a space built to house half that. The place was overcrowded and highly dangerous.

Three weeks, Danny silently repeated. *I can survive three weeks.*

Three men down from Danny, a kid with pale golden skin started crying softly.

Forty-five minutes later, Danny was still waiting. Wasting time was just one of the daily punishments embedded into prison life.

Two guards Danny had never seen before appeared through the steel sally port. One of them carried the shotgun required for all prisoner transfers. "Stand up and face the right-hand door."

When Danny rose with the others, the guard behind the booking counter said, "Not you, Byrd. Plant yourself back on the bench."

The other prisoners looked his way. For the first time.

The chains clinked and rattled as the fourteen were led through the door, out to the transfer bus rumbling in the secure garage. When the last inmate had shuffled away, the sally port clanged shut and the remaining guards went back to pretending Danny Byrd was invisible.

Not that he minded. Not a bit.

———————————— // ————————————

An hour and a half later, Escobar returned, accompanied by an older inmate with the blue trustee stripe. "On your feet, Byrd." He gestured to the trustee. "Give him your gear. Let's go."

Danny followed the guard through two more doors, past the central visitation chamber, down the windowless corridor, to the room where he met with his rotten lawyer.

Escobar unlocked the door, pushed it open, and asked whoever was inside, "You need me to stay?"

A woman's voice replied, "That won't be necessary."

"Knock when you're done." Escobar waited for Danny to enter, then shut and locked the door.

Danny faced a woman seemingly his own age. Anywhere but Hollywood, she would have been considered a beauty. She compressed her attractiveness into a tightly severe package. Her raven hair was pulled back and clenched inside a golden clasp, her makeup designed to make strong features even more stern. Her white silk blouse was sealed at the neck by a high collar, her curves masked by a boxy, dark suit.

"Sit down, Danny. That's what you prefer to be called, correct?"

Danny stayed where he was. "Who are you?"

"Megan Pierce. I'm second chair on your legal team."

"In case you hadn't heard, I've been forced to declare bankruptcy. My company is in chapter eleven. I don't have a cent to pay you."

"Our costs have been covered. Sit down, please. We don't have much time." She gestured to the chair on the table's opposite side. "Unless you'd prefer to stay with your public defender."

"Not a chance."

When Danny was seated, Megan opened a file, slid a document across the table, and offered him a pen. "This appoints us as your legal representatives. Sign on the bottom of the second page and initial all the places that are highlighted."

Danny signed. "Who's paying for this?"

"I have no idea." She indicated a suit draped over a chair by the side wall. "We found these clothes in your former office. Am I correct in assuming they belong to you?"

"My court date isn't for another three weeks."

"Answer the question, please. I have to leave in . . ." She glanced at her watch. Her wrists were strong, her fingers long and tanned. "I'm already late."

"Yes, they're mine."

"Your lead counsel has requested a meeting with the judge assigned to your case. He needs this document to proceed." She rose from the table, crossed the room, and knocked on the door. "Be dressed and ready tomorrow morning."

"Ready for what?" Danny asked.

But the woman was already gone.

———— // ————

Escobar led Danny back down the hopeless corridor into the main block. Only this time . . .

Escobar waved to the camera, then started forward. When he realized Danny had become frozen to the cement floor, he demanded, "You keeping me waiting again, Byrd?"

"No sir." Danny forced his legs to move. "Not me."

Escobar climbed the stairs and led Danny down another corridor, waved to another camera, and was buzzed through the door.

They entered the Pay to Stay wing. The place of fables and disbelief.

When the city built their jail for prisoners awaiting trial in the Beverly Hills courts, they did what only a city with extra cash on hand could even consider. They built a second structure they didn't actually need.

The Pay to Stay wing was designed by city councillors who knew all too well how easily they could step over the invisible line and enter the realm of illegality. So they established a code whereby nonviolent offenders could make an official request of the Beverly Hills courts from anywhere in California's vast and deadly penal system. Only the rich need apply.

The criminal offense had to be white-collar. As in no drugs or violence. The offender paid the daily rate of 145 dollars. In exchange he was given a Beverly Hills version of life behind bars.

Danny could do nothing about his dumbfounded expression as Escobar led him through the commons room and over to . . .

A single cell.

Danny kept waiting for somebody to come rushing up and say there had been a mistake and he didn't belong. But Escobar stopped in the doorway and pointed Danny inside. "This is your lucky day, Byrd."

The cell was just as the burglar had described. He had been

booked in here for his first few nights when the regular wing was overfull. The cell was a prefabricated steel pod. The bunk and table and stool and sink were all one piece. If Danny had stretched out his arms he could have touched both side walls. The ceiling was only a few inches higher than Danny's six-three frame. The bulletproof window was eleven inches square and overlooked the jail's interior courtyard.

A *window*.

"Look here, Byrd." Escobar waited for Danny to turn around. "The first time you make any trouble, the guards shut the door. You get fed through the slot here. You stay locked in for weeks, maybe months. The second time, you get shipped out. You read me?"

"Loud and clear, sir," Danny replied. "No trouble." He watched the guard turn and walk away. *Leaving his cell door open.*

———— // ————

At 7:15 the next morning, Danny was showered, shaved, dressed in his suit, and seated in the central hold. Waiting.

The court transfer bus left every morning at 7:30. Danny assumed there would be no more notice here than in the jail's other wing. If his new legal team had actually managed to shift the court system into a faster gear, Danny wanted to be ready.

Nine minutes later, his name was called over the loudspeaker. He rose and crossed to the guard by the exit. Danny and two other Pay to Stay prisoners were led back to the booking chamber. He was cuffed but not waist-chained. The steel access portal rose, and the prisoners were led forward. Danny entered the bus, and his cuffs were fastened to the steel panel linked to the seat in front of him. No one spoke. The normal cursing and threats and harsh commands were absent here. The reality of what awaited them if they got out of line was too close.

The Beverly Hills jail was located down an unmarked alley just off Glendale. The entire facility was rimmed by a pale stone wall that blended into the warehouses and small businesses to either side. There was no guard tower, no barbed wire, not even a sign. The only public access was a glass-fronted office on Rexford that led to the visitors' center, its windows stamped with the city seal. The bus trundled through the outer gates and down the narrow lane and . . .

Back into the real world.

Danny may have been watching the blooming trees and the fancy cars and the lovely ladies and the sunlight through wire-reinforced glass. He may have been chained to his seat. He may have been facing three to five. But today, for the first time since his arrest, he watched the world sweep past and tasted the faint flavor of hope.

The Beverly Hills courts were connected to the city's main administrative buildings, a stucco palace rimmed by palms and emerald lawns on Santa Monica Boulevard. Danny was led down the rear corridor into the holding pen where all prisoners on remand awaited their hour before the judge.

Fifteen minutes later a heavyset man with an intensely impatient air followed a deputy through the courtroom door. He crossed the concrete foyer and halted in front of the pen. "Daniel Byrd?"

"Here." Danny rose from the bench and approached the bars. He had done this twice before, then entered the courtroom and faced the judge with his rotten public defender. Each time he had felt his freedom slip one step further away.

Not today.

The man's first words were enough to assure Danny that this time was different. "My name is Sol Feinnes. As of yesterday, I serve as your principal attorney."

"How is this happening?"

"We don't have time for that. My associate has used her

firm's considerable clout to shift your court date, and what I need—"

Another deputy pushed through the swinging doors leading to the courts and said, "Feinnes, you're up."

"Coming." To Danny he said, "Follow my lead, Byrd. Your future depends on it."

2

JUDGE RICHTER was a small woman in her sixties with hair like a silver-grey helmet. She was soft-spoken and delicately boned, with features of ivory lace. But her gaze was a pale green laser and her words carried the full weight of her position. "I don't believe I've seen you in my courtroom before, Mr. Feinnes."

The attorney seated to Danny's left rose to his feet. Megan Pierce, the lawyer who had visited Danny in jail, was seated to his right.

Sol cleared his throat and replied, "This is my first opportunity to try a case in Beverly Hills, Your Honor. My practice is based in San Luis Obispo. We focus on the central-coast region."

"And yet here you are."

"Indeed." Sol gestured to Danny. "One of my clients requested me to represent Mr. Byrd in order to prevent a miscarriage of justice."

She glanced at the prosecutor, a young Latina named Suarez whose acidic words had branded Danny's public defender. When Suarez remained silent, Judge Richter said, "You have requested this change to the court's schedule, Mr. Feinnes. I

19

hope you can prove to my satisfaction that this highly irregular move was genuinely necessary."

"I hope so too, Your Honor."

"Be forewarned, Mr. Feinnes. My calendar is too overcrowded to accept any time-wasting maneuvers."

"I will be calling just two witnesses, Your Honor. I am certain they will confirm the need for this hearing."

Richter continued to glance at the prosecutor. When Suarez did not offer a response, the judge said, "Very well. Proceed."

"Thank you, Your Honor. Defense calls Greg Riggs."

Megan Pierce must have been ready for Danny's outburst. She stifled anything he might have said with a quiet hiss.

Film directors were notorious for being Hollywood's worst dressed. Greg Riggs certainly lived up to his guild. Today he wore ratty jeans, ancient boat shoes, no socks, and a vintage T-shirt advertising the Grateful Dead's last European tour. He was deceptively small, a little blond gnome who skirted around the edge of life. All that changed, however, when he was running a film set. Then Greg morphed into an individual of tornadic force, capable of joining a hundred egotistical voices into one cinematic chorus.

Greg's voice shook slightly as he was sworn in and stated his name.

Sol asked, "What is your profession, Mr. Riggs?"

"I produce and direct feature films."

"Give the court a brief overview of your career, please."

"I started as assistant director on series television. Nine years ago I directed my first made-for-TV film. I did six for Lifetime and three for Freeform. Three years ago I directed my first feature. It won the audience award at Sundance."

"How do you know the defendant, Danny Byrd?"

"He was line producer on my last two pictures for Lifetime and has worked on all my features."

"Explain for the court what the term 'line producer' means exactly."

"There is no exact. A line producer is the accountant responsible for all expenditures during the shoot. But it goes a lot further than that. Before filming, the line producer sets the film's budget. Financing depends on him getting those figures right. Once the shoot begins, a good line producer does whatever is required to keep the project on time and on budget. He is also responsible for making sure the film's investors make their payments on time."

"So you're saying Mr. Byrd is good at his job."

Greg looked Danny's way for the first time since entering the courtroom. "The best. Everybody who's ever worked with Danny says the same."

"Objection." The prosecuting attorney did not rise from her chair. "Hearsay."

"Sustained." The judge leaned toward the witness box. "Mr. Riggs, you will refrain from offering anything more than a direct response to the attorney's question."

"Sorry, Your Honor."

"Proceed, Mr. Feinnes."

"Mr. Riggs, how is it that a line producer with such a stellar reputation finds himself brought up on these very serious charges?"

Greg's head ducked down far enough for his shoulders to swallow his neck. "It's all my fault."

3

DANNY'S LIFE, career, and professional standing had all been destroyed by one word.

Escrow.

Once a film's budget and script were approved, investors placed funds in an escrow account. Contracts were negotiated and signed, establishing clear points at which the funds could be withdrawn. During Danny's early days in the film world, he watched one mid-budget film after another fall apart because the investors did not live up to their promises. As a result, he only agreed to begin production when the entire budget was placed in the escrow account. It was one of the core tenets on which Danny had built his reputation. If Danny Byrd produced your film, the film got done. Period.

Until the day everything went wrong.

Sol Feinnes proved very adept at courtroom interrogation. He was a soft-spoken bear in his late fifties, with neatly groomed iron-grey hair and a discreetly expensive navy pinstriped suit. He skillfully led Greg Riggs through a brief overview of the role the escrow account played, then asked, "So what happened with this particular production?"

"We had a great script," Greg replied. "Good enough to attract two top-tier stars. We're certain to score big at Sundance."

23

"Objection," Suarez said. She sounded almost bored. "Conjecture."

"Sustained." The judge was a Beverly Hills resident. She could smell film hype at a hundred paces. "Defense will hold his witness to the facts relevant to this case."

Sol said, "You had a script and you signed your stars, and then what?"

"I had a four-film deal in place with Italian investors. This was to be our first project. I took the script and budget and our two main stars to them. They gave their approval."

"What is their name?"

"Banco Populare."

"They are regular investors in mid-range films, correct?"

"Right. I mean, yes. They have an office and full-time team on Wilshire."

"So what happened?"

"Our production budget was 5.1 million. We received word from our bank that the first 2.7 was in escrow. Then I got a call from the investors to say there was a delay."

"What does that mean, 'delay'?"

"At the time, I had no idea. Their guy, he told me it was a temporary glitch. Another week to ten days, we'd be fully funded. He's Italian, from Florence, and when he wants he can be slick as oiled glass." Greg ran an uncertain hand across his forehead and up over his unkempt hair. "Now I know the bank was being investigated by the European Commission for underperforming loans. Their LA operation was shut down last week."

"What happened next?"

"I met with JR."

"You are referring to John Rexford, the defendant's former partner."

"Right. Our two stars were available for twenty-seven days. Not an hour more. A delay of a week and a half meant we lost the chance to shoot. The bank insisted on script and star approval. If we lost the actors, we were back to square one."

"So what was Mr. Rexford's response?"

Greg swiped his hand up his forehead and across the top of his head. "He said we should hold to our schedule."

"Begin production."

"Right."

"Without the funds actually being in place."

"That's what he said. We met with the investors' rep, he assured us the rest of the funds were coming. JR said go."

"How did the defendant respond to his partner's suggestion?"

"We didn't tell Danny."

"You're saying you did not inform the defendant of your decision."

Greg's one-handed swipe was constant now. The perspiration slicked down the hair on top of his head. "Correct."

"Why is that, Mr. Riggs?"

"JR said if we told him, Danny would have ordered us to stop the shoot."

"So you lied to my client, is that what you're saying?"

"No, it's just . . . we didn't tell him."

"One final question. When did the defendant learn of what transpired between you and his former partner?"

"I don't know. I guess now."

Sol let that bit of news hang in the air, then said, "No further questions."

"Your witness, Ms. Suarez."

The prosecuting attorney took her time rising to her feet. "The defendant is charged with willfully defrauding half a dozen local companies—everything from camera and lens rentals to catering. No one responsible for supplying these services was paid. Including the payments due in advance of your starting production."

"That's ridiculous," Greg said. "Danny Byrd is the most honest man I know."

"Can you offer any evidence to substantiate your claim that he was unaware of his own firm's financial situation?"

"JR must have suspected something was wrong and held out on Danny. And us." Greg's swipe from his forehead to the nape of his neck accelerated. "Danny's used the same catering team for four films. Ditto for lights and camera rental. Everybody wants to work with him because he's always on time with his payments. He plays it totally straight."

The judge said softly, "Answer the question."

Greg gave no sign he even heard. "We were shooting on location in El Paso. Danny got a call from the catering company's head office that their weekly check had bounced. Danny phoned JR at their office. The police answered. Danny asked me what was happening."

When Greg went silent, Suarez demanded, "How did you respond?"

"I lied. I told him I had no idea. When Danny couldn't find JR, he caught the next flight back to LA. I heard he was arrested when he showed up at their office."

Suarez tapped the blank page of her notepad. "No further questions."

The judge looked at Sol. "Redirect?"

"Just one further question, Your Honor. Mr. Riggs, what happened to your current project?"

"I mortgaged our home. We also got a check from this Chinese guy who was interested in investing in Danny's films. That plus my mortgage meant we finished the shoot. I completed postproduction three days ago."

"No further questions."

Judge Richter said, "The witness may step down."

As Greg passed Danny's table, he offered, "Man, I'm really, really—"

"You are dismissed, Mr. Riggs," the judge snapped. When Greg exited the courtroom, she continued, "I fail to see why it was necessary to request this morning's hearing, Mr. Feinnes."

Sol rose to his feet. "I called Mr. Riggs first, Your Honor, in order to supply testimony so that I might lay a necessary foundation for what my second witness will now reveal. He is the reason for this requested hearing."

"Very well. Proceed."

Sol responded by returning to his place behind the table.

Megan Pierce, still seated at Danny's right, stood and said, "Defense calls Pei-Lun Zhang."

Danny Byrd was nothing like what Megan had expected.

Her research had revealed an intriguing and possibly dangerous individual. The man's background was bizarre. But her six and a half years in Los Angeles had taught her that the film world drew the strange and the almost broken. Most such people were consumed, bones and all. Only the strongest and most determined survived.

Danny could have been a model, he was that good-looking. Dark hair falling in natural waves even when brushed. Tall and broad-shouldered with no waist to speak of. All this Megan had known in advance, of course. What astonished her was the man's nature.

Given his background, Megan had expected to find a dark and vicious streak. Danny had been born in Phoenix, and his father had abandoned the family when Danny was three. Two years later, his mother had experienced a nervous breakdown, probably induced by drugs. Danny, an only child, had been placed in foster care. Juvie records were sealed, but a pliant official had told Megan that there had been several brushes with the law. That was hardly a surprise. What did not fit into the standard model was how, at fourteen, Danny turned his life around. All by himself. His schoolwork went from barely passing to straight A's and stayed there. At fifteen he was adopted by his last of seven foster families. He ran track. He wrestled. He was class president. He gained a scholarship to the University of Nevada, graduated summa cum laude, and stayed on to earn an MBA. As soon as he passed his CPA exams, Danny moved to Los Angeles. He worked a series of low-level jobs around filmdom's periphery, then formed his partnership with John Rexford.

As Megan waited for her witness to be sworn in, she cast a glance at her client. Danny Byrd was quite possibly the most self-contained individual she had ever met. She sensed the rage lurking behind those blue-black eyes. She had noticed it immediately upon his entry into the jail's interview chamber. Megan had always appreciated the spice of latent risk in her men. Which went a long way in describing the wreckage of relationships that littered her past. But standing in court before an impatient judge was hardly the moment for such thoughts.

Her witness, Pei-Lun Zhang, was tall for an Asian, with skin of smooth and polished cedar. Megan knew he was fifty-one because she had asked him. But he could have passed for a man in his early thirties.

Megan said, "State your profession for the record, please."

"Film investor." For such a cultured and intelligent man, Pei-Lun Zhang butchered the English language with exquisite finesse. He made himself understood by speaking very slowly, isolating each word within its own bubble. "Someday."

"You are here in this country to invest in film production, is that correct?"

"Was. No more. Leave today." He turned to the judge. "So sorry. English very bad."

Judge Richter asked, "Do you understand the attorney's questions, Mr. Zhang?"

"Oh, yes. She speak very clear."

"Counsel, you may proceed."

"You are saying, Mr. Zhang, that your return to China is imminent?" Megan asked.

"Yes. Tonight fly Shanghai."

"Why is that?"

"Our money not come. Beijing take away permits."

"You are saying that you came to Los Angeles representing would-be investors who had initial permits from the Chinese government to extract funds?"

"All is correct."

"Objection," Suarez said. "Counsel is leading the witness."

Richter pondered a moment, then replied, "Given the terse nature of his responses, I would class Ms. Pierce's efforts as more in keeping with a translator." She turned to the witness. "Do you understand the word 'terse'?"

"Short."

She nodded. "I suspect your language abilities are not as limited as your speech suggests."

Wisely, Zhang did not respond.

"Proceed, counselor," Richter said. "But try not to place words in the mouth of your witness."

"Thank you, Your Honor. Mr. Zhang, how large a fund did you intend to establish?"

"First tranche, hundred million."

Megan heard Danny gasp. She wholeheartedly agreed. She sorted through several responses and settled on, "Mr. Zhang, when you first approached my firm, you said you wanted to invest five million dollars."

"Five is number for outsiders." Zhang smiled at her. "I keep secret."

"Why is that?"

"Hundred million, too many people, too many lies. Five million, nobody care."

That had been precisely the response of her law firm. And the only reason Megan had been assigned this client. She changed gears. "How did you come to know my client?"

"I hire you to investigate. I say, find me honest man. Must know film business top to bottom."

"What happened as a result of your request?"

"You bring me five names. I meet three. Choose Byrd."

"Did you inform my client he was being considered to lead your film fund?"

"No." Zhang was clearly enjoying himself. "Today big surprise."

"What did you tell him?"

"Have small funds. Me only. Eight hundred thousand."

"You selected Daniel Byrd and yet did not inform him of your real purpose? I find that remarkable, sir. Can you explain to the court why you chose to remain silent?"

"Three reasons. I meet Byrd on set. He very busy. Fourteen, sixteen hour days. I wait."

"And the second reason?"

"My partners call. They hear rumors. China central bank worried about money leaving country. So much money. New permits halted. But rumors say *old* permits halted too."

"But Mr. Zhang, you stated that the government had already issued your export permits."

Zhang was no longer smiling. "This China. Central bank say word, all change."

"I see. And the third reason?"

Zhang's gaze turned onyx hard as he focused on Megan's client. "I like Danny Byrd. I no trust partner."

Slowly Megan shifted from her position behind the defense table to the side lectern. "You met John Rexford?"

"One time. Not long."

"Did you ask me to investigate him as well?"

"Some. Not much. No need. I no do business with him."

"You intended to offer Mr. Byrd the leadership of your fund

30

on the proviso that he cease his relationship with Mr. Rexford?"

The judge interrupted with, "Do you understand the word 'proviso'?"

"Condition. Yes. Is so."

Megan asked, "But you did not reveal your concerns about Mr. Rexford?"

"No. I not tell Danny Byrd because money not come."

"And then, after Mr. Byrd's arrest, you invested eight hundred thousand dollars in his current project, is that correct?"

"This money I bring for setting up office and developing first projects." Zhang shrugged. "No more money come. No need office. Danny say this good film. I invest."

"Mr. Zhang, were you surprised to learn that Mr. Byrd's partner had stolen the firm's money?"

"Surprised, no." Zhang's gaze remained tightly focused upon Danny. "But very much sorry."

4

THURSDAY NIGHT Danny dreamed he was back in foster care. Eleven years old, small for his age, trapped in that awful system. The dream departed with a sharpish jolt that shot him from asleep to sitting up in bed. He sat there, waiting for his heart rate to ease, the memories surrounding him like a rancid cloud. Danny knew from experience that sleep would stay a stranger, at least for a while. He dressed and slipped from his room.

The moon was strong and high enough to shine full on the San Luis Obispo guesthouse's interior courtyard. Every leaf of the carefully tended shrubbery glowed pewter. Water flowing in the central fountain sparkled like mercury. Danny sat where he could listen to the liquid melody. It didn't take a genius to know why he'd had that same dream almost every night since his arrest. He tried to tell himself things were looking up. But at 1:30 on a cloudless night, the script he read in the stars overhead carried a single bitter message. Danny Byrd had lost everything.

Bankrupt, the fountain sang. *Reputation destroyed.*

Penniless, the night breeze whispered. *Dreams shattered.*

Worst of all, Danny told the night, JR had stolen his last shred of trust.

Despite it all, he missed his best friend. He smiled at the

dancing water and recalled that first crazy year. He could still remember the moment Johnny Rexford had been assigned the bunk opposite his own. Six kids crammed in a bedroom only slightly larger than a closet. A human powder keg that erupted all too often. Johnny was a year older but even smaller than Danny. That very first night, Johnny and Danny had become fast friends. Johnny Rocket and Danny Boy against all comers.

Half an hour later, the nightmare had been tucked back in its cave, and Danny returned to his little room. He cut off the AC and opened his window, letting the water's tinkling melody carry him back to sleep.

The next morning Danny woke at 6:15 sharp. He did not try to fight the lingering connection to jail time. He rose and made a cup of coffee in the guesthouse's Nespresso machine. He had never used one before and could not get over how good it tasted. Many things carried those simple jolts of pleasure so intense he actually felt guilty. As though he did not deserve a good coffee. Or how nice it was to stand in his doorway and watch the dawn gather strength.

Danny finished his cup, dressed in shorts and T-shirt and Reeboks, and went for a run. A dawn mist drifted through the streets, as vague as his whispers of fear and regret. Danny knew he could not outrun the unease and did not try. He listened to his breath and the soft drumbeat of his footsteps on the pavement. He did his best to focus on the distance—the trees and the rising sun and the endless blue overhead. All the things he had not seen for seven long weeks. Trying to claim this day as his.

The previous afternoon, Danny had been processed out of the Beverly Hills jail to find a limo waiting. The silent driver had handed him an envelope bearing the logo of Sol Feinnes's law firm. In it was a brief letter saying that Danny was booked into a San Luis Obispo guesthouse and they would meet the following day to discuss his next steps. The envelope also held five hundred dollars in cash.

The limo took Danny to his former office, where a deputy waited to unseal the door and allow him to enter. Most of the contents were still classed as part of the criminal action now leveled against JR. But Danny had turned the back two rooms into an apartment he used whenever he was forced to call Los Angeles home. The attorney's letter had informed Danny that the court had granted him permission to retrieve clothes and personal items. The deputy watched closely while Danny filled a case. He was not allowed to take anything electronic, not even his phone. It was ridiculous, but after a month and three weeks in jail, Danny had learned that complaints against the system were a waste of good air.

The deputy locked and resealed the office, then led Danny back down to the waiting limo. Danny felt no regret over leaving Los Angeles. He had never liked the city much. Part of JR's duties had been to play the local scene and dig up work. That's all Danny had ever wanted from the town. Work. He had hated LA's version of the high life from his first day. JR, on the other hand, lived for it. It was part of why they had made such a perfect team.

Or so Danny had thought.

The sun was strong and the heat rising when Danny returned to the guesthouse. He stretched and showered and dressed. Over breakfast, he worked on a list of the questions for which he needed answers. Starting with who had wanted Danny's freedom enough to pay for his new legal team? But the most important questions he did not bother writing out. As in, what was he supposed to do with a life where his dreams had all been shattered?

Danny dressed in a clean shirt and slacks. His only formal clothes were the suit and tie he'd worn for his last day in court. As soon as he could, he planned on burning them.

He obtained directions from the receptionist and set out on foot.

San Luis Obispo was his kind of town. His favorite childhood memories were all centered on families who had sought out American backwaters. Places where schools were for learning and normal teenage emotions did not inspire students to pack guns. Towns where people still forgot to lock their doors and didn't much care. Families who brought in foster kids because they wanted to try to help the least and the neglected.

Danny's film work had brought him into regular contact with lawyers. Most of the LA legal types he'd despised. In contrast, he liked Sol Feinnes's firm from the moment he entered. There was none of the pretension or aggressive gung-ho absurdity he had spent years avoiding.

When he gave the receptionist his name, she responded by offering him a handful of message slips. "A Mr. Greg Riggs has been trying to reach you. He's called seven times already this morning."

Danny felt the day's first rage. "Thanks."

The receptionist clearly saw the thunder in his expression and added, "Mr. Feinnes said to tell you he will handle this caller if you wish."

Danny was tempted but decided this was something he needed to do himself. "Is there somewhere private?"

She pointed to his left. "The first conference room isn't being used." Her phone rang. She glanced at the readout and said, "Here he is again."

Friday morning Megan was the first visitor to arrive at the offices of Sol Feinnes. The place had nothing in common with Megan's Beverly Hills firm except the law they practiced. And Megan was not altogether certain about that.

The reception area was decorated in earth tones with hand-cast ceramics on the central coffee tables and desert landscapes on the walls. Behind the receptionist opened a large central office with space for another seven employees. The entire left wall was rimmed by windows. The atmosphere was quietly frenetic, the staff cheerful and intent.

By contrast, Megan's Beverly Hills reception area was lit by lasers flashing through a central steel waterfall. The mammoth sculpture stood in a pool lined with fist-sized chunks of aquamarine. The reflection created a ceaseless electronic rhythm on the polished slate walls. Megan despised the ego-dominated atmosphere.

She pushed the useless thoughts aside and fielded a dozen emails on her phone. She typed over sixty words a minute using just her thumbs, more if she was irate, which happened with increasing frequency these days. She had taken aim at a major LA firm during her first year in law school. She had clerked, she had interned, she had earned her position on the Law Review. She had won her coveted slot in the big league. She should be . . .

Sol Feinnes entered the reception area and asked, "Ms. Pierce, are you early or am I late?"

She stowed her phone and rose to her feet. "I decided to get out of LA before the rush hour."

"Great. Come on back. You mind if I ask a couple of my colleagues to join us?"

Sol moved with deceptive ease, an aging dancer who clearly met life at double time. He ushered her into his office, directed her into the corner sofa set, asked how she took her coffee, and slipped away. When he returned, he was accompanied by two colleagues. Randolf Warner was an older gentleman who cut a dapper figure in his tailored grey suit. Sonya Barrett was a decade or so senior to Megan and encased in the shellacked armor of a full-on litigator.

When his secretary arrived with coffee, Sol made a courtly business of serving Megan. He seated himself and said, "Your firm certainly has a great deal of clout in the LA basin, Ms. Pierce."

Randolf Warner said, "To arrange a pretrial hearing on thirty-six hours' notice is a remarkable feat."

Megan smiled and sipped her coffee and pretended to accept the compliment as it was intended. There was nothing to be gained from regaling this trio with the outrage and fury she had endured as a result of her calls to Judge Richter. How Aaron Seibel, her boss, had reprimanded her for using the firm's influence on behalf of a bankrupt line producer and a Chinese refugee with a few coins in his pocket.

Sonya Barrett added, "Not to mention forcing the prosecuting attorney to drop all charges."

"Truly amazing," Sol agreed. "My hat is off, Ms. Pierce."

Megan knew the response they probably expected. She had heard such reactions often enough. Her answer to their praise should build herself up. Make herself into the star.

She couldn't do it. The unspoken words tasted so vile she almost gagged.

"Actually," Megan replied, "Ms. Suarez was expecting my call. She didn't come out and say it, but I'm convinced she had become increasingly certain the police had arrested the wrong man."

Randolf leaned back. Megan had the distinct impression he was somehow satisfied by her response.

Sonya adopted the same tone she had probably used to interrogate a thousand witnesses. Deceptively smooth and calm, backed up by a smile that did not touch her eyes. "Ms. Pierce, am I correct in assuming you believe Daniel Byrd to be innocent of all charges?"

"Call me Megan, please. And to answer your question, the moment I heard of Byrd's arrest I knew we were looking at a serious miscarriage of justice. I asked to take on his case pro bono."

"Your firm refused to allow it?"

"Something like that." The way her boss had put it was, *Do it and perish*.

Sonya glanced at Sol, who seemed to be fascinated with whatever he found in the depths of his mug. "I'm new to this case. Could you explain to me why the court jumped on Daniel Byrd over a few thousand dollars?"

When Sol Feinnes showed no interest in correcting his associate, Megan replied, "Actually, the total was 1.9 million. And to answer your question, Beverly Hills is a company town."

"Meaning what, exactly?"

"The courts are geared to protect the film world. Byrd's partner had secretly been withholding payments for months. We found dozens of past-due notices in Rexford's in-box."

"I understand some money was also missing from the firm's account."

"Not just the firm. John Rexford had power of attorney over all of Byrd's personal accounts. Danny Byrd had spent six years saving almost every cent he'd earned. He lived for his work and clearly had aims beyond just line production. Between film gigs he audited the books and did the taxes for small suppliers. Bank records show John Rexford stole almost six hundred thousand dollars from Byrd's accounts."

"Did Byrd have a particular goal in mind for those savings?"

"You'd have to ask him."

"You researched him thoroughly, Megan. I'm asking for your best guess."

"I think Danny Byrd wanted to become a player. Invest in his films. Take an active role as coproducer."

Everything about Sonya Barrett was carefully controlled. When she tilted her head, not a strand of her grey-brown hair shifted. Megan wondered if the woman was due in court that day. She could think of no reason why the attorney would take such care on her behalf.

Sonya said, "You like him. Daniel Byrd."

"I've only spoken directly with him once, the day we met at the city jail. But it's safe to say I admire him."

"Can you tell us how you came to know of him?"

"Funny," Megan said. "I was about to ask you the same thing."

Sol spoke up. "Ms. Pierce—Megan—if you don't mind, I'd appreciate it very much if you'd allow us to set your questions aside for the moment."

There was no reason why Sol's words should cause Megan's heart to race. But there was nothing she could do about it, or the sudden catch to her reply. "Sure thing."

Sonya asked again, "How did you identify Daniel Byrd?"

"It was astonishingly simple. I asked around. There is a sort of underclass of filmmakers in Los Angeles. I've worked with a number of them. They all said the same thing. Danny Byrd was the most honest man in Hollywood."

Sonya said, "What do you mean by the term 'underclass'?"

"The top-tier names are a world unto themselves. They work mostly on studio projects. The old division between television and film is basically gone these days. Even Steven Spielberg has produced a TV series for NBC. Below these major names there's a second level, and below them a third. These people are Hollywood's version of contract employees. They are constantly hunting for their next gig."

"And this is the level at which Daniel Byrd operated, correct?"

"Right. He got his start as a junior accountant for Lifetime. Then a promotion took him to Hallmark, where he operated as the in-house project administrator on a number of made-for-TV films. He switched to line production six years ago."

"How old was he then?"

"Twenty-eight." Which made him a year older than Megan.

"Tell me about Byrd's partner."

"John Rexford and Daniel Byrd were in foster care together.

Rexford is by all accounts a natural salesman. According to one person I interviewed, JR wouldn't just find an Alaskan buyer for ice. He'd arrange a bidding war."

"Why would a line producer need a partner?"

"Two reasons," Megan replied. "First, Byrd is known to despise Los Angeles. He needed a local partner to be on the watch for new gigs. But Rexford played a second important role, and this in my opinion is the key to Byrd's long-term plans."

"And that was?"

"Most of these independent films have difficulty finding distributors. Many wind up with deals that mean they never see any return. Danny Byrd and John Rexford were building a reputation for selling these rights. Rexford sold the concept, then Byrd negotiated the contracts and protected the producers' backs. It's why so many of them have become his fans."

Sol broke in with, "Seems like an odd time for Rexford to rob his partner and leave town."

Megan nodded. She had been wondering the same thing. "We're missing something."

Sonya asked, "Is your aversion to Rexford simply the result of his recent actions?"

Megan thought through several responses and settled on, "Los Angeles is a magnet for people like John Rexford."

Sonya made a process of lifting her cup, taking a sip, setting it carefully back on the saucer. "Sol?"

"You're doing just fine," he replied.

She turned back to their guest. "Megan, tell us a little about yourself."

5

THERE IT WAS. The invitation Megan could easily deflect. Asked in the same casual tone as the rest of this remarkable conversation. "I assume you're not asking about my official background."

"Of course not. Sol familiarized himself with all that before calling you. Summa cum laude, Law Review, Superior Court clerkship, the works." Sonya was as pleasant as she was intense. "What do you think of your current situation?"

Megan said as calmly as she could, "I love the work. I despise the firm."

Sol asked, "Can you please elaborate?"

Megan felt as though she had been waiting years to speak the words aloud. "The legal structure serving the LA film world is oriented toward the studios. The lower tiers I mentioned receive a very poor level of service."

Sonya asked, "What does that signify in terms of your work?"

"It's not my *work*," Megan replied. She knew she should try to match the woman's calm demeanor, but it was impossible. "It's never been about my *work*. It's all about the *attitude*. The smaller production teams are treated like riffraff. The top legal firms are all focused on landing one of the big clients. Stars, studios, major producers—they're the target. They're handled by the partners, and they are treated like spun diamonds. Everybody else is beneath contempt."

To her surprise, Sonya said, "LA's legal scene is horrible."

"You know this how?"

"Wright-Patten. Eleven years. Junior partner." Sonya's response tightened the skin of her face, aging her a decade and more. "My reward was a divorce and a ton of bad habits."

Megan lifted her mug and forced a swallow around the knot in her throat. There was nothing she could do about the way her hands shook. "My fellow associates are rewarded for padding their bills. They get congratulated for taking weeks to conclude a negotiation I could have completed in a few hours."

"They delay court cases as long as the client can still pay," Sonya said. Her smile was as hard as her gaze. "I was twice ordered by the firm's senior partners to reject a possible settlement until our client was broke and broken. The second time, I quit. I should have done so the first time around."

"I've seen my boss offer one buyer a handshake deal while his client was using our firm to mask negotiation with a second group," Megan said.

"Using innuendo and slander to slit the throat of any reputation within reach."

"Being criticized for giving a small client your best and putting their interests first."

Sonya leaned back. Nodded once. "Well then."

Sol asked his associates, "Satisfied?"

"Absolutely." Sonya's smile was genuine now.

Her male associate said, "You ask me, we've found what we need."

Sol turned to Megan. "The sort of clients your firm scoffs at are fleeing Los Angeles in droves."

"I've noticed," Megan said.

"They can't go south," Sol went on. "Even the desert counties inland from Pendleton are priced in the stratosphere."

"It's not housing that pushes them out," Sonya said. "It's the whole bitter Southern California lie. The lower-tier production groups are treated like yesterday's rubbish. Their work is consistently undervalued. The service industries overcharge, lie, steal them blind."

"A number have started heading north," Sol told her. "But Santa Barbara is gradually becoming infected by the same LA virus. So now some of them are finding their way to the central coast."

"We need someone who understands their work and values their potential," Sonya said. "Someone who will help us build a new client base."

Megan wanted to shout to the group. Scream at the top of her lungs. Tell them the whole wretched truth of her life in LA. She wanted to tell them so bad her eyes burned. Instead, she calmly replied, "I would certainly be interested in taking that on."

The phone rang before Danny had shut the conference room door. He stared at it for a long moment, but he knew he had no choice. There was no telling how long it would be before anyone else called.

Greg Riggs had deceived Danny, resulting in his taking on a film that had ruined his carefully built reputation. And dumped him here, two hundred miles north of the film world from which he was now excluded.

Even so, despite his justifiable rage, Danny knew there was an element of rightness to Greg's actions. The stars and their agents were the key behind every successful film. Having the stars back out because their time window closed meant resuming the hunt for new investors.

In Greg's position, Danny might have been tempted to take the Italians at their word and start production.

But it was easier to be mad at Greg than face the real issue. His best friend. The thief. The one who stole it all.

Danny picked up the phone. He could not keep the rage from deepening his voice a full octave. "What do you want."

"Anything. Anytime. Anywhere," Greg told him. "That's the most important thing I need to tell you. I owe you, and I want to repay." He hesitated, then added, "I guess you can hang up now."

Danny wanted to. The urge to slam down the receiver was a tremor that flowed down his arm and took hold of his entire body. Then it vanished. With the rage. All gone. "I'm listening."

Greg said, "This is totally crazy. But I have a new gig. It's real enough for me to hold off negotiating the sale of this last project. Danny, I need your help."

Danny felt another tremor take hold. But this time, he watched it from a safe distance. As though somebody else fought the urge to shout his rage into the phone, smash it down so hard the table would break. Punch holes in the conference room wall. Storm from the offices.

And then what? Where could he go? How could he start over?

His future stretched out before him, the barren wilderness of a CPA with a felonious arrest on his record.

When Danny didn't respond, Greg went on, "CBC has a project that's in serious trouble."

Chambers Broadcasting was the newest nationally ranked cable network. It was run by John Chambers, owner of the nation's second-largest radio station conglomerate. Sixteen months earlier, he had acquired a failing cable company, re-branded it, and started making inroads into the family market.

Greg told him, "Airtime is already booked. The sponsors are lined up. The schedule is set. But there's no film."

"When's the airdate?"

"Valentine's Day. Eight o'clock in the evening. Their prime-time program."

"That's . . . nine weeks."

"I know. Crazy, right? But the crew they contracted kept bluffing until yesterday. They've got nothing, Danny. Not even a working script."

Despite everything, Danny felt his pulse accelerate. This was the sort of crisis he lived for. "What's the budget?"

"Two point five. But they'll go up. I'm sure of it."

"Ask for four. Settle for three five."

"Does that mean . . . Are you in? Really?"

"I'll think about it."

"Danny, if we can make this work, it could mean a major shift for everybody involved. Chambers is in trouble. We play the white knight, we could ask for anything." When Danny remained silent, Greg said, "This is me on my knees, begging."

"What about a script?"

"Annie and I are working on it as we speak."

Annie Callow was Greg's favorite writing partner. She was sharp and fast and took no prisoners. "You're lucky she was available."

"Danny, please. I don't think I can do this without you backing me up."

"Tomorrow," Danny said. "I need . . ."

"Sure. Okay. Right. And Danny, really . . ."

"I know."

"I'm so sorry. You can't imagine."

But he didn't want to dwell on that. Not then. "Did they pass you the current script?"

"No. Wouldn't let me see it, wouldn't even tell me the concept they'd approved."

"Must have been total garbage."

"Tell me about it. The two stars they claimed to have signed never even saw it. They didn't even know about the problem until four days ago. The CBC exec responsible phoned the agent who handles both actors to say the shoot had been postponed a week or so. The agent replied, 'What shoot?' Turns out the agent had told the producer the script wasn't near ready to be passed on to the actors. That was five weeks ago, Danny. The producers never uttered a word to the channel."

"You say they've got a title?"

"That and nothing else. *A Ballad for Valentine*."

"The title carries a lot of baggage." Danny shook his head. "Valentine *ballad*. It suggests a song with sorrow attached."

"On the day when everybody is looking for romance and happiness," Greg agreed. "Annie says we can work with it. We have to."

"You'll need a location with some real force," Danny said, searching the blank wall before his face. "You'll need to balance love and distress. Romance and loss."

"A story big enough to draw in people almost against their will," Greg agreed. "Something people will actually tune in to and watch. See why I need you?"

"Tomorrow," Danny repeated, and hung up the phone.

He turned around to find the attractive woman standing in the doorway. She said, "Remember me?"

"Megan Pierce."

She pushed the door wide. "Mind if we take a drive?"

6

MEGAN WAS MENTALLY reliving her morning when Danny exclaimed, "This whole deal is totally nuts."

Megan glanced at Danny but didn't respond. She had related what little Sol had told her, handed over the file now open in Danny's lap, and left him to ponder in silence. They had been driving for almost forty-five minutes.

"None of this makes any sense. It's like I've been stuck in somebody's idea of an elaborate scam." Danny softly beat the armrest in time to his words. "Some guy I've never heard of, he dies and leaves me fifty-one percent of a hotel? And nobody can tell me who owns the other forty-nine percent?"

Megan remembered something she had not thought of in years. When she was still very young, her mother often drove them while her father sat in the passenger seat and fretted. Richard Pierce argued with himself for miles and miles. Her mother often made the entire journey to wherever they were going without saying a word.

When she was eight or nine years old, Megan had asked why her father talked like that, going on and on without her mother responding.

Her mother replied, "You know how Teddy plays with his toys?"

"Sure." Teddy was their Welsh Highland terrier. He loved nothing more than shaking his toys into submission, growling and tossing his head back and forth. He could shred a stuffed animal in twenty minutes or less.

Her mother told her, "Your father is just like Teddy when he's worried over something. He needs a chance to fret in safety."

Megan said, "But you don't speak."

"I do," her mother replied. "But only when I'm certain he's ready to listen."

Danny broke into her thoughts. "And then his widow orders some bunch of lawyers to spring me from jail? Who does that?"

Megan decided the time had come to respond. "That's not the question you should be asking."

Danny's fist froze in midair. He stared at her for a long moment. "I don't . . ."

She took the exit for Buellton and headed down the 246 toward Solvang. She could feel the intensity of Danny's gaze and decided she liked it.

"The lawyer named in these documents." He lowered his gaze to the file's cover letter. "Sol Feinnes. He's not the one speaking with me."

Megan nodded. "There you go."

"There's a reason you're driving me and not him?"

"I think so."

"You don't know?"

"Nada," she replied. She glanced over. "That's the total extent of my knowledge."

"But you know this town, Solvang."

She had already explained her connection but did not mind repeating herself. "My father was an engineer working for the California Water Authority. His last assignment based him in Paso Robles, about ninety miles away. My folks retired here a few years ago."

"So maybe that's why you're the one taking me today."

"I don't think so."

Danny went silent once more. Only this time, Megan sensed a new quality to the car's atmosphere. They were learning what it meant to move in sync.

She said, "We can keep on discussing this, just me driving and you being driven. Or I can talk to you as your legal counsel, which takes things to a totally different level. It's your call."

"I'm the guy who declared bankruptcy, remember?"

"Do you have a dollar?"

"Yes." He smiled for the very first time and pulled a dollar from his pocket. "Sol Feinnes gave it to me."

He really needed to smile more often, she thought. Danny Byrd lit up the car. "Hand it over." She accepted the bill. "Everything is now protected by attorney-client privilege."

"So what do you think is going on here?"

"There are two things we need to discuss. But this is total conjecture."

"Okay."

"First, I think Sol wants me to sign you as a client. Which means he's already accepted you as totally innocent."

"You think so too, right?"

"Absolutely. You were the victim here."

"I like him." He turned back to the front window. "And you."

"Thank you, Danny."

"I've been offered a new gig."

"The phone call in Sol's office?"

"You mean your office, right?"

"Yes. Sorry." That was definitely going to take some getting used to.

Danny related the phone conversation with Greg Riggs, then finished with, "You'll need to rep me on a contingency basis."

"I can definitely live with that."

"Ten percent?"

"Deal."

"You said there were two things."

"It all comes back to asking the right question," Megan said. "Why would Sol Feinnes send me out with a file I've not had a chance to read and a would-be client I've only spoken to in jail and in court?"

"He's hiding something."

"It's probably better to say he's protecting information he's been instructed to keep confidential. Sol doesn't want to dance around questions he can't answer. And given his representation of these other interests, he can't serve as your attorney. And I am not yet an attorney in their employ. So he's sent me."

"Wait, you're . . ."

"I am in the process of leaving a firm I've been with in LA." She had just made that decision. Declaring this to an almost stranger, she decided, actually felt right. "Please don't ask me who. I can't say until the formal announcement has been made and the offer by Sol's firm has been officially noted on record. But this interim stage means I can both help you and not be kept abreast of whoever else Sol's group is currently representing."

Danny went quiet for several miles. "He strikes me as a good man. Somebody I can trust."

"I think so too."

"How long have you known him?"

"Not long."

He went back to studying the file. "I wish I knew who this widow is. Louisa Dellacourt."

"You're sure you've never heard that name before?"

"I never forget a name."

She started to ask what he meant by that when the hotel sign appeared on the side of the highway. "This is us."

———————— // ————————

Danny wished he knew how to tell Megan what it meant, having her make this drive with him.

He slid over so that his back rested on the side door and inspected Megan openly. He had to assume she was fully aware of her beauty. The way she had designed her look and her expression spoke volumes about a woman who defied the world to treat her as eye candy. Her intelligence and her drive shone like a burnished shield.

Danny's own situation was the same, only completely different. He had grown up early and fast. The turning point for him had come in juvie. He spent thirteen months locked up with guys as nasty and vicious as he was tempted to become. The dread proved greater than the temptation, so Danny turned away. A simple act, yet also incredibly difficult. But he did it. And that had meant leaving behind a lot of temptations as soon as he grew old enough to know their names.

Now he sat beside Megan and listened to her words, and he heard what was unspoken. The desire to earn his trust. Not to mention her crystal clear perception of his world and a vivid understanding of what he faced. Gradually Danny's coiled tension and worry and fear began to unravel.

The road traced an apologetic line down the middle of a narrow valley. The day had grown overcast, the sun lost behind clouds so heavy they rested upon the hills to either side. Despite all the recent rain, many of the trees sprouted empty limbs from bone-white trunks. The houses they passed were of two very distinct types. Run-down farms bordered by derelict fences stood between newer mansions with electric gates and armed-response signs. They passed three pickups and a Bentley going in the other direction. Danny saw no other people.

Megan rounded the final curve, and the road simply ended there at the hotel's whitewashed fence. Danny read the sign aloud. "Welcome to Thrashers Ridge."

"The thrasher is a California bird," Megan said. "But I agree, it's still a bad name for a hotel."

Nailed to the post was a hand-painted Closed sign. Megan

drove slowly down the long, curving drive. Up ahead the hotel dominated a stubby rise, like a grey crown upon a head partially emerged from the valley floor. Thrashers Ridge was a child's version of the Victorian manor, with six tall gables, a broad front veranda, whitewashed railings and pillars, and stained glass framing all the windows. The entire structure was encased in grey clapboard.

The parking lot was about half full, which Danny found extremely odd for an inn that had been shut for almost a month. He scouted in every direction but saw no one. "Where is everybody?"

Behind the house stood eight smaller structures, all dressed in the same weather-beaten grey shingles. Beyond them stretched a lake, and farther still the hills curved around like enfolding arms. Quiet.

Danny rose from the car and stood listening to the silence. There was not a breath of wind. The day's grey light lay gently upon the structures, all of which were in need of work. The lawn was roughly trimmed, the paths littered with refuse and bordered by weeds. But there was nothing Danny could see that suggested structural problems. The hotel was ailing but not terminal.

He reached for the envelope holding the keys and security code. "I'm going to have a look around inside."

"I need to make a phone call," Megan said. "Then I'll join you."

His footsteps crunching across the gravel forecourt were the only sound. He thought he heard birdsong faintly in the distance. Then, as he climbed the front stairs, he heard music coming from inside the hotel.

7

MEGAN WATCHED Danny climb the hotel's front stairs, his motions uncertain. When he opened the front door she heard music. She was drawn by the sound and the mystery of who might be playing inside a closed hotel that had become her legal responsibility. But this call could not wait.

When the door squeaked shut and she was alone with the cars and the drifting mist, Megan phoned her boss on his direct line. She had been expressly ordered not to use this number unless, as Aaron Seibel had put it, a million-dollar judgment hung in the balance. Even then, Megan had been ordered to think twice. She stood in the murky light and recalled that strange first day, and how two other young associates had actually written down his words as if they were taking orders from on high. She had found it vaguely ridiculous. What kind of boss made himself unavailable to his own subordinates?

As she coded in the number, she found herself amazed at the events that had led her here. To a hotel at the end of a road to nowhere. Ready to walk away from everything she had fought so hard to obtain.

Seven years earlier, Megan had been one of nineteen new lawyers taken on by Kleber and Klaufstein, the undisputed king of Hollywood law. On their first day, Megan's boss had welcomed them with the announcement that there were slots for four of their group to advance. Within the next twenty-two months, the rest would be sacked.

Nine months after that introduction to LA law, Megan survived the first cut. A year later, she survived the second series of dismissals. She put in the ninety-hour weeks. She did without a private life. Her few disastrous dates were with men as driven and superficial as she had become. Her exercise was done in the firm's basement gym, where she dictated email and worked on briefs while she ran. Just another little rat in the cage of her own making.

A year and a half later, she made the third cut and was granted the right to print new calling cards bearing the title of senior associate. Megan began taking on a few clients of her own. But the glamour was lost now. She was finding it harder and harder to remember what exactly had drawn her to LA in the first place.

Three and a half months ago Megan had been working through a brief when her boss called her into the meeting where she met Pei-Lun Zhang. There was no need for Aaron to order her and another associate to attend. But the unspoken code at Kleber and Klaufstein was, never use one attorney when they could bill three.

Megan liked Pei-Lun Zhang from that very first moment. He was soft-spoken, direct, polite, everything her boss was not. Megan loathed Aaron's casual derision, the way he said with every gesture that an investor with five million dollars was below his radar. Megan had tried to counteract his unspoken scorn with a genuine warmth. Her boss was only too happy to assign her the client. As she led Zhang from the conference room, she saw her boss and the other senior associate share a smirk.

As soon as they were back in her office, Megan's first words to Zhang were, "You know, a headhunter would probably serve you just as well. Maybe better."

Zhang revealed an ability to bow while seated. He spoke in that slow, careful cadence she would come to know all too well. "Can you find me this person?"

"If they exist, absolutely."

"Please." He had offered his hand, sealing the deal. "Do."

Now, standing in front of Thrashers Ridge Hotel, Megan felt utterly calm about her next move. Especially after her boss answered the phone with his standard response, "Go away," and cut the connection.

If her situation had been different, Megan might have laughed out loud. She stared out over the lawn and the mist and replied, "No problem."

She had expected nothing less, but it still hurt. She swallowed against the burn and placed the call to the legal secretary responsible for dismissals. Agnes was paid an extra fifteen thousand per year to handle the hated duty.

Megan identified herself and announced, "I'm resigning from the firm. Effective immediately."

"Hold a moment, please, and let me draw up your file." Agnes typed swiftly. "I always thought you were a survivor."

Megan sorted through a number of different responses, then decided to remain silent.

"All right, dear. I am obliged to read you the following." Agnes ran through the legal requirements and warnings, then asked, "Do you understand and accept the firm's statutes on dismissal?"

"I do. But I'm not being dismissed. I'm quitting."

"The firm's position is the same. Are you seeking to take any of the firm's current clients with you?"

It was an unfair question, totally out of line. But typical of the firm's aggressive nature. "No, I am not," she said. Then, "Wait."

"Yes?"

Megan thought swiftly. Daniel Byrd had never been listed as

a client of K&K. There was no need to alert anyone to what might be developing with him. But the would-be Chinese investor was another matter. "There might be one."

"*Might* be? Dear, you have no idea how difficult they can make life if they even catch a hint that you are poaching clients."

Actually, she knew all too well. "I'm not certain he will ever actually become my client. And if he did, I don't think K&K is interested. Just the same, it's best if you check his file. The client's name is Pei-Lun Zhang."

"Spell that, dear."

She did so. And waited.

Finally Agnes replied, "I don't show any such name under the client list."

"Check billing."

"I just did. Could it be listed under the company name?"

"We hadn't gotten around to incorporating when he was called back to China," Megan replied. "There has to be something. He paid me by cashier's check the first time, and travelers' checks the second."

"Hang on a second, let me check . . . Yes. Here it is. There is a notation under payments received by you. From a Mister Pay." She spelled the name on her file. "I imagine it was how Aaron referred to him in the original notes, and accounts couldn't be bothered to correct his error." Agnes was silent for a moment, then asked, "Megan, do you have any files in your office for this man?"

"Two. Right bottom drawer. Under 'Zhang.'"

"Why don't I just mail them to your home? Clearly there's no interest here. And I'm certain this gentleman would be well served to go with you."

"Agnes, I owe you big-time."

"That's sweet, but it's not necessary." Another hesitation, then, "I don't often say this, but I will miss you, dear."

Megan thanked her a second time, then cut the connection.

She stood listening to the faint melody drifting through the hotel's entrance. There was a second call she needed to make without delay. She hit speed dial, and when her mother answered, Megan asked, "Are you alone?"

"Hang on." They had developed a terse code so that nothing that might disturb Megan's father was said in his presence. Richard Pierce was extremely observant. Any hint of tension impacted his ability to breathe. Megan heard a door shut, then her mother said, "All right. What's the matter?"

Megan took a long breath. "I've quit my job."

Her mother expelled a long breath. "When?"

"Today." She swiftly recounted the morning's events.

Sarah asked, "How do you feel?"

"Okay, I suppose. Calm. Numb." She stared out over the vague landscape to where the northern hills dissolved into shades of brown and grey. "I worked so hard to make it happen. Now I'm just walking away."

"Megan . . . Where are you now?"

"Just up the street. Literally."

"What?"

"A new client has inherited Thrashers Ridge. Part of it, anyway."

"So we're getting a new neighbor in the bargain. What is he like?"

Megan turned toward the hotel entrance. "I don't know him very well. But I think . . . nice."

"Can you stop by? I want your father to hear the news directly from you."

"When I finish here, sure. Why don't you want to tell him?"

"Honey, we've both been waiting years for you to leave that firm. Your father has been feeling low recently. I haven't wanted to say anything, given the stress you've been under. But this news will do him a world of good."

8

THE HOTEL'S FRONT DOORS opened into an old-fashioned cloakroom, a blend of entrance hall and waiting area. Wooden benches and shelves and even the coat hooks were carved with patterns of birds rising from blooming trees. The walls, floor, and beamed ceiling were all done in tongue-and-groove paneling. Glass double doors leading into the main parlor were etched with images of birds in flight. They were propped open such that the music fashioned a welcome.

The cloakroom was as far as Danny got. He seated himself on the side bench, positioned so that he could lean forward and study the musician, then settle back and stay out of sight.

The girl was stationed in the middle of a huge chamber. Her music stand held an iPad connected to a portable amplifier. Danny guessed her age to be somewhere around thirteen. Yet there was none of the coltish awkwardness of most young teens. Instead, she held herself with a womanly grace. She wore cutoffs and rope-soled sandals and a T-shirt big enough to slip down over one shoulder. Her hair was the color of polished cedar, a warm mix of dark blonde and copper. She was tall, perhaps five eight, with long, slender hands. She played with her eyes closed, swaying slightly to the music.

She was, in a word, beautiful.

She played a tenor sax, and her fingering was elegant, smooth, highly professional. What was more, she didn't seem to be following the direction of any sheet music. She was *interpreting*. She played notes from her head in time to the melody. If Danny had not already seen her, he would have assumed the artist was full-grown, a professional at the height of a successful career. She was that good.

The music took Danny straight back. Not the particular melody, but the sound and what it represented. When the song ended, he moved over a trace, staying well out of sight. The last thing he wanted was to interrupt her flow.

She hummed a quiet note as she selected a new tune. The instant the song began, Danny recognized it as from the pianist Keiko Matsui. He thought it was off her latest album, *Journey to the Heart*, but he couldn't be certain.

The girl played fusion jazz, music that had formed a lifeline for a younger Danny. His last foster father had been a retired Marine. The man had not spoken much. But he had impressed Danny with his ability to keep his own natural fury under tight control. He had arranged for Danny to take lessons in Sho Ray, the Korean form of unarmed combat. And he had introduced Danny to fusion jazz. The music had formed the basis for many of their happiest conversations.

The tune ended. Danny leaned forward to watch the girl as she placed the tenor sax in its stand and picked up a second instrument, a straight alto sax. Higher pitched than the tenor, its straight-line form gave it something of a clarinet tone.

An early love ballad by Kenny G, one of his foster dad's favorites, filled the room. Danny leaned forward to study the room. The central chamber was at least forty feet to a side and quite possibly just as tall. A second-floor balcony ran along the two sides he could see from his position, supported by alternating pillars of cedar and redwood. The room's dimensions formed a perfect baffle for the girl's music.

Then Danny spotted another woman. She was seated in an alcove directly opposite the foyer, positioned well behind the girl. Clearly her intention was to remain as unseen as Danny. The woman's features were creased with vivid agony. She wept, one hand covering her eyes. Danny felt like a voyeur, observing such naked emotions.

As soon as the tune ended, Danny coughed, rose from the bench, shuffled his feet, coughed again, then stepped through the entrance.

The young girl compressed her face into a sullen mask as she set the alto sax back on its stand, then cut off the iPad and the amp. She slipped past him and fled without a word or backward glance.

When the girl was out the door and gone, the woman approached Danny and tried to smile around her tears. "I guess this is hardly the welcome you expected."

"It's okay," he replied. He wished he could fit some better words into the moment, but he had no idea what to say. "I'm Danny Byrd."

"Robin Sturgis."

Danny recognized the name from the documents he had been studying. "You're the hotel bookkeeper."

Her nod released another tear. "Sol Feinnes called and said you were coming up. He asked me to meet you." She indicated the empty space at the center of the grand room. "That was my daughter, Emma."

"She is one amazing talent."

"She is. Yes. Emma . . ." Robin's sigh shook her frame. She was a slight woman, delicately boned but suggesting a ballerina's tensile strength. The similarity between her and Emma was unmistakable. Despite her evident burdens, Robin was a lovely woman. "My husband died the year before last."

"I'm so sorry."

She wiped her face with unsteady hands. "He was a police officer in Buellton. He was shot in the line of duty. Emma . . ."

"She's angry with the world that took him away."

Robin seemed to see him for the first time. "Yes."

"I understand."

"You do, don't you." Her gaze returned to the empty music stand. "That last song was one of my husband's favorites."

Danny nodded. "It's the only way she lets herself grieve. Now she's upset that I saw."

Robin showed him genuine gratitude. "Would you like me to show you around?"

———— // ————

There were a dozen questions Danny needed to pose. Hundreds. And this woman was clearly his best hope of obtaining answers. But just then, his brain was locked down. Completely unable to dislodge itself from an unfinished idea. Danny knew from Robin's glances that she expected him to launch into interrogation mode. And it needed to happen, sooner rather than later. But just then . . .

They were doing a tour of the upstairs bedrooms when Danny was finally able to give his unfinished idea a name. He stood by the balcony railing, looking down on the hotel's main parlor, searching for the missing fragments.

Robin asked, "Is something wrong?"

Danny shook his head. He had no choice but to move without being able to take aim. The clock was against him. "Where is your daughter?"

"Where . . ." Robin's gaze tightened. "Why do you ask?"

"I need to speak with her. And you need to hear it."

She watched him turn from the railing. "Don't you want to know—"

"Yes. Absolutely. But this can't wait. Where is she?"

"I don't . . . Probably out by the lake."

"Okay. Let's . . . No, hang on. I need to make a call."

Danny knew he was worrying her, the only connection he

had to this place and its mysteries. But the ticking clock was a drumbeat loud as thunder. He raced down the stairs and found Megan doing a slow circuit of the main parlor.

She said, "This place is amazing."

"I know. Robin Sturgis, this is my attorney, Megan Pierce. Both of you, come now, please." He crossed the boot room, burst through the front doors, and dialed as he took the steps. When Greg answered, Danny demanded, "What's the latest?"

"I thought I had until tomorrow."

"No time. How is your story coming together?"

Greg sighed. "Nothing. We got nothing at all."

"I need you to come up here."

"Where are you?"

"Solvang. A town about forty minutes north of Santa Barbara."

"Danny, now isn't a good time. Every second counts."

"That's why you need to come. Tomorrow. And bring Annie."

There was a silence so intense Danny heard the crackle of passing time.

Finally Greg asked, "So, are you in?"

"What? Yes, Greg. You think I'd ask you up so we could discuss terms?"

"I don't—no, I guess . . ."

"Yes. I'm in. Will you come?"

Greg's response was a full octave higher. "Are you kidding? Yes, of course I'll come."

"Good. Great. And bring a cameraman. Digital. And whoever you bring, make sure they're good on the sound tech side."

Greg hesitated. Danny waited for an argument, a protest, but Greg's response was almost lighthearted. "So what's in Solvang?"

"I'm not sure. But I think . . ."

"What?"

"I think I've found what we need."

9

DANNY AND MEGAN FOLLOWED Robin along a path of redwood chips bordered by railroad ties. The path rounded a largish barn, then ran along a corral missing a number of cross ties, before arriving at the lake's perimeter. Emma was seated on a bench facing the mist-clad water. The far shore was lost to the dim light.

Emma gave no indication she noticed their approach. Her expression was stony, her beauty at direct odds with her expression. She sat there, her shoulders hunched and features pinched, doing her best to shut out the world.

Danny had not been this nervous since his first arraignment, standing before the judge with his public defender. He had known that guy was a loser the moment he'd opened his mouth. Just like then, Danny had no idea what to do or say.

Strangely, he found her willful isolation actually helped him. He recognized the emotion. More than that, it forged a bond he could both understand and name.

He could see that Robin was about to say something, but he reached out and touched her arm. He said quietly, "Five minutes and you'll understand."

Before Robin could respond, Danny stepped up to where

Emma could see him without turning her head. "We need to talk."

She did not glance over. "What are they doing here?"

"They need to hear this too." Danny indicated the bench next to her. "Can I sit down?"

She gave a fractional shrug.

Danny seated himself. "Can I ask how old you are?"

"Fourteen."

He nodded as though he was taking it in deep. "When I was about your age, I got so mad at the world I robbed a bank."

Emma shot him a tight look. "Get out."

"A little younger, actually. But yeah. It's true."

She didn't want to care. He could see the struggle she put up against her own curiosity. "So what happened?"

"I haven't talked about it in years. But I'll tell you everything you want to know. Only not now. We just don't have time."

She turned back to the lake. "So go. Do whatever."

"I am. Doing." He gave that a beat. "The only reason I mentioned that is, I want you to know I've been where you are."

She huffed a dismal laugh. "Like I haven't heard that before. A billion times."

"Tell me about it," Danny replied. "Counselors. Teachers. People who keep insisting they only have your best interests at heart. And you know they're all spinning half-truths."

Perhaps it was his words. Or maybe how Robin started to protest, then went still with the words unformed. Something turned Emma around. She inspected him carefully. Maybe seeing him for the first time. Danny hoped so.

He went on, "I was in foster care for some very hard years. I made it out. Barely. I met a guy and he helped me. But it wasn't just him. It was because I was ready to listen. And that's why I'm sitting here. Because I need you to listen."

She worked through several responses. Danny could tell she

was tempted to dismiss him out of hand. But she didn't speak. He took that as a good sign.

"I'm a film producer," he said.

"You mean, like, movies?"

"Yes. Feature films."

"Mom said you owned this hotel."

"Part of it. That's why I've come to Solvang. But I'm sitting here because I'm interested in seeing if you have what it takes."

She was engaged now. "To do what?"

Danny replied, "Become a star."

10

MEGAN'S MOTHER had an abiding passion for blooming plants. She referred to working in her front and rear gardens as therapy sessions. Megan thought her mother was quite possibly the wisest woman who had ever lived.

Normally Megan's arrival meant dragging her mother out of one flower bed or another. This time, Megan had scarcely pulled into the front drive when her mother was up on her feet and shedding hat and gloves and trowel.

Sarah rushed along the front path, hugged her daughter, and said, "Tell me this is for real."

"As real as it gets."

"You've left those horrid people for good."

"You never called them that."

"How could I, when you were giving them your life?" Sarah held her daughter so tight they could almost breathe together. "No regrets?"

"Not yet."

"Second thoughts?"

"Tons." Megan studied her mother, decided her reaction was genuine. "I thought you liked where I worked."

"Proud, most certainly. Liked, never. Your father and I have spent years watching them grind you down, listening to you find excuses for how you're not getting what you need."

"Why am I only hearing this now?"

"You didn't need us telling you that we were worried." She led her daughter along the path and up the front steps. "Especially with your father like he is."

"How is Dad?"

"Fit to burst, is what. You just come with me."

After her father's second heart attack, Megan started making the drive from LA to Solvang every weekend. She took no work with her. She cut off her phone. She relearned what it meant to be part of her incredible family. Enjoying the vibrant love her parents still showed one another after thirty-five years together. Even when it reminded Megan of everything missing from her life in LA.

She had never minded being an only child, never felt deprived or missed the brother or sister who might have been. Her family was great just the way it was. She had always assumed she'd find a man like her dad, have a family that fit her like a glove. Once her dream of being a partner in LA's heady glitz was realized. Someday.

Sarah led her daughter into the den, a long room that ran the entire back of the house. Her father was in his favorite chair, in an alcove fashioned from broad windows overlooking his wife's blooming artwork. His features looked waxy in the late afternoon light. He lifted one hand in a feeble effort to embrace his daughter. Megan heard the rasp of his breaths as she held him and felt the ache of his coming departure.

Her mother must have seen Megan's distress, for as soon as her daughter straightened, Sarah gripped her with one strong arm and said, "Now you just sit down and tell us everything."

———————— // ————————

After Megan left to see her parents, Danny worked with Emma in the hotel's main chamber for a couple of hours. When it became clear to mother and daughter that more work was required, Robin invited Danny over to their home. When they walked outside, she said, "I just realized you don't have a car."

Danny decided now was not the time to describe his recent encounters with the law. "I came up with Megan."

"You need wheels. Being miles from everything is one of this place's central charms." She started down the front stairs. "You just come with me."

Robin led him around to the barn, unlocked the main doors, and revealed an ancient Jeep Cherokee. "This was used by the maintenance crew."

Emma added, "I heard the gardener say it's done over two hundred thousand very hard miles."

"I'll take it," Danny said. As Robin handed him the keys, he asked, "Why is the hotel closed?"

She looked at him strangely. "You really don't know?"

"The first time I ever heard about Thrashers Ridge was on the drive up this morning."

"The short story is, the banks. Do you want the long version, or do you want dinner?"

"Dinner. Definitely."

"See if you can get this thing started, then you can follow me home," Robin said.

The Cherokee had virtually no suspension at all. The seats were stained almost black. The interior stank of cigarette ashes and machine oil. But the engine purred and the brakes seemed fine. Danny followed Robin and Emma along the valley road and then back down the highway into Buellton.

Robin's home was fairly typical for many California small-town residences, built in the postwar heyday and repeatedly expanded until it covered almost every inch of its postage-stamp lawn. Emma's father was present in every room, on almost every wall. He was a cop in uniform, he was being decorated by some smiling officials, he was playing softball for a local league. But mostly he was pictured with his family.

All of them smiling and happy.

Here in these sad rooms lived the result of having it all stripped away. Their beginnings might have been at odds, but Danny understood this part of Emma better than he could have ever put into words.

He did not say anything. Not then. He figured at some point she would ask about the bank robbery, and he would tell her. But even though his secrets remained locked inside, the harmony was palpable. She did not lose her rage. Nor did he want her to. These hours were all about taking aim. Danny wanted her to reach down, connect with the turbulent emotions as she did when playing her music, and channel the force into words that were not her own.

Over a dinner of lasagna and salad, Danny asked Emma to name her favorite film, then describe her favorite scenes. While she and Robin cleared up, Danny downloaded the script. Then they really got to work. Hour after hour. Trying to see if Emma could do the same with words as she did with her music—reach the point where the emotions rang as true in what she said as they did in how she played. Giving the inner turmoil a new outlet.

Making her camera ready.

11

AT 1:15 THE NEXT AFTERNOON, Danny stood on the hotel's top step. He watched Greg rise slowly from the car, the uncertainty clear in his gaze. Probably gauging whether Danny was going to launch himself across the forecourt and take him down. The cameraman, Rick Stanton, had gotten his start on cheap slasher-horror films. His expression said he had spent the journey north being regaled with Danny's recent events. Rick was probably waiting for Danny to slip on the mask, crank up the chain saw, and get to work.

"Sorry we're late," Greg said. "Traffic was murder."

"Probably the wrong word," Rick muttered.

"It's okay," Danny replied. "Thanks for coming."

"We left early like you said. It still took us over an hour to make the Getty exit."

Annie Callow bounced into view. She was a pixie in her late thirties, small and lithe and taut. She possessed the energy of a woman who would never grow old. She rarely walked anywhere. She bounced or skipped or bounded or leapt. Walking slowly with Annie was like holding on to a tethered balloon.

She said, "Correction. Greg didn't show up at my place until after eight. Hi, Danny."

"Thanks for coming, Annie," Danny said.

"Wouldn't miss it. Are you really in?"

"If you want. Hi, Rick."

"Danny."

"I want," Annie replied. "I want very much."

Greg asked, "Why are we here?"

"I want you to see something. And I don't want to say anything until after you've had a chance to decide."

"Decide what?"

"Just give me time to set up a mini shoot." He waved to the three ladies who had emerged from the side of the barn, motioning them forward. "You need to meet some people. This is Megan Pierce, my attorney."

Greg grimaced. "We met in court."

"This is Robin Sturgis, the hotel's bookkeeper. And her daughter, Emma."

"Welcome to Thrashers Ridge," Robin said.

"That's really what this place is called?" Rick took a step back. "Great."

Emma did exactly what Danny had hoped—she showed the newcomers her customary pinched scowl. Her gaze skipped over the people, touching them briefly. But at least she glanced Danny's way, asking silent permission. A very good sign. As soon as Danny nodded, Emma slouched away.

Robin sighed.

Danny turned to Rick, who was reaching for his shoulder-mounted camera. Having three women appear as witnesses must have assured him they would live to breathe another day. "Let me give you a hand with your gear. Greg, Annie, why don't you go have a look around."

"How long do you need to set up?" Greg asked.

"Depends on Rick. Half an hour should do."

"Come on, Greg." Annie smiled at Robin. "Care to serve as guide?"

"I'll call you when we're ready. Don't go far." When it was just the three of them, Danny said to Megan, "This is when it gets boring."

"Why don't you let me decide that. Can I help carry something?"

"Don't ever say those words to a cameraman," Danny warned.

"I meant it, I want to help."

"In that case," he said, "absolutely."

———————————

Megan proved to be a willing helper, apparently interested in the minutiae required for a professional-grade shoot. Danny seated her on a stool in the middle of the grand chamber so as to give Rick a stand-in. He held up reflectors while Rick took readings of light and shade. Danny's explanation was as much to relax the nervous cameraman as to educate Megan.

The change to digital film, when it came, was nothing short of explosive. The transition was usually put down to George Lucas and his next-gen *Star Wars* film. At the same time Panavision, the world's leading maker of cinematic cameras, completed work on a line of lenses specially designed for digital film. The precision they offered had always before been considered beyond the realm of possible. Lucas flew to England, where the lenses had been ground by the same scientists who had worked on the Hubble Telescope's redesign. The first digital-specific lens cost 2.25 million dollars.

The result was jaw-dropping.

Lucas knew he would have to come up with something completely spectacular in order to convince his team of investors. So he developed the idea of pouring buckets of watered-down baby oil over a female fighter, then filming her shadowboxing . . . wait for it . . .

Lit only by a ring of candles.

Megan interrupted Danny's tale by turning to Rick and asking, "Does everybody in the industry know what he's telling me?"

"Some cameramen. Not many. Most people treat it as ancient history. The world has gone digital, end of story." Rick studied her through the viewfinder. "Danny, you want to have a look?"

"Sure." He waited until Rick replaced him with the reflector, then shifted over to the monitor positioned by the chairs. "Maybe a little too much shadow on the left side."

"I can shift the second reflector over closer to the window. Who's handling them for me?"

"I thought Megan would take one, Robin the other."

Rick was all business now, his former nerves left in the forecourt. "That all right with you, lawyer lady?"

"Whatever the boss says is fine by me. So the boxing film went well?"

It was Rick who replied, "Totally awesome. Lucas and his guy shot images that would have been completely impossible with film."

Danny asked, "You've seen it?"

"Only about a thousand times."

Danny said to Megan, "The camera caught the firelight in the droplets. The result was a woman in black tights encircled by flying lava. Every time she threw a punch, she shot out a stream of liquid fire."

Rick said, "Okay, we're ready. Want to check the lighting with the reason we're all here?"

"I'd rather not."

Rick waited for an explanation. When Danny offered none, he asked, "Lawyer lady, you know what's going on here?"

"Danny doesn't tell me anything."

"Liar," Danny said. "Rick, if our subject gets up and starts moving, I want you to circle in the opposite direction from her. So you'll need to shoot with the camera on your shoulder."

"That will result in shadows we can't control."

"Exactly."

Rick nodded slowly. "Makes sense, I guess."

"Okay, Megan, please go bring in the others."

12

DANNY DECIDED to use the kitchen to prep because it had the clearest lighting. The overhead fluorescents shone on spotless but dated equipment and stone floors that had to be over a century old.

Emma stood on a three-legged stool while her mother sewed a tear in her hem. She wore a silk cocktail dress of coral and palest bone. It had a high oriental collar and pearl buttons that flowed from her left shoulder to her right thigh. The fabric was gathered along her right side so that it folded up above her knee. Robin had applied a strong blush to highlight Emma's cheeks. No lipstick, of course, since it would come off as soon as Emma started playing. Dangly earrings that Danny hoped would catch the light. Hair long and unbraided, held in place by a netting that matched her earrings. Emma Sturgis was a nymph, timeless and elegant, a woman and child both.

"Wow," Danny said.

"This was one of my late husband's favorite dresses." Robin rose to her feet and tried to mask the swipe she gave her eyes. "I had no idea Emma had grown so much."

Emma's frantic gaze was almost at Danny's level. "I can't remember a thing. What's my name? Sally? Fredericka?"

Danny watched Emma's mother as much as her. Robin stood

a fraction back from Emma's left shoulder so as to hide her liquid gaze and unsteady smile.

Danny asked Emma, "Do you know who Lauren Bacall is?"

"Sure," Emma said. "Mom makes me watch those old movies."

"I don't make you do anything," Robin replied. "You love them."

"Whatever."

"You remind me of her," Danny said. "At sixteen she already had a way of smiling, as if she had heard all the lines men were going to spend lifetimes singing to her."

"I'm so scared."

"I know you are." He turned to Robin. "Can I ask you something?"

"Sure thing."

"Yesterday I showed up, this total stranger arriving on your doorstep."

"Mom knew you were coming," Emma said.

Danny went on, "All that time we spent rehearsing, inviting me for dinner in your home, you haven't asked me a thing about myself. Or, you know, what I'm doing here."

"I've known Sol Feinnes for years. He said he thought you were a good guy."

Given he had only met the attorney that one time in court, Danny had no idea what to say.

Robin looked down at the floor. Took a long breath. "I've been so worried."

That turned Emma around. "About what?"

"You, darling. You're growing up so fast. And you've been so hurt, so angry."

Emma's chin quivered. "You don't sleep."

"I spend most nights worrying about all the wrong moves you might make. I feel so helpless."

Emma's voice caught the quiver now. "You're a great mom."

82

"Thank you, dear." Robin looked at Danny. "You're an answer to a prayer."

"It hasn't happened yet," Danny warned.

Robin hugged the girl on the stool, who was now taller than her. "My baby is going to go out there and just kill them stone-dead."

Danny gave them a moment, then said, "Go tell them we're almost ready." When the kitchen door swung shut, he told Emma, "We've been over the plan how often?"

"About thirty dozen times."

"Right. So now you know what's happening and when, even though you're nervous."

"What if I, you know, flub it?"

"I told you. We can do it over as often as you like."

"They'll get bored."

"They're pros. Boredom is just part of the profession. Ready?"

"Yes." Emma reached for his hand and stepped down from the stool. "Did you really rob a bank?"

"Once we're done here, I'll tell you everything you can handle."

Emma shot him a look. "Hey. I can handle anything you can dish out."

13

THE LIGHTING was too dim for the observers to notice the faint tremors that ran through Emma's slender form. Danny knew this because the instant she appeared, his three visitors from LA just gaped. Danny led Emma over to a bar stool positioned in the room's center. The western drapes were half drawn, and the afternoon light formed brilliant pillars that could not quite touch her. Danny squeezed her hand a final time, then backed away. Only then did he realize the cameraman was frozen to the spot. He said softly, "Rick. You're on."

The cameraman jerked awake and stepped to the sound recorder. "Let me hear your voice."

At a signal from Danny, Emma said, "Test, one, two."

"And your instrument?"

Emma blew a few notes into the mike, keeping it simple, as Danny had suggested. Not giving anything away.

Rick said, "Everything is good here."

Danny said, "Let's shoot this first take."

Rick lifted his shoulder cam. "Ready."

Danny had allowed Emma to decide on the music. He wanted to shoot three songs and positioned her soliloquy after the first two. He had no idea whether she would be at her best toward the beginning and then fade, or if she could only gradually recover from her nerves.

His concerns proved meaningless. Emma nailed it. First go.

Her initial song was a bluesy ballad by Fourplay, a quartet combining Bob James and Chuck Loeb, considered by many to be, respectively, the finest fusion pianist and hollow-body guitarist alive today. Danny selected it both because Emma loved the song and because it already contained two masterful soloists. Emma played backup through the first two stanzas. On the second refrain, she let loose. Just took off and left the pros standing in her dust.

As the song faded, Danny glanced over. Greg and Annie had risen from their chairs and now stood behind the monitor, watching Emma directly and studying her presence on-screen. Annie's eyes were completely round, while Greg studied the young woman with an intense gaze and creased brow, as though uncertain whether to believe what he saw.

Megan stood between Robin and the central window, holding one of the reflectors. She caught Danny's eye and smiled. The light softened her features and deepened her gaze.

He tried to remember the last time someone had looked at him that way. And came up blank.

At a gesture from Danny, Emma moved straight into her second song.

At the end of their practice the previous evening, Danny had asked if Emma ever danced to her music.

"All the time," Robin replied. At Danny's request, she had remained present for the entire four-hour session.

"Almost never," Emma corrected.

"Never when you think I'm watching," Robin said.

Danny said, "If you feel like it, on the second song, get up and do whatever comes to you. But only if, you know . . ."

"If I'm sure my legs won't collapse and I won't fall on my sax."

"Only if you feel captured by the moment," Danny said.

Emma went quiet for so long Danny assumed she was looking for a reason to turn him down. He was about to tell her it was fine, not to worry about it, when she said, "Lindsey Stirling dances while she plays."

"Really?"

Emma gave him a look perfected by women over the past thousand years or so, equal measure gentle scorn and disbelief. "You didn't know that?"

"News to me."

"Well, she does."

"What's your favorite song by her?" Danny asked. Emma's response meant it was well after midnight before Robin insisted they quit, because she had to get up the next morning and go do her real job.

Now as the second song began, Emma slipped from her stool. Danny waved to catch Rick's attention, then swept his finger in a circle.

Lindsey Stirling's music blended rock with the soft strains of a masterful violinist. The beat was strong, the background a mix of electronic and punching brass. She had never, as far as Danny knew, used a sax as accompaniment. As he listened to Emma sweep the song up to a totally new level, he decided it was because the instrument had too much potential to dominate.

Emma did not so much dance as sway in a circle. She curved her body to fit into the line of notes.

Rick stepped in front of him. Danny didn't even notice the cameraman's motions until his own view was blocked. When the song was over, Danny stepped in close even before Emma had placed her sax in the stand. "Ready?"

She started to glance at the audience, but Danny was prepared for that. He shifted to totally fill her field of vision. She refocused, licked her lips, nodded.

"Rick." Danny's voice was scarcely a whisper. "Shoot over my shoulder."

"Got it."

Danny stepped back, taking a ninety-degree angle from the monitor where Greg and Annie stood. He took a deep breath and gave Emma the first line.

There had to be a soliloquy, a chance for the two of them to see if Emma could shine while holding to character. Danny had let her choose the film and had instantly regretted it, sort of. Emma had gone for a film that Danny had disliked from the opening credits—*3 Days to Kill*. It starred Kevin Costner as Ethan, a professional operative for the CIA. Facing a terminal disease, he decides to give up his dangerous lifestyle in order to rebuild his relationships with his wife and daughter. But in exchange for a lifesaving drug, Ethan agrees to complete one final mission. The problem is, his wife is absent, which means he must apprehend one of the world's most ruthless criminals while watching his teenage daughter, Zooey, played by Hailee Steinfeld.

There was nothing whatsoever that Danny liked about the film or the premise. Except for the fact that Emma had seen it so often she could play almost all the roles verbatim. Which, of course, was the only thing that mattered.

They played a scene where Ethan is trying to get his sullen, sarcastic daughter to do what he says so he can basically save her life. Instead, he is confronted by the blazing fury that has shaped Zooey's life without her father. The argument was something Danny had completely missed when he'd seen the film. But it formed the real reason why Emma loved it and why she wanted to play that role. So that she could act her way through an argument she had waited two long years to tell her own departed father.

Her fury was a little over the top, Danny thought. She flubbed one line, or rather, she inserted words that Steinfeld had never spoken on-screen. But the result was still powerful enough for Greg to murmur a very soft, "Wow, wow, wow."

This was what Danny had been hoping for. This was the moment he had sensed when he had first heard her play, then watched her storm from this very same room. The innate fire, the beauty, and the magnetism she did not yet realize were hers to claim. All there for her to call on. Which she just had. Danny didn't need to look at the monitor to know she had nailed it.

She sailed through her third song, captured and confident now, dancing with eyes shut as she snared them yet again.

When the song ended and Emma went still, Greg applauded with the others, then declared, "Cut and print."

14

DANNY TOOK HIS TIME shepherding Emma and her mother from the hotel. He found a weary pleasure in reassuring Emma that she had done well, that no, they didn't need to redo one of the songs, that everything was great. He helped them load the sound system and stand and instruments in Robin's old SUV, accepted hugs from both women, and stood there as they drove away. As he climbed the stairs and reentered the hotel, the sleepless night and the day's long hours felt like weights attached to his body.

He accepted Greg's and Annie's compliments, then asked, "Did you hear back from the Chambers execs about the film's budget?"

Greg grimaced. "They want to cut it to a million two."

Danny liked how Megan slipped in beside him, the silent observer. He said, "That makes sense."

"Excuse me?"

"They think whatever you deliver will be a loser. This way, the exec who's responsible for getting them into this mess can still claim a profit. They've costed it out based on a single airing and the ads they've already sold. Then they'll circular-file the project and hope everybody forgets it. Nobody loses. Except us."

Annie turned and frowned at the hotel's front doors. "This is so *wrong*."

Danny nodded. The adrenaline rush that had carried him through the hours of practice and preparation and direction was gone. All he felt now was the same leaden defeat he had carried through the past seven weeks. As though this was the only future he would ever know, no matter how hard he struggled.

Megan broke into his thoughts. "What would be your ideal budget?"

"Four million," Danny said. He didn't need to think that one through. "Three and a half as a floor."

"This could be really, really good," Annie said. "I know it in my heart. In my bones."

"Chambers would hold all North American rights, but we might sell it overseas with a limited theatrical release," Danny said. "Raise our profile."

"Can you shoot anything for a million two?"

Greg and Annie exchanged weary looks. Greg said, "Probably. We'd have to reduce the number of settings to a half dozen. Less."

"Increase the dialogue, reduce the action," Annie said. "Restrict crowd scenes to unpaid volunteers."

"Shoot in twenty days straight, no breaks, twelve-hour days," Danny said. "As few exteriors as possible."

"Work with actors who will sign on for scale," Greg said.

"Our first priority in choice of actors would be those known for getting it right first take, not who would be best in the role," Danny added. "We won't have the time or money for multiple shots."

Greg told Megan, "It's possible, sure. We've done it before. Projects like that were how Danny and I got our start. But Annie's right. We could do something special here. Emma has the potential to lift this up. We write a story around her coming-of-age."

Danny tried to put some energy into his words. "We could still do a story like that on the restricted budget."

"We could try," Greg agreed, resigned now.

Megan asked, "Would it be possible for us to meet with the Chambers executive?"

"They've already asked for it," Greg replied. "Once the budget is set, they want input on story."

"That will only slow us down more," Annie wailed. "Having to get their approval and insert their changes will be like tying anchors to our feet."

Megan said, "Can you set that meeting up for tomorrow?"

"Probably," Greg said. "They're under the same pressure as us."

Danny asked, "What's the point?"

"I have an idea," Megan said. "I'll lay it out if you like. But I'd rather have you go in cold."

Perhaps it was the spark in Megan's eyes. Or the way she refused to be held down by the burdens he shared with Greg and Annie. Whatever the reason, her words helped lift Danny at least partly from the gloom. "You want us to have deniability."

"Right. If they hate it, if it doesn't work, you can blame me for getting it wrong. I take a hike, you start over."

"Excuse me," Greg said. "But who are you, exactly? I mean—"

"We know what you mean." Danny loved the light in Megan's gaze. Like sunlight through a blue-grey veil. "Megan is on the way to becoming our new best friend."

15

DANNY HAD SELECTED the hotel cabin closest to the lake for himself, even though it was in far worse shape than the main building. The kitchenette had a Hotpoint stove with a baked-enamel finish and screws that had rusted to ocher dust. But Danny had no interest in banging around that huge, empty building by himself. From where he stood on the cabin's stubby porch, he could not see another solitary light. The hills were hulking shadows cut from a starlit night. The lake was utterly still, almost spooky in its calm, like it was listening intently, waiting for Danny to make another mistake.

Working with Emma had brought up a lot of memories. The similarity in their pasts was unmistakable. He could see the lakefront bench where she had sat. He recalled the walls of photographs in the hallway and living room and kitchen and dining area and along the stairs leading to their bedrooms. Two lonely people making the best of an impossible situation. Reminding themselves of a man who had once defined love and strength and goodness, at least for them.

Danny remembered the day he met his foster dad, the only man in his life who had actually deserved the title of father. Jack Strong had lived up to his name, an iron-hard African American who had served his country through two desert wars and a lot of skirmishes he refused to honor with names. That afternoon he had appeared with the woman from foster care, stood there before Danny and JR, and said he'd heard they were trouble with a capital T. He was there to offer them a second chance. But only if they were ready to prove the system wrong.

He took them to his bungalow under the shadow of Iron Mountain. Over their first meal together, Jack explained how his third wound had ended his military career. A forced retirement had been manageable so long as his wife kept him company. But she had been gone for two years now, and he had grown disgusted with the quiet life. So Jack had gone looking for his next challenge.

Danny and JR had certainly been that. The two of them were considered unadoptable, with their juvie records and the string of offenses that made their files almost half an inch thick. What was more, they refused to be separated. Every time it happened, they ran away, found each other, and fought until the system finally classed them as brothers just to shut them up. They were too tough and edgy to be taken in by anyone but this battered tomcat of a Marine.

Jack called them his tunnel rats and loved them with a fierce authority that finally introduced them to the concept of self-discipline. He had lived by a code molded by the military and the Bible. But he'd never attempted to jam either down their throats. He *invited* them to grow beyond all their reasons to stay tight and angry and defeated and small. The last time Danny had wept had been at old Jack's funeral.

He felt like weeping now.

Danny and JR had basically started working on their future profession while still living with Jack. Their objective had been the same since those early days. Build their opportunity to enter the big game. Make films the whole world saw.

Movies and television dramas had been their first loves. Reality shows had been tainted for them both by slatternly foster moms clouding the rooms with cigarette smoke and the stench of alcohol and drugs seeping through their pores. That, and how the kids in juvie had screamed at the television through all those shows. It was during one such reality show that Danny had finally woken up. He had watched other kids howl like teenage wolves at people acting out all the pain and rage that trapped them. There on the screen was his fate. He was terrified by the prospect of his ruined life on display so other jailed wolves could scream along with him. He didn't know what shape the exit might take, or even if one existed. But standing there at the perimeter of those teens, Danny vowed to find a way out or die trying.

Still today, ten seconds of a reality show was enough to make him feel slightly nauseous.

Danny leaned against the porch pillar and ached for his missing friend. He remembered the joy he had known sitting next to JR in the Cineplex, waiting for the big screen to light up and swallow them both. There was nothing on earth to compare to the joy he felt when the credits started, the sound built, and a different world appeared there before them. For the next two hours, their wretched pasts belonged to two other kids.

Neither he nor JR had ever felt any need to talk a film to death. Those minutes after leaving the dark space were pretty much the only time Johnny Rocket didn't have his flame on. He'd remained content and silent right there with Danny. Calm. Detached.

Danny couldn't remember who had first voiced the dream. He thought he had, but he couldn't be sure. By age fifteen, though, whenever they left the cinema, they said the word together. *Someday.* Then they bumped fists. Renewing their pact. The only one that mattered.

Danny was drawn back to the empty night by a lone wolf's howl. He breathed deep. In and out. Telling himself with each breath that he, at least, had held on to the dream.

Finally he entered the cabin and locked the door. He undressed and lay down. But he did not sleep.

16

MEGAN WOKE WHILE it was still dark and went for a run. She relished jogging the flatlands between Buellton and Solvang. Far off in the distance, the traffic rumbled and the world grudgingly began awakening to a new set of challenges. Megan often thought the sound was like a conversation, holding to a cadence all its very own. There was safety here on this empty road, something she would have never taken for granted closer to LA. The air was chilly, and she thought she tasted coming rain.

Most of her run, Megan thought of Danny. All the images that flashed through her mind carried one indelible impression. The man was so strong, so intent, it was easy to miss the fact that he was also very fragile. As the faint grey splash of light grew in the east, Megan decided Danny Byrd carried burdens he did not know how to set down.

As she returned to her front yard and began her post-run stretching exercises, Megan allowed herself to accept that she genuinely liked him. Not just as a client either. As a man. It was probably a terrible idea. But she had no idea how to stop her feelings other than walk away. Which she was definitely not going to do.

Megan returned upstairs and showered and prepared for the

day ahead. Her room and the adjoining bath were half as big as the entire downstairs. Windows faced both the front and rear—mountains and her mother's flowers and the empty road and the strengthening day. As Megan dressed in the spare outfit she kept in the otherwise empty closet, she listened to the faint sounds of her parents entering their own morning routines. She heard her father laugh, a rare sound these days, according to her mother. When he laughed a second time, Megan knew it was because she was there, their family united once again.

She walked downstairs and was greeted by her mother handing her a to-go cup of coffee, a kiss, and the words, "Your father wants to meet Danny."

"Good morning to you too."

"Invite him to dinner."

"Mom, he's a client."

Her mother's response surprised Megan. Dimples appeared, but she did not smile. Instead, she hugged her daughter and asked, "Do you think he'd like my brisket?"

———————————//———————————

Megan joined the 101 and headed north to San Luis Obispo in her secondhand Suzuki SUV. Four months earlier, she'd become eligible for a company car. She had listened to her colleagues debate the options—mostly BMWs and Mercedes, one Cadillac, a couple of Porsches—and felt nothing. As she took the downtown exit, she found herself wondering if this had been her first subconscious indication that she did not plan on staying around long enough to enjoy the perk.

She arrived at the law offices of Sol Feinnes at a quarter past seven. The parking lot behind the building had two rows of reserved spaces, eight of which were already occupied. Convenient, since Megan didn't have a key. The security agent on lobby duty recognized her name and told her to stop by later so the day crew could fix her up with an ID. The firm's reception desk was empty, but several of the staffers were already intent on their work. Two ladies smiled and wished her a good morning as if they had been doing so for years.

Megan started to ask if she had been assigned an office when Sol stepped into the central chamber. "Megan, excellent. I have court, but I want to speak with you first. Come on in." He led her around the bull pen to the corner office, waved her in, and slipped back behind his desk. "How did it go yesterday?"

She gave him a swift recap and finished with, "Danny asked me to represent him. I agreed to a straight contingency. Ten percent."

"Good on both counts. What do you think of Danny?"

"Before I get into that, can I ask for some background on the hotel?"

He shifted uncomfortably. "I'd rather you didn't just yet. I'm representing . . ." He stopped at a knock on his open door.

Sonya Barrett, the woman who had effectively interviewed Megan, asked, "Mind if I sit in?"

Sol waved her into the seat beside Megan's and said, "I want Sonya to serve as your liaison. I'm in the middle of a major court battle and won't be available as much as I might like."

Megan could not help but compare this to her previous existence, where Aaron remained isolated behind layers of associates. "Understood."

"If you need anything, feel free to get in touch. Day or night." He turned to Sonya. "I was about to explain how I needed her to remain as a buffer between Danny Byrd and the events surrounding his inheritance."

Sonya said to Megan, "Everything is legally aboveboard. But Sol was given strict marching orders by a long-standing client. It's important we not be placed in a position that leads to Sol or me divulging things before our client is ready."

Sol noticed Megan's crimped features and demanded, "What's the matter?"

"Nothing. It's . . ."

Sonya offered a knowing smile. "Different from how law is practiced in your old firm?"

"Totally."

Sonya said, "My assistant's name is Reggie. He's a gem. I suggest we share him for a while, until you get your sea legs. But if you prefer . . ."

"No, no. That's fine."

Sol said, "Recap for Sonya what you just told me."

Megan had no objection to repeating herself. She liked how they listened to her. Even with the pressure of a heavy caseload, Sol gave Megan his full attention. When she was done, he said once more, "Tell me about Danny."

"On the surface, the day was totally chaotic. The speed, this young girl, the filming, it was too much too fast. But Danny kept it all under control. More than that, he didn't impose his opinion on anyone. He wanted us to form our own impressions."

Sol said, "You trusted him."

"Yes. And so did the others." She hesitated, then added, "I think Danny's attitude yesterday basically describes who he is, even at the worst of times."

"Explain."

"The one word that describes most of the producers I've met is, they *claim*. They take what might one day be reality and claim it's theirs today. Money, rights, stars, projects, whatever. Their lives are shaped by hype."

"Not Danny."

"Right. He hasn't said anything about what might happen because there's nothing concrete to offer. But I think he wants . . ."

Sonya said, "Give us your best guess."

"The Chinese would-be investor, Zhang. He considered Danny to be singular. The fact that Danny was arrested and imprisoned didn't shake Zhang's confidence in the guy."

Sonya asked, "Any aftereffects from his recent adversity?"

"Not in his work. At least, not that I could tell. Remember, my first direct contact with him was in jail. But . . ."

"Tell us," Sonya said.

"I see why people like working with him," Megan replied. "If yesterday is anything to go on, Danny Byrd is a man on the rise."

There was another exchange of silent communication between Sol and his associate. Then he said, "What next?"

"Greg Riggs has arranged a meeting this afternoon with the executives at CBC responsible for this Valentine movie. Danny wants me to attend."

"You absolutely need to be there."

"I intend to." She looked from one to the other. "Sorry, but what is your office policy on things like billing and expenses?"

"I can run through all that with you," Sonya said.

Sol asked, "Any idea who represents the producer Riggs?"

"I asked his associate, a writer named Annie Callow. It's Wright-Patten."

Sonya grimaced. "My old firm. I doubt Greg Riggs is getting any better treatment than your Chinese investor was by K&K."

Megan nodded. Being repped by one of the big firms lent young producers like Greg Riggs a stamp of credibility. Even so, his business was treated as second-tier, fobbed off to junior associates, and discounted as unimportant.

Sonya went on, "I'll call a friend and find out who's the attorney of record."

Sol glanced at his watch. "I'm due across town in fifteen minutes."

Megan halted him from rising with, "Wait." But when he settled back, she found it difficult to express what she was thinking. Which was, in the space of this exchange, she had walked into her dream come true. It was difficult to shape the words. "I'd just like to say thanks."

17

FOR ONCE, Megan did not mind becoming caught in the LA morning snarl. She took the Westwood exit and headed inland, traveling slowly enough to ponder what lay ahead. And prepare.

The Chambers building was on Wilshire, three doors down from the Beverly Hills Ferrari and Maserati dealership. Megan had been inside several times, always playing junior to Aaron or another K&K partner. More often than not, the partner parked below the dealership so as to have an excuse to stop in and pet his next purchase.

The Chambers production studios were located eleven miles away in the San Fernando Valley. Megan's former bosses all liked how the separation kept them from needing to associate with the common people. She, on the other hand, had always thought this was a terrible mistake. The Chambers executives excused this division by describing how their parent group had acquired the Wilshire office building with the cable channel, which was now the jewel at the center of the Chambers crown.

The executives fought to be here, in the city of glitz and glamour. The problem was, they were now separated by more than just the San Fernando hills from where the real work was being done. Megan had been to the production studios dozens of times and had long ago decided that those people realized the truth. The Valley was where the real world began. They understood the tastes and expectations of the audience out in Kansas City. The Beverly Hills executives didn't have a clue. They were too busy playing their Hollywood games to pay attention to the world beyond their manicured lawns.

Which was how, Megan suspected, the Chambers group had wound up in their current mess. Nine weeks and counting from an airdate, with no product.

These execs had probably signed a production deal with a group that happened to be the flavor of the month with the Rodeo Drive flakes. But when they were caught wearing the emperor's clothes, these executives went looking for a real-world crew. Which led them to Greg Riggs. And Danny. And now her.

The problem was, Megan feared the story did not end there. Because now these same Chambers execs needed a victim. Someone they could pass the blame to. And thus save their Valentino-clad hides.

The question she desperately needed to answer was, did they see Greg and Danny as potential saviors of their project or made-to-order victims?

———————//———————

When Danny arrived with Greg and Annie an hour later, Megan thought she knew what was going to happen next.

Danny looked like he had not slept. The circles under his eyes were dark as bruises. Megan studied the three faces and saw the uncertainty of people who felt as though they didn't belong. Beggars knocking on the door of power rather than people coming to save the day. She had seen the expression often enough. Viewing it on these good people made her angry.

Megan did her best to stifle her mounting rage as she drew them into the corner farthest from the reception desk. "If I wasn't here, how would you handle this?"

"Give them a look at Emma's tape," Greg replied.

"Make our story suggestions," Annie said. "Which is bogus, because we can't work the script until we know the budget."

"But we have to dance to their tune," Danny said.

Greg nodded. "Hopefully leave with a green light. Timing is everything."

That was the logical course of action. Megan did not do what she wanted, which was to say she thought they had it all wrong. Instead she merely asked, "What if they had an ulterior motive for agreeing to meet with you today?"

All three stared at her. Danny asked, "What do you mean?"

Megan studied their weary faces and returned to what she had suggested the previous day. "Let me be on point. I will push hard for your side. If it all falls apart, you'll have the pleasure of firing me in public."

"Not a chance," Danny said.

Annie actually smiled. "I'm feeling a lot better about this than I was thirty seconds ago."

"Really?" Greg asked.

Annie pointed her chin at Megan. "The lady's a winner. I know it. I say we go with her lead."

Danny said, "I second that."

Greg hesitated, then said, "Go for it."

Danny's confidence did a lot to calm Megan's internal cauldron. Then she saw the receptionist's gesture and said, "Showtime."

———————————//———————————

Greg Riggs's contact at Chambers Broadcasting was a low-level executive about Megan's age named Rand Bethany. Rand wore skinny black jeans with a starched white blouse that draped down like a miniskirt. Her purple canvas lace-up shoes matched the streaks in her dark hair. The violet-tinted contact lenses only highlighted her nervous, darting gaze.

Accompanying her was an older woman Rand didn't introduce. Megan had to assume this was the accountant responsible for the project. She was heavyset, very still, and dressed entirely in slate grey. The older woman followed them into the first-floor conference room and seated herself four chairs removed from Rand.

Annie was at complete odds with the conference room's dismal atmosphere. She half skipped from chair to chair, giving each a little twist in passing, like she was trying to find the one that would spin her most easily. Finally she settled farther down the oval table and patted the chair next to her. "Greg, come join."

Danny remained standing by the door as Greg slipped into the chair next to Annie. Megan seated herself across from Rand and pulled out the chair beside her. Danny walked over and sat down. The action was not lost on the two women seated across from her.

Rand asked, "Who am I dealing with here?"

"My name is Megan Pierce. I am attorney of record."

"My relationship is with Greg Riggs."

"Today you deal with me," Megan replied. "I don't know what you did to deserve being handed this bomb, but it must have been really bad."

To her credit, Rand gave as good as she got. "Wait. I'm hearing this from the lawyer representing a guy who just got out of jail?"

"Correct. And allow me to finish that sentence for you. 'After being cleared of all charges and receiving a formal apology from the prosecutor's office.'"

"So why did you ask for this meeting, Ms. . . . ."

"Pierce. We need to settle on the budget."

"The budget is set. One point two."

"In that case, we are not interested."

Rand started to glance at her associate, then caught herself. "This project was agreed to by—"

"Correction. You reduced the budget below your initial offer. As a result, there is no agreement." Megan had a whole host of reasons to dislike this woman, starting with her attitude. But there were too many similarities to her own recent status. When Rand remained silent, watchful, Megan decided to go with her gut. "My clients have a concept, something that could turn the wretched vacuum in your channel's time slot into a genuine winner for everyone concerned."

"Oh, wait. Where have I heard that before," Rand scoffed. But her gaze was still now. Focused. Intent.

"What I need," Megan said, "is to know if you are able to look beyond your own current status."

"This has nothing to do—"

"Having the senior executives paint a target on your back," Megan said, motioning to the silent woman seated four chairs away. "Setting you up to take the blame for a failure that isn't your fault. Being fired and sent back to Des Moines."

Rand did not respond.

"For us to proceed, you first need to accept that we have something big. This is no longer about salvaging the situation. It's about creating a hit."

"Is this going somewhere?"

"Absolutely," Megan replied. "Moving forward on this project will cost you four million dollars."

18

THE GREY-SUITED ACCOUNTANT spoke for the first time. "Out of the question."

Megan kept her gaze on Rand. "And something else. Your group must agree that you are their on-site representative. We deal only with you. We don't have time for any more back-and-forth."

Megan had adopted the negotiating stance she had seen her former boss take any number of times. She might dislike the attitude Aaron showed his firm's junior staff. She might despise his scorn for smaller projects. But it did not make him a bad lawyer or a poor negotiator. K&K had climbed to the top of the Hollywood heap by being excellent at this. Megan had watched. Studied. Learned. Now it was her turn.

"We need one ally," she went on. "Just one. You must have signatory powers on everything to do with the project."

"Back up a second," the accountant said.

But Megan had no intention of allowing them to dictate terms or pace or direction. The longer they held back, the farther behind they fell. She focused solely on Rand. "We don't just want you on board. You have to be on location. At least one day per week through the shoot, and as much as possible in postproduction. We'll be writing and editing as we shoot.

Somebody needs to help us maintain our harmony with Chambers and their perspective. It's the only way we can deliver the project on time."

Rand said, "You're saying the story's not complete?"

Danny spoke for the first time since entering the room. "How can it be, when you won't show us what the original production group came up with?"

"We have to assume it was pretty awful," Annie said. "Total garbage. Which means some higher-up is trying to save their sorry hide by attaching the blame target to your back."

Rand did not reply.

Greg said, "There wasn't a completed script when they started shooting *Casablanca*."

"Or *Gladiator*," Annie added. "Both started with studio-approved concepts. Nothing more."

Rand looked from one to the other. She was far from being on board. But at least her hostility was gone now. And her derision. "Does this mean you have a concept?"

Danny started to pull his laptop from his case. "Absolutely."

Megan reached over and halted him with a touch to his arm. "Actually, before we get to that, you must first accept that we are no longer discussing a limited budget and a second-rate project."

"One that will probably cost you and a few of the innocent Valley guys your careers," Annie said.

"We're working on a hit," Megan said. "And we expect everyone at Chambers who is involved to treat us and our project as exactly that."

The accountant said, "And the alternative is . . ."

"My group is prepared to walk away," Megan replied. "We have something very special here. We intend to see it through. On our terms."

Rand said, "We own the title."

"Oh, please," Annie said.

"We have no objection to your holding on to the title," Megan replied. "Or your empty airdate."

When the two women didn't respond, Megan rose to her feet and lifted the others with her gaze. "If you are interested in participating in our winner of a project, you have until this time tomorrow to join us."

They were almost at the door when Annie turned back and actually sang the words, "Tick tock."

———————— // ————————

The farther they walked from the Chambers entrance, the more deflated Megan felt. Danny and Greg remained silent, their expressions almost morose. Annie was something else entirely. She half skipped a few paces ahead of them, humming what she had told the Chambers duo. *Tick tock. Tick tock.*

Greg asked, "You think they bought it?"

"Hard to say," Danny replied.

"At least they listened."

Megan told them, "If they decline, you can still dump me and go back in, say it was all my idea, try to resuscitate—"

"Are you kidding?" Annie danced back within range. "That was more fun than a day at the beach. And I love the beach more than champagne."

"Doesn't mean they bought it," Greg said.

"Listen to you," Annie scoffed. "We went in there planning to ask for crumbs. What does Megan do? All but tell those clowns we want a Bentley."

Danny watched her skip on ahead. "Annie has a point."

Annie returned and gave Danny a butterfly hug, all wings and feather-light touch and speed. "You did good bringing this lady along, D-Byrd."

"Actually, she was the one who found me. In jail."

Greg winced. "Will that ever stop hurting?"

"Not for years," Danny assured him.

113

"D-Byrd." Megan smiled. "Nice tag."

"My idea," Annie assured her. "You know, like T-Bird. Vintage cool with a sort of growl under the hood."

Danny asked, "What do you mean, 'sort of'?"

Annie gave him another lightning-fast embrace. "I've never hugged a felon before."

"Point of order," Megan said. "You're not hugging one now."

The Chambers parking lot was a multistory garage attached by an outdoor walkway to the main building. Only the top execs and their personal guests could park in the smaller basement area—another perk her former boss occasionally enjoyed. Megan was recalling that and a number of other items she would never miss when she realized Danny was unlocking the door to a truly appalling ride. "What are you driving?"

"I found this in the hotel garage," Danny said. "My car was in the company name and is tied up in the bankruptcy, remember?"

"That's not a car. It's a health hazard with four tires."

He fired the engine, revved it a couple of times, and shrugged. "It got me down here."

"That doesn't mean it will get you back."

Annie asked, "How many miles does it have?"

Danny squinted at the fractured dash. "Seven million."

"My dad isn't using his car," Megan said. "He can't since his heart attack. Maybe he'll loan it to you."

Annie said, "Just until your Bentley arrives."

Danny cut the motor. "For real?"

"Can't hurt to ask. Come to dinner tonight." Megan pretended not to see the round-eyed look Annie shot Greg, though she felt her face go crimson. She finished lamely, "My folks want to welcome you to the neighborhood."

19

MEGAN SPENT MOST of the drive north reliving her dialogue with the two Chambers executives. All she could see now were her possible mistakes. There was a very real chance she did not have the experience to use such tactics. She feared Rand and the accountant were back there now, gathered with senior Chambers decision makers, preparing to chop her off at the knees. If that happened, Chambers would circumvent her, shutting her out of any future discussions. Which meant one of them—Greg or Danny or Annie—would soon be phoning Megan. They would repeat the caustic response passed on by Chambers and apologize for needing to let her go.

Every time she felt a faint sense of hope over Annie's song and dance, she mentally turned back to the morose expressions shared by Greg and Danny. She wondered which of the three would wield the blade. Probably not Danny. She still represented him regarding the hotel's ownership. Not to mention her instrumental role in freeing him. No, it would be one of the others. Greg was the obvious choice, but Annie might handle it with a humming sympathy. Megan drove through Santa Barbara hoping desperately that it wouldn't be Danny.

By the time she took the Buellton exit, no one had called. Ditto when she turned down the road leading to Thrashers

Ridge. Her heart raced in a frantic battle to stamp down on hope when she parked.

Danny arrived twenty minutes later. He was on the phone as he rose from that wretched Jeep. He was too far away for her to make out the words. But his face was creased with weary strain and his free hand pumped in time to his words.

He cut the connection and carried his frown across the lot. "We've got a problem. What am I saying? If only we had just *one* problem."

Megan swallowed, hating how it had to be Danny to tell her. She had finally gotten used to the glass-half-empty emotional state. She was finally accepting that there would be no happy ending for her, no man who could put up with all her jagged edges. But standing there and waiting for Danny to say the words and wound her anew, she missed him already. Maybe in a few more years she could find a way to separate her professional existence from her heart. But all she could think at the moment was how much she secretly hoped they might have had a chance at . . . something.

Danny went on, "Chambers wants another meeting."

"I . . . What?"

"They were insisting on Greg coming in alone. Which forced our hand. I wanted you to be on point. But I couldn't . . ."

Megan had spent her entire adult life assuming she never cried. It was a defining trait. And yet here she was for the second time in two days, swallowing against the burning lump. Wishing she could turn away, just for a moment, and wipe her eyes. When she was certain her voice would remain fairly steady, she said, "You couldn't tell him or Annie to take this step. They had to reach the decision on their own."

"Right. Greg has an attorney he's used for two years—"

"Wright-Patten. I know."

"He's complained about them ever since he signed. Even so, his knee-jerk response was to bring them in. They're the last firm we should be working with on this. They'd take a week to wind their watch."

"But you couldn't tell him that."

Danny fought against the weary burdens dragging down the edges of his face. And smiled. "Annie did it for us. I wish you could have heard her hit those high notes. She didn't actually strike Greg. But it was touch and go for a while."

"Remind me to thank her next time we meet."

"Which will be tomorrow. They're back in LA packing. And fretting over what comes next." Danny swiped his forehead. "We don't have a story. We've got a fourteen-year-old actress who's never stood in front of a camera. Emma has no idea what it means to work a sixteen-hour schedule."

"Danny, back to Chambers."

"Right. Sorry. It means you've got to turn around and head back to LA tomorrow." He waved his phone. "I just heard that our project has been kicked up a level. The guy's name is Lawrence Abbott—he's number three on the programming totem pole. Greg and I have both checked. Nobody we've spoken with had a single nice thing to say about the guy."

Megan resisted the urge to rush forward and hug the man. "So . . . Greg agreed."

Danny looked momentarily confused. "To what?"

"To my being made attorney of record for the project."

"Didn't I already say that?"

"No, Danny. You missed that point."

"Right. Sorry." He rubbed his face. "Long day. Bad night."

She was so relieved her legs felt weak. "Of course I'll go."

"Megan . . . we don't have any ammunition."

"What's the worst that could happen?"

"Lawrence apparently likes to turn the screws."

"What does that mean?"

Danny turned in the direction of the eastern hills. His neck corded up like he was going to yell the words. "He'll punish us for pushing. He'll cut the budget. Again. Force us to take actors of his choice. 'This or nothing'—apparently that's a favorite phrase. 'This or the door.'"

It amazed her that he didn't add how their current state was her fault. The only thing she could think to say was, "Go have a shower. Change your clothes. Then come have dinner with my folks."

20

MEGAN WAS SURPRISED by Danny's response to her parents. Gone was the confidence, the suppressed anger, the boxer's readiness to battle the world. Instead, Danny entered her home with an uncertain tread.

Equally unexpected was how her parents responded. Her mother showed him an almost courtly grace, grasping his hand in both of hers, smiling from the heart, and saying what a joy it was to have him join them.

Sarah led Danny through the house and onto the broad rear porch. Her father closed his Bible, set it on the side table, and rose from his chair in stages. He then waited for Danny to walk over. Richard's speech had become increasingly fragmented. He held Danny's hand a good deal longer than politeness required and said, "Sorry."

Danny seemed confused. "For what?"

Richard motioned to the oxygen tank, the plastic tubes that snaked up his back and plugged into his nostrils. His voice was muted, almost robotic. "My state."

Danny shrugged, clearly uncertain how to respond.

Sarah asked, "Danny, will you have something to drink?"

"I'm good, thanks."

"Dinner will be just a few minutes. Megan, why don't you give me a hand."

But Megan lingered in the doorway and watched as Danny turned toward the screens and said, "Wow."

Her father asked, "You like gardens?"

"Never been around them much. Not like this."

"This is Sarah's gift. One of many."

Megan sensed her mother step up beside her in time to hear Danny say, "I was raised in the Arizona foster-care system. The families who took me, they weren't into flowers."

Megan listened to her father's raspy breathing. "It was bad?"

"Some, yeah. Awful. But the last guy, he was great. A Marine." Danny glanced at the Bible on the table by her father's chair. "He was a believer. It didn't take."

Her father shrugged. "There's time."

Danny smiled and stared out the rear screen. "You know the names to all of these?"

"Most." Another few breaths, then, "What happened to your parents, Danny?"

"My dad was a gambler—my mom used to say he was addicted to losing. Which was pretty much the pot calling the kettle black. The state took me into care when I was six."

"I'm sorry."

Danny nodded. "My mom passed away when I was twelve. When they brought me the news, I went totally off the rails. I mean, it was touch and go before. But the week after they told me, I went looking for the worst trouble I could get into. Me and JR, my best friend, we stole a gun from our foster folks' closet and robbed a bank."

Megan heard her father make an unfamiliar sound and thought for a moment he was choking. Then she realized he was laughing, so hard he had trouble drawing breath.

"How old was your buddy?"

"Thirteen."

Richard gripped Danny's upper arm and motioned toward the rear door. "Let's go sit in the shade."

Danny took it slow, allowing her father to lean on his strength. The screen door slapped shut behind them. Megan heard Danny say, "They sent us to juvie. Fourteen months. It was the best thing that ever happened to me . . ."

Sarah took a long breath and touched Megan's arm. "Come away."

Megan shrugged off her mother's hand and followed the men into the back garden. She stood at a distance and watched as Danny helped ease her father onto a bench beneath the Lebanese cedar. They faced a quilt-work of dahlias and sat there in silence for a time, until her father said, "What happened in juvie?"

"I woke up to where I was headed. It scared me. Bad."

"Remarkable," her father rasped. "So young, with so many reasons to stay angry and blind."

Danny responded by leaning forward and planting his elbows on his knees. "JR came out kind of half broken. And it was my fault. I was the one who knew where the old man kept his gun. I led. JR followed. They split us up when we got back to juvie. That lasted maybe five months. Then we ran away and met up. Twice. Soon after, the old Marine offered to take us. JR never did tell me what happened to him. But I know . . ."

"You can't blame yourself, son."

Danny remained as he was, crouched like he was ready to spring up and fling himself away. Instead, he said to the ground, "Megan told you how we met?"

"Beverly Hills Jail. Because your best friend stole everything." Richard patted Danny's shoulder. "I'm sorry, son."

Danny's gaze remained planted on the ground. "The only reason I'm not angrier with JR is because he at least waited this long to pay me back."

Megan stood there long enough to be certain her father was

not going to respond. Then she turned around and walked toward the house.

---//---

After dinner, Megan stood to one side and observed the almost formal farewells. She had spent much of the evening in observation mode. Listening to her parents talk with her new client as if they had been friends for several lifetimes. Danny was more than just at ease with them. When he spoke, it was with the quiet confidence of a man who knew he belonged. The stains from jail time and bad sleep and new stress lessened considerably. His fatigue was still there, of course. But it no longer defined him.

As they stood by the door, Sarah said, "The Buick. Richard, where are your car keys?"

Megan watched as her father fiddled the key off his ring and handed it over. Danny's response was very subdued. Sarah hugged him. Richard shook his hand a final time. Danny offered them both a very solemn, softly spoken thanks. As he followed Megan outside, Sarah called, "Don't be a stranger."

She and Danny crossed to the garage. Megan opened the doors to the second bay. For the first time in eight and a half months.

Danny stared at the Buick. "I never talk about myself. But that's all I did tonight. Talk."

She saw his wounded state and decided to tell him something that had occurred to her during dinner. "My favorite professor taught third-year contracts. He was a master at making the companies and the people and the conflicts come alive. I became his assistant for the second half of the year—unpaid, of course—and in return he used his influence to land me a clerkship."

Megan found it easier to talk if she turned away from Danny. She watched the moths circle the carriage lights. "This evening

122

I thought of something he said once, and it really blew me away at the time. He said the best contract lawyers were the ones who heard the unspoken. The hopes and dreams and fears that both sides held, sometimes so tightly they didn't even know it themselves. A good contract attorney has to be a mediator first and foremost. And the best mediator is someone who can translate conflicting emotions into some form of harmony. But to do that, they have to look beneath the surface. See the unseen. Hear the unspoken."

Danny stared at her now, so intently his dark gaze held a fire all its own. Megan heard herself add, "Daddy has been increasingly cut off. Your talking to him meant the world."

"Really? He didn't say much."

"He talked more tonight than he has in weeks. You made him feel . . . needed."

Danny was silent a long moment. "It's been a while since I was reminded to look beyond the problems of today."

"I don't remember Daddy saying that."

Danny walked over and gave her a brief, strong hug. "It's what I heard."

She stood at the point where the drive met the street long after the night swallowed the car's rear lights. Feeling his arms.

21

MEGAN SKIPPED her pre-dawn run and left Solvang when the sunrise was merely a faint grey wash over the eastern hills. She drove first to the San Luis Obispo offices, signed forms piled on her desk, and had a quick coffee with Sonya Barrett. Megan found a genuine sense of professional comfort in discussing her situation with the former Wright-Patten attorney. Even when she had to confess, "I'll be entering Chambers without any ammunition."

"You have your clients' backing and their confidence. That's a lot."

"I wish I could hand them the world. They deserve it."

"Your affection for them is probably the best thing they could ask for, given the circumstances." Sonya walked her to the elevators. "Lawrence Abbott is not a nice man. I once handled a dispute where he was part of the opposition. That was before he joined Chambers. Don't go in there hoping to appeal to his good side. He doesn't have one."

Several of Megan's former colleagues at K&K had been as close to friends as they could afford, given the fact that they all competed for the same corner office. Gary Landis had been foremost among them, a running back from Iowa State. It was easy to forget that the massive build and easy grin and good-old-boy manner hid a fairly brilliant mind.

When Megan called Gary on the drive south, he answered with, "Tell me we're not breaking up the happy home, doll."

"Point of clarification," she replied. "I'm nobody's doll."

He laughed with the ease of a good-hearted kid. "The folks I like here at K&K are all walking around with black armbands. Nobody can explain why the best of the lot suddenly left the building. Off chasing Elvis is my guess."

"If you wanted to know so bad, why didn't you call?"

He lost his good humor. "We've been officially ordered not to have any contact with you."

"Wait, what?"

"For real."

"Have you ever heard of them doing that with somebody else who left?"

"No, but you're the first senior associate anybody can recall who volunteered to walk the plank."

She pondered that a long moment. "Something more than my departure is at work here."

"I assumed one of our main competitors made an offer you couldn't refuse."

"Actually, I'm joining a firm in San Luis Obispo."

He gave that a beat. "Did you steal a client?"

She thought of how they had misfiled her one guy who was not actually a client since he was ten thousand miles away and without funds. Even so, she made a mental note to drop Zhang a line. "No."

"For real?"

"I walked away clean."

"Then I don't get it."

"If you hear something, will you let me know?"

"Sure thing. I'll probably do it from a throwaway phone at midnight. You understand?"

"Yes. I owe you."

"Dinner at the Ivy, dessert at my place?"

"I don't owe you that much." She waited through his laugh. "Can I ask about a Chambers exec?"

"Hang on a sec." There was silence, then the sound of a door closing. "Which one?"

"Lawrence Abbott."

"You're dealing with him?"

"Let's just say I'm headed into a meeting with him, and I have no intel. Nada."

"Then you're moving up a step. The only confabs I've been party to with Mr. Abbott have been in the company of our betters. Don't call him Larry. He hates the name. Not that you'll ever be on familiar terms . . . Now, that's interesting."

"What?"

"I just remembered something. Your old pal mentioned he was on point for face time with Abbott. Today."

Megan felt a chill run through her. "Brandon Lee is working on a project with Lawrence Abbott?"

"That high up the Chambers food chain, one of the partners will claim the account. Brandon is just their hired gun. It's the role he's born to play."

"That doesn't make any sense." Even if her old firm had a client who was competing for the project with Danny, the current budget would not spark that level of interest. Not at K&K.

"With Brandon involved, you need to watch for the unseen blade." Gary sounded worried. "Take care, you hear?"

Megan pulled into the Chambers satellite parking lot a little after eleven. She drove up the curving ramp to the top deck. Her car would be an oven by the time she returned. But the cell phone signal was strongest up here, and the deck was virtually hers.

She parked where she could look out over the LA skyline and phoned Danny. "I've arrived."

"Wait, let me patch in the others."

There were a couple of clicks, then Greg came on. "I hate how you're going in there alone."

Annie said, "Greg, enough with the frets. That's not what she needs to be hearing."

"I vote we go for the gig. Say yes to their terms, however awful."

"Coward," Annie said.

"Let's recap here. We got what, exactly? Wait, I know. We got nothing."

"We've been handed an incredible setting and a wonderful young actress," Annie pointed out.

"So we turn this into a decent project, we deliver on time, we make a name for ourselves with Chambers. There are worse endings to a hard week."

"We've still bent ourselves into servile positions. And everybody will know."

"It's the first time for us to work with Chambers," Greg said. "They're buying most of their product from the top names in the business."

"We're saving their bacon when one of these so-called top people completely failed. Now they want to apply the screws. How exactly is this going to get us anywhere?"

Greg went silent.

"Well?"

"I still say it's our best chance. We tried for the big ticket. They called our bluff. It happens."

Annie snorted. "Danny, don't you have anything to say?"

"I'm waiting for Megan to give us the word."

Megan said, "And I'm waiting for somebody to say how this situation is all my fault."

Annie actually laughed. "Nobody thinks that, do they, Greg?"

There was enough steel in the way she spoke his name that Greg came back with, "You tried to do what we all wanted but didn't know how."

"There," Annie said. "That didn't hurt, did it?"

"I need for you to decide how I should respond to Abbott's offer if he does lowball us," Megan said.

"You have my answer," Greg said.

Annie pleaded, "Danny, tell him he's wrong."

"I would, it's just . . ."

"Danny?"

"I have an incoming call. I need to take this."

Greg was in full-fret mode. "You're switching to another call? *Now?*"

"Everybody just sit tight. Megan, don't move."

The phone went quiet until Annie asked, "What just happened?"

Megan didn't respond at first. But she was thinking that Danny's absence was a genuine void. She liked that. How this man she was coming to know just a little was the rock everybody needed to rely on. "Danny said wait. We wait."

Early in his career, Danny had served as gopher on a low-budget shoot for Curtis Rhodes, a former A-list star. Curtis had loved the art of acting too much to give in to the sorrow of losing his top rank. He'd stayed off the booze, avoided on-air rants, and kept silent when the LA knives started carving slices from his reputation. Danny now knew there were a few such stars in every generation—actors who endured the roller-coaster ride of their fickle profession and accepted the hard years of mediocre scripts, new directors, and wannabe production companies as just part of the craft.

Danny had done his best to treat Curtis as the star he had known in his childhood days. Back when the man and his roles had represented the world Danny and JR had both yearned to join. Someday.

At the end of an exhausting sixteen hours, Danny was seated in the minuscule dressing cubby as Curtis stripped off his makeup. Danny asked about how it had all started. The big chance. How the actor had separated himself from the crowd and soared into the LA stratosphere.

He expected to hear about the big role. When Curtis had been selected to play a college student who set up a party center in the basement of his dorm, fell in love, blackmailed the college president, won a Maserati in a rigged card game, and came out on top of the world. Danny knew all of that because he had researched it just in case such a moment as this arose.

Instead, Curtis told him, "Watch for the moment when the angels sing."

Danny didn't know how to respond to that.

"When I was starting out, I played second to a Broadway star in a musical," Curtis said. "The star never missed a show, which is good for everyone concerned because I can't dance. I asked him the same question. And that was what he told me."

"The angels sing," Danny said.

"The impossible event. It comes silently, a quick snippet of opportunity, there and gone in a flash. So secretive it would be easy to claim it never happened at all." He watched Danny in the mirror rimmed by lights. "You know what I'm going to say next, don't you."

"You have to be ready."

"Most people trying to make it out here become so embittered by the process that they don't prep. They don't grow or learn or build their repertoire. They just spend their time complaining. It's all too easy to hide from the wounds and the rejections and the people who tell you the chance will never come." He turned back to the mirror and inspected the face that had flamed a hundred million romances. "Once in a very rare while, the angels sing twice in one life. It's what I keep reminding myself on days like this. That I have to walk through this day with heart and eyes and ears open. Just in case."

Danny had seen the event come to others. The silent arrival of the impossible opportunity. And as long as it had been him and JR against the world, he had managed to hold on to the hope that their time would come. Which was another reason why jail had been so harsh, the loss of his best friend so bitter. The unspoken terror was that his hope of ever rising to the top of the Hollywood heap was gone as well.

He was thinking about all that when he switched to the incoming call and said, "This is Danny Byrd."

A young man spoke the impossible words, calm as ice on a stick. "Hold, please, for Lane Pritchard."

Lane Pritchard was a legend in a town made for fables. She had started as just another mail-room drone but within ten years had risen to be the only female managing partner of a top-tier LA agency. Eight years after that, she had lost a boardroom battle that was still discussed in awestruck tones. Lane then set up her own firm. She named it Boutique, which was the name Danny had seen on his phone.

The big agencies were the only ones capable of performing their new role, the work that defined successful Hollywood agents from the nineties to today. These agencies packaged. Only a huge agency representing every major component of the talent pool could bring together script, director, producer, cinematographer, and stars. Only they could sell it as a package ready to be shot. All the risks and delays were taken care of in-agency. Only then could studio execs stay shielded from selling a concept and then watching their careers fade in a torrent of holdups and impediments and scandals and legal disputes.

Lane Pritchard defied the trend. Her stars were big enough to demand their inclusion. Not since the death of Swifty Lazar had a lone agent managed to represent such an array of A-list talent.

Lane now kept him waiting for ten long minutes. Danny received five frantic texts, first from Greg and then from Megan and another from Greg and then two from Annie. He hesitated to respond because he could scarcely believe what was happening. To text the name meant accepting it was real. But five minutes after Megan was supposed to be in the meeting with Larry, Danny finally texted who had phoned him. The trio went silent.

Lane came on the line and demanded, "Is what I hear true?"

"If it's bad," Danny replied, "then probably."

"Your erstwhile partner and lifelong friend skipped town with that platinum-haired loser?"

Danny had listened to Lane's legendary blunt bark on any number of stages and behind-the-scenes TV shows. Even so, he found himself amazed by the energy in this one-on-one. "I hadn't heard who the lady was, other than she acted."

"That's too strong a word. She's a reality-show clown. The most real component of her body is her ego."

Danny did not want to talk about JR and his choice in ladies. "Why are we having this conversation?"

"Word is, the Chambers group has dumped a trainload of garbage in your collective laps. And your response was to claim you're polishing a diamond."

Danny hesitated.

"I'm waiting."

He decided this woman deserved the raw and unvarnished truth. But first he needed to know something. "Who am I talking to here?"

It was Lane's turn to go silent.

"If it's Lane Pritchard and nobody else, I want to give you exactly what I have. But if I'm talking to the LA scene . . ."

"This is you and me and one client. I'll tell you before it goes any further."

"In that case, we might have a good thing. But we're still operating on smoke and mirrors, basically. We have a concept in its rawest form. And one additional component that could actually turn this into a major hit."

"Define major."

"There's no chance timewise for Chambers to plan a cinematic release. But if this is as good as we think it might become, our project could potentially go to the big screen overseas. Then become a mainstay of the CBC annual schedule."

"Aired numerous times," Lane interpreted. "Then brought out every year for a repeat performance."

"That's what my gut is saying."

"How long is your shoot?"

"Hard to say. Airdate is Valentine's Day. We need to complete it in time for edits and scoring. We don't have a finished script or a budget."

"Ballpark."

Danny had spent many nighttime hours running through this very issue. "Twenty-two days. Twenty-five tops."

"Is the girl as good as I hear?"

That rocked him back a step. "How did . . ."

"I live and breathe on the strength of my contacts. Tell me."

"Lane, the girl is incredible. She reminds me of the first film Lauren Bacall made. That same punch-to-the-gut power."

"You'll let me see her test?"

"Of course. And Lane, it was just one take. No reshoot."

"She's not trained?"

His phone chirped, signaling another incoming message. Danny did not need to check the screen. "Lane, excuse me, but our attorney is late for her meeting with Lawrence Abbott."

"That schmo. That waste of a perfectly good corner office."

"I agree. But she's being called into his office as we speak."

"Tell her to go in and tread water."

"You'll stay on the line?"

"Absolutely, darling. You and I need to talk about twenty-two tomorrows."

22

MEGAN RUSHED into the Chambers foyer at one measure below a full sprint. The receptionist-guard was a tall man who observed her entry with a vast grin. "Anytime you want to run like that for me, I'm available."

She was so jazzed from what Danny had just told her, she could smile, tap the ring on his fourth finger, and say between pants, "Be sure to let me have your home number."

The guard winced. "What can I do for you?"

"Get me back the fifteen minutes I'm missing. I'm late for a meeting with Lawrence Abbott."

"Somebody with your spark deserves better." He lifted the phone and dialed. "Mr. Abbott, I have . . ."

"Megan Pierce."

"Ms. Pierce is late because I got held up with a . . ." He lifted his gaze to the distant ceiling and shook his head. "Right away, sir."

As he printed off her visitor's badge, Megan asked, "Am I correct in assuming Lawrence is not your all-time favorite executive?"

"It would be highly inappropriate of me to reply." He peeled the back off the badge and passed it over. "Ninth floor. Sorry, we're all out of flame-retardant gear."

Megan entered the double doors marked Programming and gave her name to a slender young man with a beautiful face and superior expression. He sniffed and pointed his pen at the waiting area. For once, Megan was more than happy to cool her heels.

Greg texted, then Annie, both asking how it was going. When they heard she was still stuck in leather-bound limbo, Danny came back with a text.

Danny
Hang there as long as you possibly can.

The texts were directed to them all, so Megan read Annie's response.

Annie
Dannnnyyy??????

Danny
Stay tight.

Greg
Ninety seconds more and I'm going to be smeared by exploded writer.

Annie
Oh, and the two-step you're doing is to music I'm not hearing?

Megan
I believe I'm listening to Greg's tune.

Greg
There, see?

Megan
Problem is, I think Larry is tone-deaf.

Annie

Don't call him that, he's probably tracking our texts.

Danny

Okay, people. We are a go for launch.

23

WHEN DANNY RECONNECTED with the agent, her first
words were, "You were saying she's not trained."

"Well, she is. On the sax. Her name is Emma Sturgis, by the
way. She's had no acting lessons of any kind."

"You're working with her?"

"Four hours before the take, and a couple more times since."

"Your impression?"

Danny took a breath and gave it to her straight. "This first
film, the stars with experience must play off Emma. We need
to use the core emotions she has boiling inside, basically build
a character that lets her be as she is. The camera loves her, so
that should work. But that's not what you're asking, is it?"

Lane responded by changing direction. "You know the cause
of these emotions?"

"Her father was a police officer. Two years ago he was shot
in the line of duty."

"Poor kid." Lane gave that a beat, then asked, "Her music
is classical?"

"Jazz. Contemporary. Fusion. Sax mostly, but she also plays
flute. She's already improvising. At fourteen."

"Jennie is a jazz fanatic."

Danny felt an electric quiver in his gut. "Jennie French?"

139

"Right. She has a firm commitment to a Lionsgate project that's been pushed back to early February."

Danny plopped down on the bottom step, glad it was there to catch him. His legs had just lost all their strength. "You're offering me Jennie French?"

"There are conditions."

"Of course there are. I accept them."

She chuckled. "Young man, you are a breath of fresh air. Executive producer status, name above the title, scale, closed set, and thirty percent of all residuals."

"Done."

"And script approval."

"Lane, we can't. We just can't. We'll be writing as we shoot. Any delay, even an hour, and we miss our target date."

"You can't expect Jennie to accept a role in a film written by unknowns."

"Greg Riggs and Annie Callow have worked on their last four projects together. Annie is beyond gifted. Greg's input results in a script that is ready to go straight to film. Their partnership has generated screenplays that go far beyond the quality they've been able to achieve, given their budgets."

"I like the way you stand up for your team, Danny Byrd."

"With them, it's a cinch."

"Even after Riggs landed you in jail?"

"Greg was misled by JR and pressured by his stars' tight schedules. He did wrong. But for the right reasons."

"Well said, Danny Byrd."

The way she spoke his name sent the electric current through his entire body. Tight bursts of energy, causing him to jerk slightly, then freeze.

Danny said, "Back to story. I'll send you their last three scripts so you can see for yourself—"

"No need. Jennie's watched all the films they've done together."

"I . . . What?"

"You can have her for nineteen days, starting Saturday. Not one second more."

"Understood."

"Who's handling your legal?"

"Megan Pierce."

"I know that name."

"She just left K&K."

"That's where I heard about her. Formerly a senior associate, right?"

"Something like that."

"Marked for partner, just walked out the door. First in history. Good for her."

"Lane, I have to ask."

"Haven't you heard? It's dangerous to inspect a gift horse too closely."

"Just the same, I need to know. I really do. Why is Jennie French even talking to us?"

"Because she's impressed. And Jennie doesn't impress easily. One day you're the talk of LA for having been dumped in the deep by Johnny Rocket."

"Jennie knows JR?"

"People like your erstwhile friend are a dime a dozen in this town. They show up at the hyped events like slime mold. Jennie has met him often enough to dislike him. Do I need to say anything more?"

"No. Definitely not."

"So of course she hears about how you were left hanging and how you've somehow managed to spring back to life. Two rules she and I have both learned about this town: Hollywood prefers to bury their corpses while they're still breathing. And they expect their victims to stay dead."

Danny had no idea how to respond. He just sat there, staring at the gravel by his feet, while the electric tremors continued to race through him.

"Jennie has survived some burials of her own," Lane went on. "She likes survivor tales. She had me check around. Despite the fact that you were arrested for fraud, everyone I spoke with declared you were both honest and good at your job."

"Thank you, Lane. A lot."

"You're welcome, Danny Byrd. A lot. Now go get to work. Jennie will expect to hit the ground running."

An idea struck. "Lane, it's completely within your rights to say no. But we could use your help right now."

24

MEGAN'S PHONE CHIMED just as she was directed into Lawrence Abbott's office. She read Danny's instructions and had to stop in the doorway and text back.

> I want to jump for joy, but I can't. Larry is watching.

Lawrence Abbott had a triathlete's build, lean and big-boned and tough. He halted her from reading Danny's response by demanding, "Is that text more important than this meeting?"

"Absolutely not." Megan stowed the phone away, but not her smile. As a result, she met the smirk of her former associate with a warmth that was alien to them both. "Hello, Brandon. I wish I could say it was a pleasure."

"I'd ask how you were doing out in the boonies, Megan, but I really don't care." Brandon turned to Lawrence and explained, "Ms. Pierce recently—"

"Your petty feuds have no place in my office. I get enough of that from my own staff. Can we proceed?"

Megan took the chair directly opposite Lawrence. "Most certainly."

"Mr. Lee represents a production group that seeks to take

over the Valentine's Day project. I am inclined to accept their offer. Explain to me why I shouldn't. If you can."

Megan drew her phone back out and touched the number Danny had sent in his text. She hit the speaker button and said, "I'd like my associate to join this discussion."

"It won't help you, Pierce," Brandon said. "Nothing will."

He was seated to her left, not quite behind Lawrence's desk. But his position suggested he was already on the buyer's side. Megan met his gaze as a young man's voice said, "Boutique."

"Megan Pierce calling for Lane Pritchard."

Brandon took the words like a body blow.

Lawrence sat up straighter. "Lane Pritchard is involved in this?"

The agent responded herself. "Why else would I be taking this call? Hello, Larry."

"Ms. Pritchard."

"Is anybody else present?"

"Brandon Lee," Megan replied. "Senior associate at Kleber and Klaufstein. Mr. Abbott has just announced that Brandon represents a different production group that wants the project."

"Who's the competition?"

Lawrence turned to Brandon. The attorney swallowed hard and replied, "Legend Partners, Ms. Pritchard."

The agent barked a laugh. "Let's get real here."

Lawrence's gaze resembled an iron griddle, dark and burning hot. "Mr. Lee assures me—"

"Come on, Larry. You know that group couldn't hit your target date if it were Valentine's next year, much less in eight and a half weeks. They don't wipe their noses without board approval."

"They are offering to bring in a major talent."

"Let's set that aside for a moment, shall we? Legend is strictly feature. Why are they even talking to you?"

Under the strength of Lawrence's glare, Brandon had no

choice but to reply, "I was sent over to deliver the offer, Ms. Pritchard. The details are being handled by my boss."

"Which means the real power is hiding behind this guy. And they've got some secret they can't let out until you've signed. What could that possibly be, I wonder?"

The two men remained silent.

"And another thing, Larry. You're in this current mess because of some headline group that couldn't deliver. So why don't you send Junior back to his overpriced office and let's get down to salvaging your project."

Lawrence protested, "I have no assurance this other group can do any better."

"Oh, please. Now get rid of the hired gun."

But Lawrence refused to let Lane Pritchard take charge. He insisted on Brandon staying. Which was both good and bad as far as Megan was concerned. Brandon was rendered toothless and silent, which was good. But she had to make the deal on her first-ever project while enduring Brandon's constant glower.

Then again, that also held a certain secret pleasure.

Lane said, "What's the budget?"

"One eight was the original offer," Megan said. "But we've requested more."

"Not happening," Lawrence said. "In fact, I ordered this meeting to announce a significant reduction."

"Don't even start," Lane snapped. "What did Legend want from you, Larry? Five?"

Lawrence glared at the phone, hot enough to melt the device. "A no-name production group run by a Lifetime director and a convict doesn't deserve a dime, much less a budget increase."

Lane asked, "Megan, do you want to respond?"

"It's probably best if I don't." But she now matched Lawrence glare for glare.

He went on, "Not to mention how I've not seen any hint of a script."

"And you won't," Megan snapped. "Script approval disappeared when you tried to stiff my team on the budget."

He looked ready to crawl across the desk. "You've got some nerve."

"Allow me to respond," Lane said. "Larry, either you behave or I'm taking this straight to Harvey Chambers. And you know I'll do it."

Lawrence squinted. Megan leaned forward, ready to meet him midway across the desk. Almost wishing he'd try.

"Megan?"

"My team receives five million. Four for the production, one for your insults."

"The door's right there behind you," Lawrence snarled.

"I'm sure Megan would settle for three five and an apology. Wouldn't you?"

"Only because you're the one asking," Megan replied.

"My dear, I do like your style. Well, Larry?"

"This is ridiculous."

"I take that as a yes. Megan, perhaps you should share with Larry who is going to star."

Megan turned so as to offer Brandon a hint of her rage. "Jennie French."

The name jammed Lawrence back in his seat. Brandon's complexion shifted another degree toward chalk.

"Now here's what is going to happen," Lane said. "You will agree in writing to our budget."

"The three five buys you airtime for this one season only. Full share of residuals on all future airings," Megan said. "And no interference from headquarters during production or post-production. Rand Bethany remains our sole contact from now until airdate. All CBC authority rests with her."

"Either you agree now," Lane said, "or I am calling Harvey and telling him you've just lost the chance to have Jennie French, one of Hollywood's hottest stars, feature in her only television special this season. Leaving you with a title and no project, and probably resulting in your being shown the door. Is that what you want, Larry?"

"I'll wait outside while you put all that in writing." Megan would have handled it more smoothly had it not been for the slur on Danny's reputation. That and her smoldering heat, hot enough to match Lawrence's gaze. As it was, she rose, picked up her phone, and said, "You have an hour."

25

GREG AND ANNIE each took a second-floor room overlooking the lake and the western ridge. Robin arranged for a cook and three cleaners. The cook brought in two helpers. Gradually the little hotel was coming back to life. Danny didn't know what he thought about it. He still did not feel as though the place was even partly his. But all such issues had to wait.

After a preliminary discussion with Greg and Annie about story, Danny drove to San Luis Obispo and spent the afternoon working through the first pile of contracts. He and Megan labored side by side in the smaller of two conference rooms. She was in full legal mode now—pushy, intelligent, taking no prisoners. She interrupted her line-by-line assessment of the contracts with numerous phone calls to correct issues on the fly. Her conversations came out in tight bursts, demanding movement in no time flat. She even handled Lane that way. And apparently Lane approved.

Repeatedly that afternoon Danny felt at war with himself. Wanting to retreat from Megan, wanting to grow more intimate still. Not knowing what to do with either urge. Twice Megan asked if something was wrong. Danny held to a silence because he could think of nothing to say.

That evening Danny returned for another dinner at Megan's

parents' house. Sarah and Richard greeted him as they would an old friend.

Danny helped Megan set the porch table. Then he asked if she would join him in the back garden. She must have assumed something bad was coming, because by the time they reached the bench under the Lebanese cedar, she had shrunk inside herself like a child seeking to hide by making herself smaller.

When they were seated, Megan asked, "Did I do something wrong?"

Danny could only manage, "No."

"Will you tell me what's the matter?"

He wanted to. So much. Starting with how he had not been in a relationship for almost three years. Before, they had all followed the same pattern. Temporary, flaming passion had swiftly reduced to bitter cinders. Always Danny had found himself unable to take the next step. Unable to commit. Unable to . . .

And now he feared the pattern was laid out before him all over again. Helpless and angry and scared and . . .

The words remained trapped inside him, until finally Megan's mother called them in to dinner.

But as Danny followed her up the stairs and through the rear porch, Megan's father waved him over. Richard waited until Megan entered the kitchen, then said simply, "I saw how you were sitting. Trouble?"

There was something about this man and his wife, their calm and gentle ways, that managed to pry open the doors Danny had assumed were welded permanently shut. He sighed. "So many."

He saw how Richard glanced at the Bible open on the side table, the heavy notations on the pages. But all Richard said was, "You've made it on your own for so long."

"I had JR."

"Alone," Richard repeated. "Relying on your own strength. Danny, I am impressed. I don't impress easy."

Danny stood there, uncertain how to respond.

Richard seemed pleased with the silence. He reached up, inviting Danny to help him stand. As they walked toward the dining table, he said, "You're a better man than you know, son."

———————— // ————————

The next day Megan returned to San Luis Obispo while Danny and Greg and Annie made sorties through Solvang and the surrounding areas. There was little need for conversation. They knew the rhythm of each other's creative process. Greg frowned at everything. Annie hummed and bounced to a tune in her head. Every now and then she pointed out something and spoke a few words. Like a kiss scene or a breakup. Greg usually responded with a grunt. He was not thinking just story. His primary purpose that day was to structure the concepts into a form that engaged the audience on the screen. Which meant worrying about everything.

Danny remained locked in silence. Neither Greg nor Annie seemed to feel any need to draw him out, which was both good and bad. Good because it gave him time to reflect on the previous evening, and bad for the exact same reason.

Thinking about Megan was like watching a storm rise over the Pacific, brooding and mysterious and frightening in its power. Time and again Danny recalled what Richard had said. Wishing he was indeed a good man. Someone who knew what to do. Someone who might truly be ready for Megan.

That afternoon they drove to the Refugio Beach Park. Danny stayed in the car while the other two walked the shoreline path. Annie chased a pair of gulls like she was six again and the most important part of her afternoon was reveling in the sea and the sunlight. Greg watched her with a bemused expression.

As Danny observed them, he remembered something from his early days. A director reaching the end of an illustrious career had repeated one expression almost daily: "Background makes foreground." It was an adage that dated from the silent-film days, when the early greats transported audiences without the crutches of either color or sound. The motto had mostly been forgotten, especially among the film-school crowd, who liked to think they could make a name for themselves by re-inventing the wheel. But Danny thought it still carried a lot of weight. *Background makes foreground.* Paying attention to the details no audience ever noticed was what set the film's emotional cadence. Get the details right and the story fit into place. It breathed. Became real. Supplanted the outside world for tens of millions of people around the world.

Danny watched Annie dance and Greg fret and knew this was why the three of them made such a great team. They were all after the same thing. They wanted to create the feel of a feature film, regardless of how tight the budget and how many ridiculous barriers stood between them and success.

He watched the pair start back to the car and rolled down his window. He took a long breath of the sea and the afternoon, wishing he could say the right things, *do* the right things, and build a successful relationship with Megan. The kind she deserved.

———————————//———————————

Wednesday arrived with rain and wind and a torrent of fresh work. The best thing Danny could say about the day was that every specialist he contacted leapt at the chance to work with him again. Even the ones JR had stiffed. They did not ask for back payments. They did not express rage over what Danny's best friend had done to them all. This was LA. They knew where the risks lurked. Welcome to the world of film and broken promises.

When the film crew started arriving that afternoon, most offered him a weary smile and a word about paying dues. Treating him as one of them. Still a man they could trust.

Robin went full-time for them, handling all payments and accounts. As far as she was concerned, numbers were numbers. She let her friends in Solvang know what they were doing and how she and Emma were involved. As a result, when Danny drove into town for lunch and a visit to the supermarket, several people offered him a California welcome. Easy, familiar, casual. It wasn't just because he was making a film in their hometown. These were native Californians, fairly immune to film crews. They were being nice because Danny was becoming friends with some of their own.

And in two days, their first major actor was arriving.

--------------------//--------------------

Danny spent the afternoon coaching Emma through the initial scenes Annie had completed. It was the first time Emma had even seen pages of fresh script. She did not do well at all. Danny was mildly disappointed by the level of her performance, but not overly so. She listened, she tried, she stayed determined to improve. For today, it was enough. Almost.

Everything was overlaid by the electric tension everyone felt but did not address directly. To speak the words would only have made it worse.

Alex Cross, their male lead, was arriving on Friday. Jennie French on Saturday. It was showtime. And the story was nowhere near ready.

While Danny coached Emma, Greg walked through the hotel and grounds with Rick Stanton, the cinematographer. Trailing behind them were the assistant cameraman, two lighting techs, and the soundman. Now and then Annie danced along the fringes, her fingers trailing handwritten pages like they were paper wings. Rick was an integral part of the group, offering suggestions as they talked story, framing shots even before the decisions were made. This was how Greg worked, and one of the things Danny most liked about the man. Greg took counsel from everyone on his team, treating even the interns as having valid opinions. But once he made his decision, he expected everyone to fall in line.

Thursday morning they gathered in the kitchen at five. No one complained, not even the cook, who shuffled sleepily about, making breakfast burritos and strong pre-dawn coffee. Anyone who had ever worked behind the camera knew the hours were long and would soon grow longer still.

They drove through empty roads and halted in the middle of Solvang's main street. Rick and the soundman spoke in awestruck whispers, discussing camera angles and directional mikes. Mist caught the first tendrils of daylight, a golden veil that seemed to breathe in time to the rise of birdsong. The sight was so incredible, Rick brought out his shoulder cam and started shooting.

When they returned to the hotel, Greg and Annie hunkered down in the room that Greg was turning into his office. The roadies shifted the room's bed into the basement, brought in a long trestle table and four office chairs, and rimmed the walls with whiteboards. Gradually the boards became filled with a day-by-day shooting schedule. Danny stayed in the background, fielding calls and making arrangements. The closer they came to the first actual shoot, the more Greg would be taking charge. Once the cameras started rolling, it became Greg's show. Danny was just another guy playing backup.

Thursday afternoon was the first time Greg worked directly with Emma. They were both nervous, but for different reasons. Annie hovered in the background, making frantic notes and skipping about while the guys set up lights, taped background mikes into place, and laid tracks for the cameras. Robin emerged now and then from her second-floor office, surveying the scene and observing her daughter, then returned to her numbers. The presence of all that quietly frantic movement only made things worse for Emma. But neither Danny nor Greg responded to her pleas for a chance to work in private.

Finally Danny called a break and led Emma back to the kitchen. But the cook and her assistants were in there, cleaning up after lunch and preparing a buffet dinner. So Danny led the young woman upstairs and into Robin's office. The room held two chairs and a battered desk that Robin had pulled over to the window. Two new filing drawers and a second desk for Danny fronted the side wall. His desk was piled with ledgers and a stack of bill trays. He pointed Emma into the chair he normally used, then went down the hall and returned with one of Greg's office chairs.

Emma greeted him with, "I'm just awful."

"You're missing the point." Danny closed the door and seated himself. "Today isn't about your acting. Well, it is, but . . ."

"What? Tell me! It can't be worse than what I'm thinking."

"Emma, they all expect you to be bad. To flub your lines. To get it totally wrong."

"But I was so good during the first take! Everybody says so!"

"You were mimicking. You've seen that movie how often?"

"I don't know."

"Six thousand times," Robin said quietly.

Emma glared, or tried. But she was tired and she was weak, and the internal rage had a new outlet. It was no longer necessary to flame at her mother. And both women knew it.

"This is totally different," Danny said. "And saying the words right is less than one-tenth of the battle."

"I'm scared of doing this in front of Jennie French."

"I know you are. But you need to understand something. So long as you try as hard as you are right now, she won't be upset over any mistake you might make."

"Really?'

"Yes, Emma. Really."

Robin asked, "What is the other nine-tenths?"

"Framing the character's internal world," Danny said. "You need to listen to Greg. He'll help you with that."

"But so much of what he's saying is . . ."

"Conflicting. That's why I wanted to talk with you. Greg doesn't know who your character is yet. A lot of that depends on you. So he and Annie are trying out different directions. Seeing if they can fit you comfortably into one mold or another. Then they'll write around this."

Emma stared at him. Danny could see she was rocked and heard it in the smallness of her voice. "They'll do that for me?"

"Everybody on set knows you're giving it all you possibly can. Greg sees that you're trying to listen, even though you're in the process of learning a totally new language. They like this more than you can imagine. They want you to succeed, Emma. And something else."

"What?"

Danny wasn't sure whether he should even mention it. But he went with his gut and talked to her like he would a highly trained artist. An adult. Someone who was ready for the raw truth. "They don't have a story."

"What about all the lines I'm reading?"

"They have *scenes*. They have *concepts*. But they don't have a hook."

"I heard Annie say that word like it was dirty."

"It's what's keeping us up at night. Annie is watching you, hoping you'll connect with one emotional core or another. And then . . ."

Robin was the one who said, "They can start building the story's heart."

"That's it exactly," Danny said.

Emma asked, "So what does it really mean, 'hook'?"

"It's easiest to explain with an example. What's your favorite line from a movie poster?"

She replied without hesitation, "The coast is toast."

"See? Four words and you know it's Armageddon for LA. A hook is why people stay locked in their seats. The core foundation of the story. Annie and Greg are desperate to find this before . . ."

"Before Jennie French shows up," Robin finished.

"The clock is ticking," Danny said. "Your training is one small part of a very tight race. See?"

Emma nodded. "I won't let you down, Danny."

"That's my girl. Ready for round two?"

"No."

"Good." Danny rose to his feet. "Let's go. Greg is waiting."

26

FRIDAY MORNING their first star arrived.

Alex Cross was typically offhand in his greetings. He sneered at the entire team when they did not offer the bended knee. He yawned over the unfinished script. He smirked from behind his super dark Ray-Bans when introduced to Emma. While the assistant camera operator served as Alex's stand-in, the actor retreated to a lonely corner of the front porch. Tinny music, probably hip-hop, sounded from his earbuds.

The first few takes went well enough. The problem emerged on take four, when Emma flubbed her lines. Again. Alex left the lighted front parlor, and as he stepped around Greg's chair, he told the film director to call him when they got a real actor on set. Somebody who actually knew what she was doing.

Emma waited until Alex had exited the front door to vent. "He's *awful*."

Danny turned to the crew and said, "Why don't you all take ten."

Emma stood with arms crossed and face set in concrete lines. Her hair shone like a fresh new penny under the lights. "He's *gross* and he *smells*."

Danny could see the crew had no interest in missing a moment of this. Truth be told, he didn't mind. When Annie walked over to shut the window between the unfolding drama and Alex's corner chair, Danny shook his head. The actor needed to hear this.

Danny told Emma, "He's your new dad."

"*No!* He's a total creep! Did you see what he tried to do with his hands? Ewww! Gross me out!"

Danny clamped down on his fury and the urgent desire to walk outside and hammer Alex like a bent nail. Touching Emma inappropriately sounded very much like something Alex would try. Danny breathed slowly, waiting until he was certain his rage was totally under control. He liked how Emma's mother did not rush up and offer the unwanted comfort. Instead, Robin remained behind the camera, watching. Trusting him.

"Are you done?" Danny asked.

"No."

"I'll wait."

"This could take years," Emma replied.

"Humor. A good sign."

"I wasn't kidding, Danny."

"Neither am I. Emma, to make it in this trade means dealing with the impossibles. And you need to believe me here. Alex Cross is neither the last nor the worst."

She kicked at the leg of the sofa where she had been seated with her supposed dad. Hard.

"Alex Cross is part of the package. He is actually named in the Chambers contract. The only way this film gets made is by us using him."

"But *why?*"

"I can't say for certain, but I think I know. And I'll tell you, once you're ready to listen."

Emma stopped kicking the sofa leg and released the grip on her middle. She offered him a fraction of a nod.

"Okay. Five years ago Alex Cross was a star on the rise. Then he shot himself in the foot. He insisted on producing two films where he had a hand in writing the script. It's a problem with a lot of people in LA. They assume writing a good screenplay is nothing more than putting words on a page. But Alex can't write. If you don't believe me, go see his last two films. Together they cost almost fifty million dollars to produce and made less than twenty at the box office."

Emma continued to glare at the wooden floor, but she was listening now.

Danny went on, "So he raged against the system. He fired his agent. Sued his manager. Then he spent six spectacular months basically stoned out of his tiny mind. He was in court three times."

"Four," Annie corrected.

"Whatever. His booking photos became hot-ticket items on the cable entertainment shows. He was flameout of the year with some rag."

"*National Enquirer*," Annie offered. "The ugliest photo ever."

Emma moaned. "But why is he here?"

"I'm guessing Chambers bought him for a song. Then they probably tried to put him into some project or another. Their thinking was, even if he acts badly, he's still good for some publicity. Alex probably gave them the worst performance on record. He saw it as an act of revenge." Danny paused long enough to offer Emma a chance to vent. When she remained silent, he continued, "Between them, Megan and Lane put the screws on the Chambers programming deputy chief, Lawrence Abbott. Larry's idea of revenge was to dump Alex on us. Because Larry wants us to fail."

Emma said softly, "We're not, though, are we?"

"Not if you give us half as good as I think you can."

"I'm going to do more than that, Danny." She lifted her gaze. Solemn now. Determined. "I'm going to give you great."

That was good for a hug. "That's my girl."

As he started across the foyer, Emma called out, "But if

he *ever* tries to touch me like that again, he'll lose a hand. I *mean* it."

Danny walked down the porch and around the corner to where Alex sat with his feet propped on the peeling rail. He had his earbuds in, but Danny suspected he had not turned on the music. The afternoon was so quiet, he probably would have heard even if Alex had turned it down low. Which meant Alex had listened to everything that had just gone on inside. And that, Danny decided, was very good indeed.

Alex wore a pair of professionally torn jeans, seven hundred dollars at a Rodeo Drive shop. An untucked dress shirt beneath a silk suit vest. Hair an extremely styled rat's nest. Ray-Bans dark as his expression.

Danny walked over and leaned against the porch pillar. He saw Greg and Annie step up to the other side of the window. Emma slipped in behind them. Then Robin.

All good.

Alex finally accepted that Danny would wait all day if necessary. "What a dump."

Danny gave no sign he had even heard.

"If I'd known they were going to send me out to the sticks . . ."

"You'd what, turn down the gig?" Danny indicated the gravel drive. "So walk."

"You'd like that, wouldn't you?"

Danny shook his head. "No. I'm not like the others. I know you're a good actor. And I think you can still salvage your career."

"Oh, and you're such a hotshot producer you can give me advice, is that it?"

"I'm the only producer who's interested in giving you a chance."

Alex snorted. "What a joke."

Danny didn't respond.

The silence finally got to Alex. "What?"

"Same as I told Emma. I'm waiting for you to really listen." Danny gave that a beat, then said, "Take off your shades."

Alex wanted to refuse. Danny could see it. Doing anything meant bowing to the will of a man he already despised. But in the end he lifted a finger and dragged them down his nose, letting them slip to where they hung around his neck. Revealing the guy's incredible gaze, the smoky green of a pasture seen through a dawn mist.

Danny said, "I remember the thrill you gave me in your first film. *Rebel Base*, remember that one? I've probably watched it a dozen times. You are a great actor. Notice I didn't say you *were*. You still are. When you let yourself give your best."

The guy sneered. "Nice windup, ace."

But Danny detected the hunger now, and the pain. So that was what he aimed for, ignoring the truly awful attitude. And Alex's slightly slurred speech. And the way his gaze drifted off center.

Danny squatted on his heels, letting Alex look down on him. "I want to give you a choice. All I ask in return is honesty. Either way, I think we both win. So here's the deal. If you want to stay on whatever it is you're stuffing up your nose or down your throat, just say the word. We'll write your character to reflect your decision."

Alex stared at him. "So this daddy gig . . ."

"They were all throwaways. Discarded scenes. Practice sessions. We weren't certain until we saw the lack of chemistry between you and Emma. Now we know. We won't shoot any backstory. The only connection Emma will have with her late father will be in the photographs."

A quietly hissed "yes" drifted through the window. Alex clearly heard it but pretended he hadn't. "So my character . . ."

"Is the dead guy's brother. A complete waste of perfectly good air. Emma's father was a cop working undercover. You were facing jail time for possession with intent. He argued with the DA, got you a break, and in return you were setting them up with your supplier. But that night things went south, and he died. Emma's mother, Jennie French, down deep still considers her loss to be all your fault. And you half agree with her." Danny picked at a fleck of old varnish. "You claim the guilt is more than you can take. You hide in whatever chemical you can get your hands on. Emma tries to forgive you. Maybe she can, maybe not. Her mother despises you. Her hatred eats at her like an acid."

Danny rose to his feet. Made a process of dusting off his jeans. "Emma's character knows how her mother feels, and disagrees. She thinks you deserve a second chance at life and family both. She tries to forge a bond, create an atmosphere that isn't so poisonous, even though her own bitter knowledge threatens to overwhelm her because of the wreckage you are making of your life. She sees the truth. That the reason you stay high most of the time isn't guilt over your part in wrecking these three lives. In truth, that's just your current best excuse. You'll use whatever reason is closest to indulge in your next chemical cocktail."

When Danny started to walk away, Alex dropped his feet to the floor. "Wait. That's my choice?"

"Of course not." Danny walked on.

"So . . . what?"

Danny reached the corner and paused long enough to look back and offer Alex some heat of his own. "It really doesn't matter, does it. Unless you commit to staying clean for the entire shoot and behaving yourself with the crew. *Especially* with Emma. She deserves a lot better than what you're giving her."

Alex did not respond.

The heat had him now. The rage he'd been carrying since forever. "Yeah, that's what I thought," Danny said. "Why bother with building a hero? You've made your choice. So we'll shoot you as you really are. The wreck who might have been great and ran away from it all. And uses women with the same careless abandon that he does his drug of the day. Who even tries his moves on a fourteen-year-old actress who will soon be a star on the rise. It should make a great story line. Who knows, it might even resurrect your career."

27

DANNY RETREATED to the bench by the lake's shoreline. It had become his favorite place to sit and ponder all the things he needed to do next. But not today. Now that the confrontation was over, Danny felt nauseous. He knew the rage was always there. He could not lie to himself about the scars he carried. But it shocked him how close it was to the surface, how easy it would have been to release it.

Danny was still tempted to go back and pound the actor into the ground. He had not seen Alex actually grope Emma. But he believed the young woman's claim. It was good he had missed it. The smoldering ashes of his rage left him utterly convinced he would have lost it.

He did not hear the approaching footsteps. When Emma sat down beside him, Danny jumped. He prided himself on being constantly aware. But here he was, so wrapped up in the might-have-beens that Emma managed to approach unnoticed.

He was trying to stow away the bitter remnants when Emma curled up beside him, pulling her legs under her in a coltish fashion. Danny found true comfort in her gift of silent thanks.

They were still seated like this three minutes later when two sets of footsteps approached. Danny turned and saw Robin and Greg walking the path toward them. Emma took their approach

167

as her cue and rose and walked away. Danny followed her with his gaze, taking in how Robin reached out and stroked her daughter's hair as she passed, and then how Greg smiled at her. As though he fully understood what just happened.

Robin remained where she was and said, "I have a couple of friends who would like to meet you. Locals." When Danny didn't respond, she went on, "These people could be really helpful, Danny. You need to do this. I wanted to introduce them earlier, but they asked me to wait until I was certain."

"I don't understand."

"You will. I've invited them for dinner. It has to be early. They . . . work nights. My place in an hour and a half. Say yes."

Danny recognized he had no choice. "Yes, all right."

"Good." She turned to Greg. "You and Annie need to come too."

"Anything for a home-cooked meal."

"Great. Okay if I leave now and take Emma with me to get things ready?"

"If you're sure this is important," Danny said.

"It is, and I am. You'll like them. A lot. And they will like you." She flashed a rare smile, then turned and walked away.

Danny waited until the barn blocked her from view, then told Greg, "I owe you an apology."

"That's my tune."

"No. Really. I should have spoken with you. And Annie. I was totally out of line telling Alex we weren't going to use Annie's backstory. Or how Alex—"

"You were right. And Annie agrees." Greg's attention appeared to be elsewhere. "Look, man. I'm glad you did it . . . No, that's not right. I don't . . ."

"Just say it, Greg."

"I want you to have sole producer credit."

Danny was rocked back so far he almost fell over the bench's arm. "What?"

"You heard me."

"Greg, that doesn't . . . CBC came to you. You brought me in."

"Okay, so give me exec producer credit. Five percent of the residuals above the director's share. Deal?"

Danny had no idea how to respond. Greg seemed to find nothing wrong with his silence. He reached over, started to pat Danny's shoulder, then thought better of it and walked away.

The irony was hard to swallow, how Danny had just been handed his lifelong dream by the same guy who had landed him in jail. Sole producer credit meant the world of Hollywood movers and shakers would see Danny as the engine behind the film. The guy who was responsible for making it happen. A film by Danny Byrd.

He was still sitting there, staring out over the water, when another set of footsteps alerted him to more incoming fire. He did not need to look around, however. Only one person could walk and skip at the same time.

Annie settled onto the seat next to him. "We're friends, right?"

Danny nodded, having no idea where this was headed. Which was pretty much par for his day thus far.

"Friends tell friends when they're acting like total dodos, right?"

Danny straightened.

"You need to forgive Greg."

"I don't . . . We're working on a film together."

She made a fist and swung it at the air between them. "Don't even try to pretend at stupid."

Danny slid back out of range. "Ohhh-kaaay."

"Greg feels terrible about what happened. He's doing his best to say sorry with more than just words. You need to tell him you understand and the whole jail thing is behind you."

Danny nodded slowly. Hearing it only solidified something

he'd been working through at gut level. She was right, of course. But still there was . . . the jail thing.

Annie rose to her feet and put some distance between them. Like she wanted to get a running start before she launched her final blow. "When Greg heard about you being arrested, he started calling around. Well, actually, first he closed the set and got stinking drunk, a real crying jag. But the next day, when he managed to stand upright and fasten two words together, he phoned his buddies. People you both have worked with, mutual pals, like that. Greg put together a legal war chest. He begged, he argued, he wouldn't take no, not even from people who'd been stiffed by JR."

Danny rose and backed away. It wasn't that he didn't want to hear what Annie was telling him. But the news was scalding.

Annie tracked him step for step. "Remember, Danny, this is while he's in the final weeks of filming on a project that might go under because the money's not there. He's also arranging a mortgage on his house and juggling all the production balls. Then Zhang shows up and decides to invest in the project and in the war chest. Basically because of how he sees Greg trying to help you. Or at least that's how I read it. But Zhang's English is so bad, I might have gotten that part totally wrong. Of course, Greg called those legal losers at Wright-Patten about taking on your case. But they wouldn't even discuss representing you until Greg had placed all the money they demanded in their account. Fifty thousand dollars. So Greg keeps hounding his pals, scraping together your war chest. And what happens but he gets the call from Megan, asking if he'd be willing to stand up for his pal Danny in court."

Danny knew she was waiting for him to feed her the next line. "So the money Greg raised . . ."

"It's still there. Waiting for you to thank Greg, confirm the nightmare is behind you both, and tell him he can give it all back."

Danny stared at her and realized he had never seen her so still. Or looking so grave. "How much . . ."

Annie closed the distance and yelled straight into his face, "*Forty-seven thousand dollars!*"

Then she stepped back, spun around, and walked away.

28

ALEX GAVE NO RESPONSE when Danny invited him to join them for dinner at Robin's. He just sat on the porch, staring at nothing, the wires from his silent earbuds dangling down his chest. Danny could not decide whether it was good for him to come or not. He simply said they'd be leaving in half an hour, and if Alex didn't want to come, the cook would make him whatever he liked.

Thirty-five minutes later, the entire crew piled into three vehicles. As Danny started the Buick, Alex slunk down the stairs and fitted himself silently into the rear seat. His sullen slump would have been an irritation had it not been for Megan, who simply chose to ignore him entirely. She had brought a sheaf of papers with her from San Luis Obispo, the two dozen questions marked with yellow sticky-note arrows. She kept up a barrage of questions until they halted in front of Robin's home.

As she stuffed the pages back into her briefcase, Danny said, "Don't you dare bring that into the house."

"Then when are we supposed to talk about everything else?"

"We'll find a time."

Alex snuffled a laugh at that, rose from the car, and slunk away.

Megan watched him through her open window and asked softly, "Is he as bad as he appears at first glance?"

"We don't have to like him." Danny spoke as much to himself as her. "We just have to get the best he has to give."

"I'm sorry I let Abbott saddle us with him."

"You didn't *let* anything. Abbott was spoiling for a fight."

"That's how it seemed to me."

They had covered this ground twice before, but Danny didn't mind the repetition. "Your agreeing was the only way we got the contract."

"That was what I thought too."

Danny saw Annie turn at the front door and wave them forward. He asked Megan, "The money has been turned over?"

"All 3.45 is in escrow," she confirmed. "The bank manager himself called a few minutes before five. I'm sorry I couldn't get us the full four."

"Three five is enough for a solid project." He did not add what he was thinking, which was, if they could come up with a decent story. "Naturally Abbott waited until the last possible moment, the final banking hour on the Friday before Jennie French arrives."

"What time is she due?"

"Midafternoon."

"Are you ready?"

Danny sighed. "We're so far from that word, you might as well be speaking Martian."

Megan glanced at the house. "Any idea why Robin wanted us here?"

"None whatsoever." He shrugged. "Still, the crew's got to eat."

Robin's friends were from Solvang and now lived in Santa Barbara. Robin introduced them as Michelle Cassick and Consuela Reyes, speaking in the easy manner of bringing old friends into a new circle. Michelle was a statuesque woman with a piercing gaze. Consuela was a stunning Latina whose nature was to flirt, just as Annie's was to dance. Alex naturally made a pass at her, but Consuela handled him with the ease of a professional flame thrower. The former A-list star found himself a seat far from the others, nursed a beer, and sulked.

Emma's response was what most interested Danny. She did not just like the two women. She showed a touching eagerness, clearly hoping they would like Danny and vice versa.

They dined on marinated chicken grilled over a mesquite fire and a whole host of cold side dishes supplied by the two women. Throughout the meal, Michelle and Consuela kept scrutinizing Danny and the film crew.

An hour and a half later, Danny was still no closer to understanding why Robin had insisted this meeting was important. Even so, it felt nice to set aside the day, even if the lighthearted banter only partly masked their burdens. Even if it was just for a couple of hours.

Finally, Michelle said she and Consuela needed to get to work. As Danny joined the others and started clearing up the remains, Emma walked over. He wished there was some way to capture on film how she looked just then. But he didn't say anything, because Emma's solemn expression held such a sweet vulnerability. As though she was ready to show him her secret heart. All there in her young gaze.

Emma said, "I want you to meet my dad."

Robin froze in the act of stretching plastic wrap over a salad bowl. All those within hearing range glanced over. Michelle and Consuela turned from the home's side gate and started back toward them.

Emma touched Danny's arm. "Let's go inside."

All the home's light angled slightly, or so it seemed to Danny. Emma became encased in an intense glow. She did not merely reflect the home's illumination. Her entire form shone. It was a star's ability to carry such a magnetic force and bend the power of shadow and brightness to suit her.

Emma walked him through the kitchen and into the cluttered living room. She led him to the side wall and started pointing to the multitude of photographs. Danny had seen them all before. But not like this. Not standing next to the daughter of a man whose loss remained an open wound, whose absence defined this household.

Danny let Emma set the pace. Her voice was bell-like, the music of a young woman revealing her true nature. Robin followed close behind, saying nothing, punctuating most of Emma's explanations with quiet sniffles. The whole film crew came inside, even Alex. Michelle and Consuela were with them too. Danny glanced at them a couple of times and liked what he saw. Their gazes glistened brightly. He saw Michelle step away and twice wipe her eyes as she texted something. He liked that too, how this incredible moment was clearly more important than something as mundane as a work schedule.

They started down the hallway, Emma continuing with her soft recollections. "This was Daddy winning an award."

Robin had started playing chorus to her daughter's words. "He was named Officer of the Year and promoted to detective."

"The youngest gold shield ever." Emma pointed to the next photograph. "This was Daddy teaching me to water-ski. It took forever before I could stand up."

"It took less than two hours, and you did great."

"This is us camping. Daddy always brought his guitar and always sang. Or tried to."

"Graham was born tone-deaf."

Danny glanced back and saw how Annie was making frantic notes in her pad. Doing her job, even here. And how Michelle and Consuela were watching.

They arrived at the point where the hallway met the stairs. A large family portrait hung all by itself, the only stylized photo in the entire lineup.

Emma stood there a long moment, then said, "I hate this picture."

Robin said, "You used to love it."

"That was . . . before."

Danny expected to hear something like, before the night they got the news, or before they draped the photograph's frame in black and positioned it by her father's coffin.

Instead, Emma went quiet. It was her mother who said, "Before the party."

"Party," Emma muttered. "Ha."

Danny said, "Excuse me?"

"It wasn't a party," Emma said. "It was an excuse for people to be sad."

"We should never have gone," Robin said.

"I warned you."

"I know you did, darling. And I should have listened."

Danny said, "What are we talking about?"

"Four weeks ago Mom got together with all these people who wanted another reason to be miserable."

Robin said, "It was my support group. They decided to have a Christmas party for their children."

"They sat around a Christmas tree and moaned. For hours. They didn't even *notice* how their kids felt."

"Everybody brought a picture. The idea was to make the kids feel like their loved ones were still part of the family."

Everyone but Alex had moved in close. Wanting to catch every word, every nuance. Danny wondered if they felt the same thing he did. That there was something here, something important, hiding in plain sight.

He asked, "Support group?"

Michelle addressed him directly for the first time. "Local

churches have counseling groups for families who have lost a loved one. There are special sessions for victims of violence."

"They're all over the place," Consuela offered. "They have to be. We're surrounded by military bases."

"Not to mention the Lompoc prison for violent offenders south of San Luis Obispo," Robin said.

"Solvang is still this little quiet haven," Consuela said. "But go fifty miles in any direction and it's a different story."

"A Christmas party for Mom's support group." Emma glared at the photo. "What a totally rotten joke."

Danny looked at Greg, then Annie. He saw in their faces the same fire he felt in his gut. It was just the three of them now. "This is it."

Greg said, "The support group. They all thought the same thing. Or most of them, anyway."

"Their Christmas party should have been more than it was," Danny said.

Annie added, "A few of them turned it into just another crying jag, and they brought everybody else down to their level."

"But now they're talking," Greg continued. "Now it's coming up on Valentine's. And they want something else."

"They want what they didn't get at Christmas," Annie said. "A chance to love *through* the sorrow."

"They want to heal and hope and make it a special day," Danny said.

"Turn the corner," Annie said. "Stop making it about yesterday. Make it about tomorrow."

Emma asked, "You're talking about the hook, aren't you?"

Greg turned to Robin. "Can we bring together those in your support group who would go along with this?"

"It would help make it real," Annie said. "Having them play extras."

"This isn't about playing," Greg said. "Well, it is, but we're after a real setting."

"I'll ask," Robin said.

"Great," Greg said. "How many can you possibly get together?"

"How many do you want?"

"Enough to fill the hotel's big front room."

"We'll need more than my group, then."

Michelle said, "I can help with that." She looked at Emma. "And you want her to play for them, right?"

"The Valentine ballad," Greg said. "A song for tomorrow."

"As fractured and imperfect as the party may be," Annie said, "it's still a reason to hope for new beginnings."

"To try," Robin said, reaching for her daughter.

Emma asked, "Can I decide what song to play?"

Greg seemed to have expected that. "I'll have to hear it before we can give you the green light, you understand? The entire film will be leading to this big moment. But sure, if you want to try, you can. Long as you understand."

Annie said, "We can always use it somewhere else in the soundtrack, right, Greg?"

"Absolutely," Danny said.

Michelle glanced at her watch. "We're late. Danny, would you walk us outside? There's something you and I need to discuss."

For some reason, those words were enough to cause Emma to bounce up and down and see him off with a soft, "This is going to be *great*."

29

THE SUN WAS SETTING when the call finally came, and Jennie French's assistant said they had made the turn onto Thrashers Ridge Road. Danny walked down the front steps and did a slow circuit of the forecourt. There were a dozen or so cars and pickups parked by the far fence, and now Danny knew why. The locals had been worried that the start of filming would mean they'd be barred from parking here and hiking the hilltop trail, all of which was on hotel property. When Danny had assured them the only time Thrashers Ridge would be off-limits was when they were actually shooting an outdoor scene, he and the entire crew had taken another giant step toward being accepted as temporary members of the community.

Danny had no idea what Jennie French would be driving. A-list stars came in all shapes and sizes. What made her singular was her shunning of LA society. She rarely gave interviews. She never appeared on the cable-show lollipops, not even when doing a publicity tour. She kept an apartment in a secure Westwood high-rise and owned a small cabin on the Aspen ranch of her favorite director. But where she lived the rest of the year was a closely held secret.

Jennie had starred in her first feature at the ripe old age of fifteen, playing an American runaway in Paris. The role had made her a cult icon. At sixteen she starred opposite Robin Williams in the comedy smash hit of the year. At seventeen she played a genetically enhanced CIA assassin. At eighteen she was nominated for her first Academy Award. At nineteen she turned her back on Hollywood, earned her GED, and then enrolled in Georgetown, where she studied political history and graduated cum laude.

When she returned to LA after four years at Georgetown, the cynics crowed and the on-air pundits claimed her time was past. One cable lollipop announced her return by saying Jennie French was back to play tourist. She responded with her customary silence. She took several secondary roles, then four years ago J. J. Abrams tapped her to lead an all-star cast in the summer's biggest blockbuster. Nine hundred million dollars in global box office sales later, the cynics had gone strangely silent. She had no patience with the press. She refused point-blank to discuss her personal life.

Danny waited for her in the hotel's forecourt, liking her already.

A black Infiniti QX60 pulled through the gates. The SUV's windows were all shaded, so Danny could not see inside. But he knew it was her, and he liked her ride. It was a fine luxury vehicle, but one that attracted no attention whatsoever.

Danny stood in front of the hotel and waited as the driver's door opened and a woman in a slate-grey suit stepped down. "Mr. Byrd?"

"That's me."

She glanced at the parked cars. "Where is everybody?"

Danny pointed at the western ridgeline. "Locals park here and hike the hills, watching the sunset. My team is on set. We're alone."

She gave him a cop's hard-eyed measure. Her dark hair was chopped very short. She was slender but appeared both strong and extremely aware. "Ms. French is on the phone. She asks that you give her a minute."

"No problem."

"Where will Ms. French be staying?"

"Here, if she likes. Otherwise at a Solvang inn. It's her call."

"Show me the rooms, please."

Danny turned and started up the stairs. He held the door for her. "Can I ask your name?"

"Kate."

"How many others are in her security detail?"

"Depends on the circumstances, Mr. Byrd. It's just me for the moment. But that may change at any time."

"Understood." Danny led her up the main staircase and through the double doors leading to the hotel's finest suite. Nothing could hide the fact that the entire hotel was in desperate need of renovations. But the parlor's domed ceiling held three original hand-blown Tiffany lamps, and the bed's four posters were carved from the same redwood as the broad-planked floors.

Kate inspected each room, checked out the bath, then declared, "I believe Ms. French will be quite comfortable."

"Great."

"How many others will be based here?"

"The entire crew—that's nineteen including me."

"What about Mr. Cross?"

"I've put him in one of the cabins."

"Jennie has heard some things. Will he be a problem?"

Danny decided she would prefer to hear it straight. "He might try. But I imagine if Ms. French comes down hard on him one time, he'll fold his tents and creep away."

Kate liked that enough to smile. "Why don't we go back outside and meet the lady herself."

------ // ------

Jennie French stood beside the rear passenger door when Danny emerged from the hotel. She waved at him, then pointed at the phone still attached to her ear. Beside Jennie stood her personal assistant, whose name Danny knew was Evelyn. Danny had dealt with her several times and thought Evelyn was going to be a true asset. Many PAs to the stars expected to be treated like power players themselves. Their egos were bruised by the slightest hint of disrespect. If that happened, they made the set as miserable as they possibly could. Plus the PA was normally in charge of managing a star's entourage during a shoot. This could include a cosmetician, hairdresser, manager, agent, personal vet for the pets they insisted on bringing along, and one or more petulant lovers. To have a star like Jennie French show up minus limo and hangers-on placed her in a very exclusive group indeed.

Danny wasn't certain, but he thought Evelyn belonged to an equally rare breed. He hoped the PA would prove to be a professional whose primary job was to smooth the star's path. Simply having a star like Jennie French on set did not mean all her other responsibilities were going to go away. Lane Pritchard had outlined some of the urgent matters Jennie needed to juggle—a cover shoot for *Vanity Fair*, negotiations on a book whose film rights she wanted, an unsatisfactory screenplay for the film going into production four weeks from now, issues regarding a three-film production deal with Universal, and so forth. All in the next nineteen days.

Danny liked having this opportunity to study her. He had never been this close to a major star, and Jennie French was most certainly that. Two Oscars and currently nominated for a third. Three films completed last year, at least that many this year. A power in the industry. His for almost three weeks.

She was five feet seven inches tall and could not possibly weigh more than 110. She was fine-boned and had the sculpted features of a long-distance runner, or a bird of prey. Her beauty was simply one component of her unique draw. She shared the hunting bird's intent stillness, able to focus completely on whatever was being said over the phone. Danny felt the woman's kinetic power like it was plugged directly into his chest. He would have been intimidated by her force had he not already been dealing with a younger version.

Emma shared a number of traits with this woman, enough to make it believable that Jennie French was indeed her mother. The same tensile strength, the narrow bones and perfectly carved features, the piercing brown-gold gaze, the age-defying beauty, the copper hair. Jennie wore her age with the same awareness and comfort as every other aspect of herself.

She said into the phone, "I agree with all those conditions except the first. That's my final word, Bart. Are we good? . . . Excellent. Write it up and send it to Lane." She cut the connection, handed the phone to her PA, and said, "No more calls."

"*Cosmo* is still asking about the shoot."

"I haven't decided. Tell them to get back to me next month." She offered her hand. "You're Danny, correct? Nice to meet you."

"Likewise, Ms. French."

"Let's go with Jennie, okay? Tell everybody on set."

"Will do."

"I'm sorry we're late. Traffic was unbelievable." She turned to where Kate was coming down the stairs. "We good?"

"I think this residence will suit you well, ma'am."

"Excellent." She offered Danny a professional smile. "I hate commuting. Especially with early hours on set."

"I'm with you."

"Where is everybody?"

"Setting up in Santa Barbara."

Jennie showed surprise for the first time. "We're shooting a location scene?"

"In ninety-three minutes," Danny replied.

"Where are my pages?"

"You don't have any lines."

"Costume?"

"If you don't mind, I'd like to shoot you dressed exactly as you are right now."

She looked down at herself. "I've been in these clothes since daybreak. I'm a mess."

"They fit the scene perfectly." Danny glanced at his watch. "We don't have a moment to lose."

30

MEGAN WAS STANDING outside Santa Barbara's Soho Music Club when her old pal from K&K pulled up. Gary Landis rose from his dark grey Mercedes E350, waved the script pages she had sent him, and said, "This is real? You've got me hooked up with a speaking role?"

"Unpaid."

"Girl, pay is not the issue. Screen time is." Gary looked as excited as she had ever seen him. "I am definitely in your debt."

Gary Landis had been passionate about acting since childhood. He acted in the local LA theater and took whatever paying roles he could land. His winning smile had been featured in four different toothpaste ads. He was, in his own way, holding on to whatever shred of his dream came within reach.

None of this, however, was why Megan had invited him up. She circled his new car because it was expected of her. "Nice ride."

"The notice that I could order what I wanted just dropped out of the sky. Nobody's saying, but it appears your departure had its benefits for those of us still surviving the place." He studied her. "You look good, Megan. Relaxed."

"I'm too busy to relax, but thanks."

"You know what I mean." Gary wore what probably passed

for weekend casual back in Des Moines—light-blue jeans, a dress shirt, and a silk and wool jacket. Hand-stitched cowboy boots. He nervously fingered his collar and said, "I had always hoped, you know, we might have a chance."

"You need to move beyond that," Megan replied. "We don't have much time and we have a lot of ground to cover."

He frowned. "I don't follow."

"First I need to know that you can really hear me."

"Megan . . . Yes."

"I mean it, Gary. This is maybe the most important conversation we'll ever have."

His sky-blue gaze was clear now. "Okay. What?"

"There's a woman who's serving as my intro into the San Luis Obispo law practice. Her name is Sonya Barrett."

"Wait, you brought me here to talk about a *job*?"

"Just listen, Gary. Sonya was formerly the chief litigator at Wright-Patten. A junior partner. She almost lost herself in the process, so she left. And now she's a partner in the firm I've joined. And what I've learned from her . . ."

Gary was focused now. Intent. "What?"

"There's a different legal arena than what we've been led to believe is the only one dealing with film. And it's fun."

The bitter humor they all developed in order to survive surfaced now. "Girl, what drug are you on?"

"My new firm is made up of some very good people. And the work is incredible. There are no layers. I was told to go out and do whatever is required. I've spent my first week here negotiating a three-and-a-half-million-dollar film deal. No oversight except for what I request. They *trust* me."

Gary stepped back until he collided with the car. "Megan, we're talking San Luis Obispo. I mean, how much farther in the sticks can you get?"

"How happy has LA made you, Gary? How fulfilled are you at K&K?"

"This *is* a job offer. I don't believe it."

"Actually, it's not. It's too early for that. The business isn't in place yet. But I've been talking with these people. My new friends. Exploring the next step. And I've discovered . . ."

Gary's voice softened. "Tell me."

"I'll do better than that." Megan reached for his arm. "I'll show you."

———————//———————

Jennie French was clearly a woman comfortable with silence. She had not spoken since they'd left the hotel. Her gaze swept Santa Barbara's State Street scene. Finally she asked Danny about the alternate accommodation he'd had in mind.

"It's the only place in Solvang that offers anything like a suite," he replied. "The building was recently gutted by its new owners and turned into large studios. It's nice. Nothing fancy, but the best this town has to offer."

Jennie said, "Kate?"

The security woman caught Danny's eye in the rearview mirror. "How many doors open onto the street?"

"Seven." It was a standard question from stars and their retinues, one Danny had fielded many times before. "There's also a private parking area and pool behind the main house."

She turned to Jennie and said, "I can guard you better where we are now."

"Let's stay with Thrashers Ridge for the moment," Jennie said. "What a name."

Evelyn spoke for the first time. "The thrasher is a bird."

Jennie did not show any surprise at her PA having the answer at hand. "Really?"

"Native to California. It prefers thick brush and often goes unseen even by people who know where to look." Evelyn's voice was pleasant enough for a monotone. Danny suspected very little could shake this woman's calm. "Solvang used to have thousands of the birds living in neighboring forests. Now the flock is restricted to the ridge owned by the hotel."

Jennie went quiet and did not speak again until they were driving along the Santa Barbara Harbor. "So how does a young film producer come to own a hotel?"

"That needs to wait," Danny said. There was nothing to be gained by adding that it had to wait because he didn't have any idea. "You're on in less than half an hour."

31

THE SOHO MUSIC CLUB was becoming known as the premier live jazz locale between Los Angeles and San Francisco. It regularly pulled in acts that went on to become huge international sensations. The food was good, the atmosphere relaxed and electric, the stage and music systems and lighting all professional quality.

They entered the club by way of the kitchen. The staff was gone, and the steel counters were filled with remnants of a buffet-style dinner. Michelle had laid out a special meal and invited only longtime customers. Danny had agreed to pay for the meal and the bar bill, which was going to be substantial but far less than what renting a restaurant and filling it with extras would have cost.

Then there was the matter of their unexpected bonus, which was the result of their dinner at Robin's. The reason Michelle had wanted to speak with Danny after the meal. The reason he kept wanting to break into song.

Danny had expected Greg to be in the kitchen, ready to prep Jennie. But as they entered, Annie rushed through the doors leading to the restaurant and said, "Hi, Ms. French. Annie Callow, writer. Danny, Greg needs another fifteen minutes. There've been issues with the lighting."

Danny didn't care about that so much as what Jennie thought about not being properly greeted. If Annie noticed his concerns, she didn't show it.

"The run-through looks great. Consuela is a natural. The locals are behaving." She started back through the swinging doors. "Greg asks you to start prepping."

As the door swung shut, Jennie demanded, "You're using locals as volunteer extras?"

Danny felt her displeasure and agreed. "They've all signed waivers, and they're being paid. Sort of."

"And this Consuela?"

"Consuela Reyes is the focal point of this scene. She's been acting in commercials and local theater since she won a beauty contest as a teen. She worked most of today with Annie and Greg and Alex, getting ready for your arrival. It's good, Jennie. Really a solid scene."

Jennie crossed her arms. "I didn't agree to this gig for a dose of community theater."

"Something major and totally unexpected is happening out there," Danny replied.

She could have melted the swinging doors with her glare. "I'm listening."

"Word is spreading through this entire region about our project. The response has been . . . well, incredible is the only word that works for what's going on out there."

"I hate working with local extras," she said, still glaring at the doors. Danny decided that was better than enduring her heat directly. "They're unruly. They insist they know better. They grow impatient. They chatter. They blow scenes."

"We agree. But this is different. Jennie, they're not here because of you."

She turned to him. Silent now.

"Emma and her mother are genuinely loved around here. We're only now learning what that means." Danny gestured at the door. "Michelle has turned her restaurant over to us for free. On a weekend night. We're paying the locals with a quick buffet and some drinks. Anybody who doesn't behave is expelled. But that's not the best part. Michelle is lifelong friends with Randy Willis."

"Willis, the jazz pianist?"

"Right. He's agreed to accompany Emma tonight. We're doing it now because Randy leaves tomorrow for two weeks, touring in Canada."

The news eased Jennie's tension. As well it should. Randy Willis was one of those rarest of breeds, a jazz musician whose fan base crossed all sorts of divides. He had written three scores for films, one of which had been an Oscar finalist and another that had won him a Grammy. The last time he and his band played in Los Angeles, it had been to a sellout crowd in the Hollywood Bowl.

Jennie asked, "Where is Emma?"

"In an apartment upstairs. Consuela and her husband live there."

"Why?"

"Consuela is both the head bartender and assistant manager." Danny waved that aside. "Greg thinks it's important from the story's standpoint that you not meet Emma until after tonight's scene."

She circled back to, "So Randy Willis is doing a cameo. Tonight. And you don't want me to have any lines?"

Danny nodded. It was the right question to ask. "Get ready for round two."

32

MEGAN WATCHED GREG move about the restaurant, ordering people and lights and camera placements with quiet authority. She had come to know several directors because she had begged and pleaded to be allowed on set. Most K&K attorneys had laughed at her request and assumed she was starstruck. But that wasn't it at all. Megan wanted to make film her life, and studying what happened on set was all part of the package. She shared what film professionals knew and never talked about. That there was an energy to the process of bringing a story to life. So strong it survived the tedium and the exhaustion and the stress.

Megan thought Greg handled his job with the skill of a good football quarterback. The guy who relied on everybody and made them feel equally vital to the success of their next play. He talked calmly, he repeated himself until he was certain things were getting through, then he moved on. When he stepped over to where she and her friend were seated, he asked, "What's your name again?"

"Gary. Gary Landis."

"Megan has vouched for you, Gary. She assures me you can carry the scene. You'll be front and center, and we don't have time for multiple takes. Understood?"

Gary swallowed. "I'm good to go."

"Okay. Watch for my signal." Greg moved on.

Gary glanced at Megan, both nervous and excited. "I wish there was some way to tell you what this means."

Greg addressed the group encircling the bar. Steady, calm, defying the storm he was in the process of creating. "We're going to shoot a scene based on the history of Thrashers Ridge, which Annie has turned into script. Consuela will tell the story, supported by several others around the bar. Your job, Gary, is to respond like it's the first time you ever heard what Consuela is about to reveal. And Alex here will serve as Consuela's goad. So you follow his lead even though you're front and center. Is that clear?"

"Crystal."

"That's my guy." Greg turned to Alex. "The second camera will play off you the whole time. You're a pro. Tell me you know what to do."

For once, Alex rose to the occasion. "You're asking me to play the weary local. Man, this is what I live for."

"Just don't over-egg the custard. We need to get this in one take." He looked across the bar at Consuela. "What's the first rule?"

"Don't ever look at the camera," she said.

"Right. Now here's what I want you to do. You're going to flirt with Gary here, right in front of his date. And to make this real, you're going to treat Megan just like you do the camera. She's there, but you ignore her entirely."

Consuela smiled at her. "Sorry in advance."

Megan smiled back. "You little thief, you."

"Pay attention, Consuela. Here's the key. I want you to focus all your energy, all your powers of flirtation, at the people beyond the camera lens. That's what makes a great scene. No matter what the line or who your partner is, you're really trying to get the audience to dance with you."

If Consuela was the least bit nervous, she did not show it. "I can hear the music already."

Greg turned and raised his voice. "Okay, everybody. You know your roles. Waiters, serve the tables. Michelle, go manage. Patrons, talk and flirt and have a good time. What's my first rule?"

The restaurant spoke with one voice. "The camera isn't in the room."

Greg clapped his hands. "This is a take."

33

THE CLUB was a brick-walled cube, with a forty-foot ceiling and the acoustics of an old-fashioned music hall, which it once had been. Back in Santa Barbara's first heyday, when the stars retreated here to escape the spotlight's glare and the newshounds' cameras and do whatever, the Soho Club had been one of their favorite haunts. The stage had seen numerous impromptu late-night sessions starring the likes of Sammy Davis Jr., Harry Belafonte, Frank Sinatra, Dean Martin, and scores of others.

Gary delivered his first line just like Greg had instructed. Talking casually, his arm draped over the back of Megan's chair. With his gaze locked on Consuela, tracking the lovely bartender's every move. Megan's job was to stay silent and fume.

Gary asked, "So what's the big deal about Thrashers Ridge?"

Consuela picked up the shaker and began mixing a drink, taking the time to flash a look Gary's way. The entire restaurant was lit for the cameras, but the spotlights were all directed upward. The ceiling was high enough to spread out the illumination, diffusing and softening the effect. Even so, Consuela's gaze flashed with the sheer pleasure of knowing she had another captive male. "That's a locals-only sort of story."

Alex was seated on the horseshoe-shaped bar's opposite side. He snorted and tossed back the rest of his drink, which was supposedly bourbon on the rocks but was actually iced tea. He supplied his line on cue. "In case you hadn't noticed, this is California. Take away the folks from someplace else, the tumbleweeds would be rolling down Main Street."

The next time Consuela danced back in front of Gary, she pointed to Alex and said, "Allow me to introduce Signor Escalofriante."

"I have no idea what you just said," Gary told her.

"Mister Spooky there," Megan said. "His family owns Thrashers Ridge."

Gary was into it now. "You're actually telling me you think the hotel has a real live ghost?"

"I don't think, I know," Consuela retorted.

Alex asked, "Are we actually having this conversation?"

"I am," Consuela replied. "Don't know about you."

Alex demanded, "So have you seen this thing?"

"Don't call Skipper a thing," Consuela replied. "It's disrespectful."

"Which means your answer is no."

"I haven't ever seen an atom either. But I know it's real."

"Here we go."

Gary asked, "Who's this Skipper?"

Consuela snapped at Alex, "You give me that face one more time, I'm gonna dump you on the street."

"I didn't say a thing."

Consuela huffed and turned back to Gary. "Look here. Back when this place was young, there was this ship's captain. His name was . . . oh, what was it now . . ."

Alex rattled the ice in his empty glass. "Wainwright. Richard Wainwright. And he wasn't a captain. He was a smuggler."

"They were pretty much the same thing back then. Those were lean times. Very lean. Wainwright smuggled because he had to." Consuela sparkled with the simple joy of having all eyes on her. As she moved to refill Alex's glass, the entire bar shifted with her. "The Skipper worked the California coast, but he kept coming back to Solvang because he'd fallen in love with a local girl."

"Amaya," Alex said. "A real looker."

"Amaya's descendants are still down there in Monarch Valley," Consuela said. "There was this one guy, a rancher's son. Maybe ten years older than me. But a real heart stopper when he was young."

Alex offered, "That would be Rinaldo."

Consuela turned her martini shaker into cymbals. "Aiyee, Rinaldo. *Pedaso de cielo.*"

"Piece of heaven," Alex offered. "Not anymore. He's still got the ranch next to Thrashers. Doubt he's been in a saddle recently. Hard to find a horse that'll carry three hundred and fifty pounds."

Megan studied the man seated around the curve of the bar. It was astonishing how Alex had become transformed by the presence of cameras and lighting. There was no flamboyance to his gestures, nor much inflection to his voice. Even so, his every word carried a magnetic draw.

Consuela lifted two iced goblets from the freezer, set them on a tray, added fruit, then poured the shaker. "Anyway, Amaya got tired of waiting for the captain to leave the sea. She married the rancher."

"Named Rinaldo too, as it happens," Alex said.

"So when the skipper finally came home, he discovered his *amante* had married somebody else. Which bent him totally out of shape."

"Wainwright bought this big stretch of land not far from Amaya's new home. Two hundred acres. Plus the lake and the ridgeline."

"Then he built himself that huge place."

"Pretty much a palace," Alex said. "Nicest home south of San Francisco at the time."

"Then he just sat there all by himself."

"All those bedrooms rimming that huge parlor he designed as a ballroom. For a party that never happened."

"He liked to climb the ridge so he could look down over the ranch where his Amaya lived. Never went back to the sea, by all accounts."

"Never set eyes on the ocean again, is what I heard." Alex shook his head. "Wainwright stayed landlocked for the rest of his life. Because of a woman who didn't love him back."

"And he waited, year after year," Consuela said. "He's still waiting."

Alex snorted. "Come on."

"A hundred and eighteen years he's waited," she insisted. "He died there after living down the road from his beloved for forty-one years."

"Who stayed happily married all that time," Alex said. "To Rinaldo."

Gary delivered his final line. "That is just wild."

Greg stepped forward. "Cut. Great job. That's a wrap."

The whole restaurant applauded.

34

WHEN GREG FINALLY entered the kitchen, Danny thought he handled himself very well. He was too busy and too involved in the evening's shoot to be deferential. He spoke to Jennie as if they were just working another scene, one of many. "Your role tonight is crucial. It's the turning point at the start of act two. Up to this moment, you've been pretty much swallowed by the loss of your husband. Emma is the glue that's held you together."

Jennie thought that over, then nodded. "Go on."

"You weren't going to come tonight. Emma begged, but in the end you refused. Going out in public is just awful. People care for you around here. They all offer you sympathy and want to help, and they're kind and they—"

"Make things worse." She nodded again. "I believe I've sung that tune myself."

"Right. So Emma told you she was going to come here and play—her first public gig. And you said no way. You actually didn't want her to come. You argued with her."

"She came anyway." Jennie gave a tight smile. "I like her already."

"The lines are Annie's, but the attitude is totally Emma's. So she's going to carry her sorrow up onto the stage. Despite your refusal to come watch her breakout performance, she's excited about this incredible opportunity."

"Randy's playing himself?"

"Right. Back before he broke into the big time, Randy and Michelle used to be an item. Michelle owns this restaurant. Randy plays here from time to time, the sort of secret gig that's passed around between old friends. He uses these visits as an opportunity to return to his first love of jazz."

"Modern renditions of big-band swing. I read about that somewhere," Jennie said. "We all need a time to remember the reality of small-time roles."

They shared a quick smile before Greg said, "Thanks so much for the chance to work with you, by the way."

"You can thank me when it's in the can," Jennie replied. "But you're welcome."

"Right. Back to tonight's scene. Randy has accompanied Emma several times, thanks to Michelle. In our story, he has arranged tonight to help Emma learn how to handle audiences, which is where she belongs. On the stage, in the spotlight."

"She's that good?"

"That's what drags you down against your will. Needing to see this for yourself and decide."

"So how do I respond?"

Greg shook his head, refusing to answer. "There's a place for you at the bar, beside your brother-in-law. You sneak in and sit beside him."

"Alex. The wastrel. The guy who . . ."

"You both love and hate. Right. He waves you over."

"And then?"

Greg smiled. "Annie and I have gone back and forth. We can't decide."

"So . . ."

"Play it as it lays," Greg said. "We'll shoot a couple of takes and see what works best."

35

MEGAN WOULD HAVE PREFERRED to have this conversation outside, in the open. Away from the myriad of eyes that now tracked Gary. Everyone in the restaurant now assumed Gary was one of the actors. But she had to go with what she had. She touched his arm, drawing him back to earth. "We need to talk."

He sparkled with adrenaline. "What do you call this?"

"I call you a guy flying about as high as he possibly could without pharmaceutical assistance."

He laughed. "You got that right."

"I want you to land, Gary. As soon as we finish the next scene, I'm going to have to go back to work."

"We're not working now?"

"No, Gary. For me, this is an interlude. The only one I'll have tonight." She poked a finger into his shoulder. "Pay attention."

"Ow, girl."

"Oh, get real." But she saw he was smiling now, his gaze alert and with her. "Two things. They're not connected. You do the first or not, it's okay. The second, my offer, still stands."

He lost the smile. "Offer?"

"First my request. Remember, if you don't feel it's workable, I understand. Truly." She sketched out the mystery of Brandon's appearance in Lawrence Abbott's office.

Gary was intent now. Frowning. "Legend Partners doesn't do television."

"That's why we're discussing it at all," she said. "Trying to understand what's below the surface."

"There have been rumors Legend wants to branch out. You know how it is. Everybody's trying to ride the Netflix train."

"But this isn't Netflix, Gary. We're talking about a project with Chambers, the new cable kid on the block. Low budget, small audience, super tight timeline."

"You want to know if there's an ulterior motive."

"There has to be. I want to know *why*. And who is actually behind this, both in the firm and inside Legend."

He pondered the ancient brick wall. "I might be able to check into that."

"But only if you can stay safe." Megan saw Greg emerge from the kitchen and knew she was running out of time. "Back to what we talked about outside. I want you to think about coming to work with me."

"Megan . . ."

"I know all the reasons why this isn't feasible, believe me. Two weeks ago I would have recited them all myself. Well, maybe not. I was ready to leave."

"Could have fooled me."

"I hated the place. And I suspect down deep you do too."

"Hey. Arrogant bosses, actions that skirt the fringes of legality, hyper-competitive associates, LA-size egos, backstabbing, high attrition." His smile was canted now. "What's not to love about K&K?"

"What I want you to understand is, none of those things you just listed exist in my new professional home."

"You haven't been there long enough to be certain of anything."

She nodded. "You're right. It could all be a ruse. One day soon I'll walk in and the evil genie will spring out of the broom closet. Then I'll be back in the same-old. Only now I'm trapped in San Luis Obispo." Megan leaned forward. "But what I'm seeing is a totally different approach to law and to serving our clients."

"Service," Gary said. "I remember that word. They mentioned it in law school."

"And something more," Megan said. "My new firm expects me to *define* my role. If there really are film production companies moving north, I'll need help to make this happen. I want you to be part of my team."

Gary studied her with the same focused intensity he brought to trial work. The reason why she had loved partnering with him on cases. The reason why they were having this conversation. "I'll think about it."

Greg chose that moment to clap his hands and call for quiet. He ran through his instructions quickly this time, clearly trusting his actors and all the volunteers to get it right. He positioned the actors, checked the camera positions a final time, then called for action.

When the two people emerged from the stairwell, Gary was almost knocked off his bar stool. He waited for the trailing camera to pass him to whisper, "That was Randy Willis."

"Right. Shh."

The world-famous musician appeared centered and calm and utterly professional. A number of the locals applauded as he and Michelle approached the stage up by the bay window. The welcome was totally unscripted, but Megan thought it suited the moment very well.

Randy kissed Michelle before seating himself behind the piano. Michelle leaned over, rested a hand on his shoulder, and spoke into his mike. "Tonight we have a special guest . . . I'm sorry, what was your name again?"

Randy waited until the laughter faded, then launched straight into his first song, a solo rendition of Bobby Darin's hit "Beyond the Sea." He was then joined by a couple who rose from the front table. The woman took a companionable hold on a double bass, and the man seated himself at the drum set. Together they swung smoothly into a song made famous by Judy Garland, "Come Rain or Come Shine."

In the middle of that song, Megan saw Alex wave at someone in the restaurant's entrance behind her. She did not turn around, but the knowledge of what was about to happen caused her heart rate to accelerate. It was silly being so excited over a star's arrival. But she couldn't help it. She pretended to focus on the music as Jennie French slipped through the tables and approached Alex. When Gary let out a faint whuff of surprise, she was ready. She prodded his arm with one finger, a subtle gesture but enough to draw him back into focus on the music. And just in time, for trailing behind Jennie was the close-up camera, there to capture the moment when Alex slipped from his chair, embraced his sister-in-law, and offered her his stool.

The song ended, and Megan watched as Alex said, "I'm glad you came."

Jennie was not scripted to respond, but she glanced in confusion at the crowd and the applause, then asked, "Why am I here?"

Alex showed a pro's ability and reacted as the broken brother-in-law, the guy who was rendered only half a man by the guilt he carried and the drink he held. He took a slug of his iced tea and pointed his sister-in-law's attention back to the stage.

At that same moment, Randy gestured to someone at the restaurant's far end. A second rustle of anticipation filtered through the rooms.

Emma stepped forward.

Normally such low-budget projects only used one camera crew. Costs grew exponentially when employing a second team because it heightened both the technology requirements and the staff. Even so, Danny and Greg had hired two additional teams from Santa Cruz who made their living shooting advertisements. Using locals as extras, having Randy Willis play, and being given the Soho Club for one night meant getting this scene in the can with a minimum of takes.

Three cameras were in action now, one stationed upon Jennie's face, positioned so that it captured Jennie's astonishment and Alex's slightly canted smile. Rick's main crew trailed behind Emma as she walked calmly through the crowd and stepped onto the stage. The third camera swept back and forth, panning the audience as they whistled and applauded.

The first camera operator then lowered himself to floor level, there to watch Randy as he handed Emma an alto sax. She wet the reed, positioned her fingers, then nodded. Together they gave the audience Kevin Cole's "All of You."

Megan was tempted to lose herself fully in the music. The sight of that young girl playing with three professional musicians was magnetic. The group formed a seamless flow, four instruments in sync. The restaurant lights gradually dimmed. The strongest illumination came from the table candles and a pair of spotlights over the piano. Randy's two accompanists remained in the shadows. When he was not singing, Randy leaned back so that he too became a half specter. It was a remarkable feat, this star's ability to reduce himself to a mere silhouette, as though what really mattered was not the man at all but rather his music. And the young woman. The night's real star.

As she played, Emma's gaze shifted back and forth between Randy's hands and his face. She did not even glance toward the audience. Her concentration was total. Then Randy looked at her and nodded once.

Emma turned and fastened her attention on the bassist. The woman's upper body rocked slightly, offering encouragement in time to her thumping melody. Emma began nodding in time to the woman and took flight. She played with such an emotional resonance that Megan did not realize she had gripped Gary's arm. Emma did not merely play her solo. She revealed her heart. She sang her youthful fire.

The solo's end was greeted with a spontaneous eruption that rocked the Soho Club.

Megan used the applause to look at Jennie. The camera was less than three feet from the left side of the star's face. She occupied the last stool around the bar's far side. Jennie's features showed an incredible blend of anguish and shock. Megan thought she knew exactly how the star felt.

Randy waited through the tumult, then offered the audience a rousing rendition of the Jimmie Rodgers hit "Kisses Sweeter Than Wine." Midway through, Megan saw Jennie reach up and clear her face. Her hands were incredibly unsteady. The streaks on her cheeks caught the light, smearing her skin with subtle rainbows.

The script called for Michelle to step forward and settle one hand on Jennie's shoulder. It was the simple gesture of a close friend. What was unwritten, yet totally worked, was how Consuela reached across the bar and gripped Jennie's arm where it rested on the bar. Alex stepped a bit closer and lifted his arm, but his gesture halted in midair, then he let his arm drop back down. They stood like that, the four of them, ignoring how almost everyone nearby watched them now. Megan found it incredible how such a silent act could bind the audience together, all of them sharing a supposedly secret tale.

Randy and his companions swung into Nat King Cole's "Almost Like Being in Love."

There had recently been a time when Megan had made a profession of never revealing her emotions. Sometimes late at night, when she had lain in her lonely bed and waited impatiently for another empty night to end, she had felt as though her heart held too many tears to weep. Now, as she found herself needing to clear her eyes yet again, it seemed as though this was not just a new job and a new place and hopefully a new love. Rather, she was being forced to redefine who she was. She felt as much as saw and heard Gary glance over and ask if she was all right. It was an uncommon act as far as LA went. But here the gesture carried the subtle flavor of new beginnings. Two friends swept up in music strong enough to seal out the world's problems. For this brief instant, the most real element was the manufactured sorrow of Emma's supposed mother.

When the song ended and the applause and whistles erupted, Megan watched Jennie rise from her stool, shrug off the hands of her friends, and slip away into the night. Megan did not follow the woman's departure. Instead, she focused on how the camera remained tight on the three faces Jennie left behind. Michelle and Consuela and Alex watched Jennie's exit with knowing sympathy. Megan found it astonishing in its force.

Then her attention was drawn back to the stage as Randy and his companions performed Keely Smith's "That Old Black Magic."

———————— // ————————

When the set ended, Emma left the stage the same way she had entered. She drifted through the restaurant, supposedly blind to the applause and whistles and smiles and accolades cast her way. She gave no sign she was even aware of the people who watched her passage. If anything, Megan thought the ovation somehow made her sad.

As Emma approached the exit, Megan saw Jennie step from the shadows behind the hostess station. Everyone in the restaurant watched as she draped an arm over her daughter's shoulders. Together they departed the restaurant, two shadow figures bound by a mystery that pulled at Megan's heart.

Then Greg stepped forward and clapped his hands. "Cut! That's a wrap."

Megan felt Gary jerk in surprise and was pleased to learn she was not the only one shocked by the forced return to reality.

"Thank you, everyone," Greg said. "Great job. You have fifteen minutes, then we'll shoot a second take."

36

AFTER THE THIRD TAKE, Greg declared himself satisfied and thanked the extras for a fabulous job. Randy Willis and the two accompanists hugged a smiling Emma. As the Soho Club emptied, Danny wound cables and remained at the periphery of the action. He watched Jennie accept the crew's greetings and congratulations. He watched Alex offer Emma what appeared to be genuine compliments.

He watched the handsome blond man hug Megan, who laughed at something he said and hugged him back.

The exchange lasted a few seconds at most. Danny knew if he asked her, Megan would have a perfectly good reason for having invited Gary to play a role in their first scene. She could no doubt explain the easy affection they showed one another. Perhaps it was a relationship that had come and gone. It didn't matter.

Danny knew his jealousy and fear weren't really connected to what he witnessed. Not at all.

He watched Megan bring the man over to where he stood. He heard her say something about them having worked together. Gary complimented him on the project, on Randy Willis, Jennie French, Emma's performance. Danny kept smiling as Megan guided Gary across the street and accepted another hug before he slipped into his Mercedes, started the car, beeped the horn, and drove away.

Danny watched the taillights recede into the distance and knew with utter certainty he wasn't ready. He couldn't handle love.

Over the next two days, Danny occupied a nether space. He was physically present for the twelve-hour shoots. He took care of everything that arose with calm efficiency. But a robot would have been more emotionally involved.

To make matters much worse, there were problems with Emma.

No one came out and said anything. But everyone knew. They spent the days shooting secondary scenes. Greg and Annie retreated each evening to his office, where they quietly rearranged the next day's schedule. Holding back on any deeply emotional work. Waiting.

Emma was pliant. She listened. She did what was asked. She followed Greg's directions. She hit her marks, she said her lines, but . . .

The scenes were flat. Dull. Changing the lines did not alter the result. Watching the dailies—the raw footage of a scene— was an endurance contest.

Danny had not slept more than an hour each night since the restaurant scene. His eyes felt grainy, but otherwise he was okay. In fact, the lack of sleep helped somewhat. It granted him a numbed space from which to observe himself as well as everyone else. Especially Megan.

Even when she was away, Megan's presence hung in the air, right there alongside the fact that Danny's past had come back to haunt him.

Dinner that third evening was a morose event. Emma and her mother left for a quiet night at home. Jennie was upstairs in her suite, fielding calls and handling work she had put off during the day. Alex was off somewhere being Alex. The rest of them gathered at the broad kitchen table where the hotel staff had formally eaten.

Megan was in San Luis Obispo, handling the myriad of legal issues surrounding any shoot. Everyone's eyes drifted occasionally to the kitchen wall clock. No one said anything. Speaking their thoughts out loud would only make the pressure worse.

The meal over, Danny bid the crew a good night and walked back to his cabin by the lake. The lights in Alex's cabin were on, and Danny saw a lone silhouette pass in front of the side window.

The fatigue was a massive weight he carried down the path and up his three steps and into the front room. He lay down on his creaky bed and stared at the ceiling. Waiting for the sleep he knew was not going to come.

When his phone buzzed, Danny was tempted not to answer. He was afraid it would be Megan and he would say the wrong thing. Or the right thing. He could not even say which it was anymore. What he wanted, what he should do, how he should handle things . . . The list of impossibles stretched out into the night.

The readout said it was a blocked number. So he answered.

When Danny heard the voice, he felt as though he had been waiting for this call ever since getting out of jail.

JR said, "Let me explain."

37

WITHIN THE SPACE of those three words, Danny's night crystallized with a hard brilliance. He carried the phone outside, went down the walk turned pewter by the rising moon, and stood at the lake's edge. Studying the dark liquid mirror.

JR asked, "You there, bro?"

"Don't call me that."

Johnny Rocket responded with a hyena's laugh. "You gonna hear me out?"

"Go ahead."

"Truth is, man, I got tired of waiting."

Danny was fairly certain JR was stoned. The words emerged with a slight twist, like they were puzzle pieces JR had set into the wrong positions. He did that sometimes, showing up at the office after an all-night party, pretending he could hide his inebriation behind laughter and words that did not quite connect.

JR went on, "That screenplay I sent you."

"You were always sending me scripts."

"I'm talking about the last one. The only one that mattered. *Night Express*. You remember?"

"Yes." Danny had a near-perfect recollection of movies. He could see a film once, even one he thoroughly disliked, and ten years later he could recall every segment. Characters, scenic structure, much of the dialogue. "It was lame."

"See, man, that's the thing. I'm out there all the time, scoping the scene, finding us the gig that will put us on the map. And you act like your only job is to shoot me down."

Danny nodded. He had figured this was the issue, the reason why JR did what he did, and why it happened now. "We had an agreement."

"Sure, okay. But—"

"We would only move on projects that we both wanted to move on. And we would only move together."

"But you were *never* going to move, were you." A hint of the frantic rage surfaced. The filament at the core of JR's being. The one that burned so hot he hid it from everyone, most especially from himself. "Long as you kept shooting me down, you didn't have to risk a *dime*. You could sit there on your safe little sets, doing your little gigs, banking your safe little salary."

Danny saw no need to respond.

JR panted three times, building up. "You were *never* going to green-light a project. You ran from the risk. That's your job. Risk avoidance. When it came to *taking* a risk, you were a . . ."

Danny waited to see if JR was actually going to finish his sentence. But his former partner swallowed his last word. *Coward.* The unspoken thought hung in the night, as brilliant as the moon.

Danny said, "Why are we having this conversation?"

It was JR's turn to go quiet.

"You're in Cabo with our money. What were you going to spend it on anyway? Not even you could stuff close to a million dollars up your nose."

"I didn't . . . I went ahead with the project."

Danny felt as though he had just slipped away. Out of his body, away from the stress and the problems and all the impossible issues.

JR went on in a rush, "I set up a dummy corporation and

acquired the script. I started preproduction. Things were looking good, man. I signed two stars and a director, I had the green light from the Italians, the distributors at Sony gave me a preliminary offer. I was going to come back to you with all the pieces in order. All you had to do was sign."

Danny floated in disembodied ease out over the lake. He glided through the silver light. Weightless. Leaving his physical form and all the burdens there on the shore. Paralyzed.

"You know what happened, right? The Italians didn't just let you down. I was *this close*. Then they just . . . vanished. One day we were having lunch and talking terms. The next day they were *gone*." JR panted hard. Running the race of his life, all the way to Cabo. "What can I say, man. I freaked. I couldn't face you. I couldn't . . ."

Danny flew back and settled into his body. Trapped all over again. He repeated, "Why are we having this conversation?"

JR's swallow was clearly audible. "I'm back."

"You're where?"

"Here. LA. In every sense of the word. I was tracked down by Kleber and Klaufstein."

"Wait, what?"

"You know, K&K. The big-league law firm found me in Cabo and offered this lifeline. One of their major clients has made a firm offer for the project. Danny, I'm looking at a letter promising an initial up-front payment of a cool mil. Which means I can put back everything I . . ."

"Stole."

"But it's only valid if we both stay on as producers."

"That doesn't make sense."

"There you go, playing the assassin. Danny, they like us. This is our *chance*. We're being offered a producer's gig for a film with a budget of eight million dollars."

Danny turned from the moonlight and the night's freedom. "Who is K&K fronting?"

"They haven't said yet, and won't until we sign. I know this is a major ask. But man, if you could just set this aside . . . You can have my take. But you've got to talk with the prosecutor. Get her to drop the charges. Do that, sign on with me, and your money is back in the bank, Danny. We can pay off all the outstanding debts, leave us ready to step inside the big tent."

Danny cut the connection. He stood gripping the phone with both hands, trying to sort through the tempest and find not just the answer but the truth. Because one thing he was certain of above all else.

He was missing something major.

38

MEGAN DID NOT LEAVE the San Luis Obispo offices until after nine that evening. The day's stress felt wrapped around her like a concrete overcoat. She had brewed a cup of green tea for the journey, but it rested in the central console untouched. She had not eaten anything since breakfast.

The ribbed asphalt ran straight through fields for a time before winding its way around the Santa Rita hills. Megan liked coming home this way. She probably needed to sell her condo in Westwood and find someplace in San Lu, as the locals called it. But Megan felt no great rush. Her parents clearly liked her being home, and the drive between Solvang and San Lu was manageable. She also knew it was good not to need to worry over this now. Her dance card was already too full.

Her phone rang as she was on the final approach to Solvang. "This is Megan."

Gary asked, "Where are you?"

"Almost home. It's been a long day."

"Is this phone secure?"

Megan pulled up to her parents' home and reversed into the drive. She wanted to focus on the outside world for whatever came next. "I have no idea."

"Is this your company phone?"

"I kept the number, but I turned in the device. This is a new one." When Gary remained silent, she demanded, "What's the matter, Gary?"

"Something's going on. I asked one lady about the project Brandon put forward, and it was like I poked a stick into a hornet's nest."

Megan stared at the night. Hills cut a sloping silhouette from the eastern skyline. She rolled down all her windows and sat thinking.

Gary went on, "Here I thought I was being careful. I only asked my first supervisor, someone I thought I could trust to be discreet. The next thing I know, Aaron is in my office, breathing fire."

Aaron Seibel. Her former boss. "What did you tell him?"

"The only thing that came to mind was that I'd heard a rumor about something big going on with Legend Partners. And if it was true, I wanted in."

"Nice move."

"Yeah, it's amazing how fast the brain works when overdosing on adrenaline and fear."

"What did Aaron say?"

"He freaked. Demanded to know who had talked. I said I couldn't be certain, it was just office gossip. He asked if it was Brandon. I've got to tell you, I was tempted to say yes. But I couldn't do it. Aaron warned me that if I wanted to keep my job, I wouldn't speak about this to anyone, and left."

"When was this?"

"About an hour ago. Long enough for me to stop shaking."

A night bird called and another responded. Quick bell-like chirrups. "I don't understand."

"That makes two of us." Over the car's speakers she heard a gunning engine. She assumed Gary was on the freeway, heading up Mulholland Drive's steep incline. He had a hillside condo overlooking Studio City. "One thing I know for certain.

Aaron wouldn't get this worked up over a small-time television gig."

Megan liked how Gary was not running from the threat. It said a lot about the man. "I agree."

"When the office went quiet, I did a little trolling through our database. Legend's average budget for the features it shot last year was twenty-eight million. It has a new television arm, but right now it's working on just one pilot for NBC. The budget is six mil."

"Chambers would never put up that kind of money," Megan said. "Or come anywhere near the audience numbers that sort of budget would require."

"The number I'm calling you on is a throwaway. You're the only person who has it. Call me outside office hours."

"Gary . . . this is above and beyond."

"Hey, the acting gig you set me up for was just off the scales. And then your offer of a job—"

"It's not a job yet."

"I know. But still. Someday I hope I can tell you how much it meant, having you single me out."

"I think you just did," Megan replied. "Be careful. Stay safe."

39

MEGAN WAS SO TIRED she left her phone downstairs in the front hall. She did that on rare occasions when she assumed someone would try to interrupt her rest, which she desperately needed. She made a salad of easy colors—as in, everything handy—and ate standing by the rear windows, staring at her reflection in the dark glass. She was half asleep before she started climbing the stairs.

Megan woke the next morning ready to face the day. She glanced at her watch and saw it was not yet seven. She'd hoped to sleep longer, but the hours had done their magic and she felt rested. The banked-up fatigue was still with her, but she had been living with that ever since moving to LA.

She entered the kitchen, greeted her parents, and accepted a mug of coffee. Hummingbirds flittered about the three backyard feeders, their wings flashing gold in the sunrise. The flowers glistened like an Impressionist oil, which meant her mother had been out already, watering them before the sun grew too hot.

Her mother said, "Your phone's been buzzing like an angry hornet."

"Which is why I left it downstairs." Megan drank more coffee. She felt as though she was trying to listen beyond sound. Her awareness was often like this before entering the courtroom.

At such times, being able to detect the unseen foe was vital. The opposition was constantly trying to upend her case, attack from the high grass. Megan could not yet see the hunters. But the conversation with Gary had confirmed that they were out there. Her job was to find out why, discover their weakness, and turn them into prey.

When her phone buzzed with another incoming call, Megan was ready. Which was very good indeed, because when she picked up the phone, the readout said Aaron Seibel.

She stood looking at the screen. Her former boss had never phoned her. Not once in four and a half years. If he'd wanted her, he'd used the nearest minion to issue a summons.

She touched the screen. "This is Megan."

"What is this, you're playing hard to get? With *me*?"

"What can I do for you, Aaron?"

"Look, I'm going out on a limb for you. The partners were adamant that we deposit your career in the nearest dumpster. But I know a good thing when I see one. So I fought for you."

Megan saw her mother step into the kitchen doorway, no doubt drawn by the sudden shift in the home's atmosphere. The subtle charge before the storm erupted. Megan waved her away, then seated herself on the stairs leading up to her bedroom. "I'm listening."

"Junior partner. Your own client list. Two associates assigned to you full-time. How does that sound?"

"It sounds like I'm missing something."

"Excuse me?" Aaron sounded impatient. "This is the point where you thank me."

Megan pondered the carpet by her feet.

"You're too good to lose, Megan. I did my magic and convinced the partners—"

"If you want me back, I'm going to need some answers," Megan said. "Call it a good-faith measure. To show me this is a real offer."

It was Aaron's turn to go quiet.

"Starting with Legend Partners," Megan said. "They're one of your clients, right?"

Aaron did not reply.

"I want to know why one of Hollywood's biggest independent studios would be fighting over television scraps. With Chambers Broadcasting, of all people. And with a timeline that—"

"I will *bury* you. Is that what you want?"

Megan lifted her head. Sunlight and shadows glinted off the windows on either side of the front door. A breeze caused the tree limbs to shiver such that they scripted a dark message over the glass. There and gone.

"Take my offer or don't. That's your call. But if I even *think* you're going after Legend, I will ruin you."

This was the boss as she knew him. Aaron Seibel was a brawler by nature. He thrived on conflict. He lived for the chance to take down an opponent. This was why the associates assigned to him lived in a state of perpetual fear. Knowing he could turn on them at any time.

"You do *not* want me as an enemy. I will—"

"Thank you for calling," Megan said, and cut the connection.

When she did not move, her mother returned to the doorway and asked, "Everything all right?"

"Thinking."

Her mother walked over. "Give me your mug. I've always found coffee helps the brain accelerate."

"Thanks, Mom." When her mother retreated, Megan phoned Rand Bethany at CBC. They had been talking a couple of times each day. Rand had visited the site twice and mostly remained a silent presence throughout. In return, Megan did her best to keep Rand in the loop. "Is our meeting with the ad execs still on?"

"Eleven o'clock, two days from now. Head of marketing is going to try to be there as well."

"Could you check on something? I need to know if Legend Partners is still trying to muscle in on the Valentine's Day project."

"So . . . you're asking a favor."

Megan smiled. She liked dealing with a woman who laid it out in black and white. "A big one. And there might be blow-back if somebody learns you're asking."

Her mother returned down the hallway with a fresh mug. But as she handed it over, something outside their front door caught her eye. Sarah straightened and crossed the foyer, still holding the mug. "Danny's here."

Rand said, "In that case, I need some specific reason why I'm nosing around."

"I don't have one." Megan stood and stepped up next to her mother. Danny stood where the front walk met their driveway. Staring at the house. Not moving. "Find out what you can. And be careful."

When Megan pocketed her phone, Sarah asked, "Why won't Danny come in the house?"

"I have no idea."

"Did you two have a fight?"

Megan didn't bother responding. She opened the door and started down the walk.

Then it hit her.

This was another element from her courtroom days, when she detected vital bits of information long before there was any logical reason or concrete evidence. Megan knew she was a good trial attorney, and she also knew this sixth sense was part of the reason why. Once, when she was waiting to take evidence from a police detective, the woman had referred to it as a spider sense. Megan's spider sense was working overtime as she walked down the front path. She could see the shadows in Danny's gaze, identical to the ones he had revealed in the San Luis Obispo conference room and again outside the Soho Club.

By the time she halted in front of him, Megan knew exactly what she had to do. The message was clear in his expression.

If she let Danny speak, it was over.

Megan said, "I have something to say, and I want you to stay silent until I'm done."

She found a distinct assurance in how calm she sounded. Somehow her racing pulse and electric tension were utterly masked. She had to remain detached here. That was her role. To be the person who remained untouched by the storm Danny had brought with him. She knew she was being manipulative, and she didn't care. She would do anything to hold on to a shred of hope. She already cared for him that much.

"There can never be anything romantic between us, Danny."

The shock of hearing Megan say what he had clearly come to tell her shoved him back a step.

Megan did not give him time to recover. She tracked him move for move. "You show up here after another episode of whatever it is that's rocked your world. I don't know what happened, and I won't *want* to know."

"Megan—"

"Be quiet, Danny. I'll tell you when it's your turn to talk. Right now your job is to *pay attention*." She moved in closer. "I'm falling for you, Danny Byrd. Hard. But I can't be in a relationship with a child."

"I'm not—"

"Yes you are, and I told you, be quiet and listen. You've said it yourself, how you battle against problems you've carried since childhood. And that's what brought you over here today. It's not me. It's your past. That makes three of us in this relationship, and that's one too many. Do you understand what I'm saying? If you want to be involved with me, you need to *be a man*." Megan jabbed a finger back at the house. "Do you think my parents would call their love perfect? My mom lives with the uncertainty that there might not be many more tomorrows . . ."

The emotions almost caught her then. Megan had to turn away, clench herself up tight, and gasp for control. When she was certain she could maintain an exterior calm, she turned back. And in that instant, she knew she had done right. The shadows were gone, at least for the moment. And Danny's raw pain was revealed.

"I know you're hurting. I know you carry scars. And I want to help you. But to do that, you need to *let me in*. Not just when things are going your way. In the hard moments too. When it's rough, and you're scared, and the world is against you. I can't make you do that, Danny. And I can't shout against all the noise in your head."

He whispered, "It's so hard."

"You want hard, you march inside my home and see my dad and my mom struggling against reality. That's hard. This is just part of growing up. And that's what you've got to do, Danny. I'm here for you, but only if I know, I *know*, that you're there for me. You have got to move beyond these barriers and *commit*."

Megan knew it was time to stop. It was like a courtroom drama. Leave the jury wanting more. She stepped back. "I'll see you through this project, and then we're done. Unless you decide to change, Danny. For good. And for *us*."

40

DANNY DROVE STRAIGHT back from Megan's home to Thrashers Ridge. He entered the main room as Greg was finishing up with the first scene's preliminary work. Cameramen, sound, lighting. Evelyn and Robin and one of the grips were serving as stand-ins. Annie waved to him from the doors leading to the kitchen and started over. Everything normal, save for the fact that Megan had completely obliterated his internal world.

Danny felt as though his brain had been frozen in neutral by what she had just said. He had struggled with himself outside her front door. He had mentally repeated the words and the reasons why they needed to hold to a professional relationship and nothing more. And then she had marched out and blasted him where he stood by giving him exactly what he had come looking to say. Leaving him so numb even his thoughts had gone silent.

Annie said, "Emma is freaking out."

Danny opened and shut his mouth twice. No sound emerged.

"You know what's about to happen. We're shooting the first highly charged scene today. Emma is terrified."

Danny reached for the mug Annie held. He took a swallow and grimaced. He forgot Annie used coffee as merely a vehicle for sugar. But at least the shock reconnected him with his voice. "Greg is director. He's in control."

"Come on, Danny. Get real." Annie glanced behind her, making sure they weren't being overheard. "Greg can't handle her. You know that as well as I do. He needs your help."

Danny nodded slowly. Not so much at Annie's words as at the realization that he should have already seen this for himself. That was what he was best at. Handling problems before they surfaced.

His mind circled back to Megan's confrontation, and the simple fact that she was the one who had just handled things.

While he was coming to terms with the new reality, Annie steered him around. "Now go work your magic and let's save this thing."

Danny slowly crossed the main room, disconnected from everything, including himself. Megan's absence formed a vacuum at the core of his being, one so huge it threatened to swallow him whole. The loudest sound was that of her voice, the one that was no longer part of him. She had shut him out. Her face was there before him now, the disappointment and hurt and longing eating at his empty space like acid.

The love.

She had been forced to speak of a growing love for him. Because he would not, could not, do what she wanted and needed.

Open up.

Greg waved the cameraman away and tried to smile at Danny's approach. But his smile was strained and his gaze was tight. "Missed you at breakfast. You go see Megan?"

Hearing her name caused the empty space to burn. Danny shifted to one side in a futile effort to dodge the incoming blow. "Annie says Emma is having a hard time."

"She . . ." Greg sighed. "You've seen the dailies."

"Yes."

"Then you know. And so does she."

"Where is her mother?"

"Working from home."

"And Jennie?"

"Upstairs. I told her to kick back, let us go through a couple of runs with Emma on her own. Maybe, you know . . ." Greg sighed and ran his hand through his hair.

Strange how Danny could be standing there talking about one thing, yet his heart was resonating with an absolute certainty that the two things were actually one. The problem with Emma, the situation with Megan—they were the same. Which was impossible. But logic played no role here.

Danny said, "Maybe I could help."

Greg only revealed his frantic state now. "Would you?"

"Greg, you're the director. I'm breaking all the boundaries even suggesting this."

"We're in new territory for us both."

"So, if she's willing . . ."

"Do it. Whatever you can. Green light all the way."

"Where is she now?"

Greg pointed at the stairs. "In her room with the door locked."

As Danny started up the stairs, the cosmetician met him with, "You going to see Emma?"

"Yes."

"She told me to go away." The woman was in her early sixties and bore a veteran's unflappable air. Even so, she glanced up to the second floor and shook her head. "Poor kid. She said nothing I did to her face would help make things right, not where it mattered."

As Danny walked along the upstairs balcony, he glanced down to see all the eyes on set tracking his progress. He knocked on Emma's door.

"Go away."

"It's me. Danny."

There was a longish pause, punctuated by an absolute stillness down below. Then the door opened a crack. Emma's tear-streaked face peered out. "What?"

"Can I come in?"

She stood there for a time, then opened the door a fraction more and looked behind him. "Who else is out there?"

"I'm alone."

She turned away. Danny followed her inside and watched her make a teenager's boneless slide onto the carpet.

Emma moaned. "Just shoot me."

He pulled over a chair and seated himself. The loudest sound he heard was the echo of Megan's refrain, demanding that he let the world in.

"Here's what I think," Danny said. "We've got two possible tracks we can follow. The first is, you stay at the same level you're on right now. We reduce the number of lines you're required to deliver. We play off you rather than keep you in the spotlight. The only time this would shift is when you're playing music. Then you're front and center. The result will be a solid piece. It won't win awards, but it will be more than anyone could realistically expect, from you or from us. We will deliver as promised."

Emma did not move. She did not even appear to be breathing. But Danny was fairly certain she listened intently. He glanced over and saw that Annie had taken up a position in the doorway. Not intruding but letting them both know they were not in this alone.

He went on, "The downside is clear. We came into this expecting to launch you into stardom. Having a lackluster early effort won't stop you from making it later. But it won't be the vehicle that we were hoping to create. The surprise that blows everyone's socks off. Yes, that's a disappointment. But as far as the outside world is concerned, we've still delivered. You need to understand that, Emma."

"I'm letting everyone down."

"No one feels that."

"Yes they do."

"Emma, look at me. Please."

Danny waited. Finally she rolled over, cushioned her head on one elbow, and looked his way.

"Remember what I said earlier. Everybody on set is a pro."

"Everybody but me."

"They see how hard you're trying. They like you, Emma. They want you to succeed."

"I can't make it work like I want."

"I know. Will you sit up, please?"

She unwound and slid over to where she could rest her back on the bed. "I want this so much."

"That's exactly what I needed to hear."

"But I *can't* . . ." She was halted by Danny's upraised hand. "What?"

"Acting is a terribly difficult process. Most people simply can't make the transition. What you're being required to do is leave your definition of reality behind. Right now you're trying to do this from the outside in. That's what my gut is telling me."

"Maybe you should take an antacid."

"Humor. That's good. What you need to do is take a different approach. Accept that the Emma Sturgis reality does not work under the lights. Walk away from it entirely. Become this other person."

"But Greg keeps telling me—"

"Forget Greg. From this point on, it's just you and me."

"Really?"

"If you want."

"Yes, Danny. I want. A lot."

"Okay. Good." He rose from the chair. "Let's get to work."

41

DANNY LED EMMA DOWN the stairs and between the behind-camera people. He halted in front of the canvas chair with Emma's name pinned to the back. As he passed Greg, he asked, "Can I borrow your chalk?"

"What? Oh, sure."

"Thanks. Come on, Emma." He waved to the cosmetician and said, "You need to start on her right now." As the woman rushed for her kit, Danny said to Greg, "Go ask Jennie to come on down here."

A voice from behind the lights replied, "No need."

Danny turned back to Greg. "From now on, you shoot the practice take. You get one more. Max three, and only if Emma asks. Otherwise it's two and done. All close-ups except hers are handled after she leaves the set."

"But . . . Okay."

Danny turned back to Emma. The young woman's eyes could not have been any bigger. "Did you hear what I just said?"

"Greg has me practice my lines six or seven times."

"And that's not working. So we're going to take a different course. There are some really famous actresses who shine brightest on their first take."

"Really?"

"Yes, Emma. I've been watching you, and I think that's part of who you are. So before you come downstairs from now on, you and I will run through your lines."

"I'll help," Jennie called.

"See? There are a whole host of people here who want you to shine. No, don't you dare cry. You'll mess up all that work she's doing on your face."

"You're mean."

"Tell me about it." Danny knelt and drew a circle around where Emma stood, big enough to include the canvas chair. He rose and asked the cosmetician, "Are we about done here?"

"Sounds to me like an order."

"You were listening. Good."

"You're right, hon. Mean as they come." The cosmetician sprayed Emma's hair and whispered, "Just knock him out for me, will you?"

Danny waited until Emma was focused intently on him. There was a visceral connection between them now. Danny saw his own hollow core echoed there in her young gaze. It hurt him doubly, sharing this sense of absence. He shook himself mentally and pointed at the chalk line. "This is you. Emma Sturgis. You are locked inside this circle. Every time you feel like Emma starts to resurface, you return here."

"I don't get it."

"You will. Remember what I said upstairs?"

She scrunched her face. "I'm acting from the lines in. Or something like that."

"Precisely that. And it ends now. We both know it's not taking you where we all want you to go."

"So . . ."

"Now we're going to change things around. No, Emma. Don't look at Greg. From this point on, it's just you and me."

"And whoever I'm acting with, right?"

"No, because Emma is not going to be out there at all."

Danny saw the realization register and liked how it added to her intensity. "First things first. Behind the camera, outside the lights, it's just you and me. Any question, you ask me. Any concern, you discuss it with me. Tell me you understand."

"Yes, Danny."

"Okay. Good." He turned to Greg. "Where's her mark?"

Wordlessly Greg walked over and stood at a point midway between the reception desk and the first line of sofas. "She enters from the kitchen and stops here."

Danny turned back. "You and I are going to start a new rhythm. We'll come downstairs and run through the scene together. Not the lines. You have the lines down pat. That's never been the issue."

"But I keep flubbing them."

"The issue is not the lines," Danny repeated. "What's bothering you is how you don't *own* them. You're speaking something Annie wrote and not living them." He pointed at the circle. "All those problems are here. Inside this circle where Emma stays. What we're going to do now is build a new you. The character who lives *outside* this circle. Out there in the lights. Ready?"

"I think . . . Yes."

Something caught his attention. A brief shift in the space beyond his field of vision. A change in the unseen winds. Danny looked over just in time to see Megan enter the front doors. The pain was so intense he almost lost it. The control, the focus, the young woman who trusted him to make things right. He breathed deep, then again.

When he was ready, he turned back to Emma and said, "Now close your eyes."

The set was astonishingly silent. A good film crew developed the ability to turn off every possible source of sound, even breathe quietly, when the cameras rolled. During a take, all their collective energy was focused on the actors and the set. They were bound together like that now.

Danny said, "I want you to think of a secret that has recently rocked your world. Something you haven't told anybody. But you know it's had a major impact on who you are." He gave that a beat. "Now open your eyes. Do you have that in mind?"

She looked at him and nodded.

"Okay. Now I want you to look out there where the lights are brightest. Out there, it's only your character. So what I want you to do now is take your secret and change it. Make it into *her* secret. Something that has rocked *her* world. Ready?"

"Yes."

"Good. Now close your eyes and make it happen." Danny waited through a half-dozen heartbeats. When Emma reopened her eyes, he walked over and stood beside her mark. "As you exit the circle, you leave Emma behind. Once you leave that circle, everything about who you are stays in there. You make this transition by thinking about the *new* secret. The one that is hers, that forms your link. Your job is to be your character. When we start shooting, *your character* will enter through the kitchen doors and come over and stop here. By the time you hit this mark, the change is complete."

She watched him. They all did. Careful, cautious, focused. The energy was intoxicating.

Danny went on, "Every day, before we start shooting the next scene, we're going to build another segment of this bridge between the you inside Emma's circle and the new you. Each scene only has time for one emotion. There is room for just one secret thread. So before each scene, you and I are going to do an exercise like this one. Gradually you'll build a new emotional state, one to replace everything that you're about to leave inside Emma's circle. You're creating a new tapestry of emotions and the past. The lines you speak will be a natural outflow from this new you."

In his peripheral vision, Danny saw Annie cover her mouth with both hands. Greg reached over and draped one arm over her shoulders.

"Do you need to run through your Emma secret again?" Danny asked.

"No." Her voice sounded stronger now. More certain. "I know it."

"Good. So close your eyes. Think about your character. There is a secret she carries. Something she's only just discovered. Something she's never told anybody. But it has rocked her world. *Your* world." Danny gave that a long beat. "When you're ready, open your eyes, take a firm grip on the secret thread that you use to weave the new you. Then step outside the circle and go make a movie."

42

MEGAN'S NEXT FOUR DAYS were a blur of frenetic action. Danny's plan was working. Everybody on the set remained almost afraid to say anything, even think that they might have turned the corner. But with each take, every passing hour, and all the new dawns, the certainty grew. Emma made mistakes. A lot of them. But the flavor of a real story grew into something very real.

They were making movie magic.

Since their confrontation in Megan's drive, she had not spoken directly with Danny. Her work brought her into the hotel every day, but she dealt exclusively with Robin. It had become clear in the manner of movie osmosis that she and Danny had argued. People knew. Anyone with half a brain could see the wounded looks the two of them shared. But the clock pushed them all so hard, everyone silently accepted it and moved on.

The third day after their driveway confrontation, Greg pulled Megan aside to report that Rick and Annie and the soundman had all been contacted by their agents and offered hugely lucrative new gigs starting immediately, but only if they broke off their work for Greg. The offers had come through K&K, who claimed the new project was a feature film financed by Chinese money.

Greg went on, "Annie wouldn't dream of walking away. The others . . ." He rocked his hand from side to side. "Probably not. Since you've got them tied up with contracts, they had no choice but to refuse."

"Interesting," was all she said. But what she thought was, *First the carrot, now the stick.*

———— // ————

The story Annie had written was centered upon reality. When she heard this, Megan took the structure to CBC's legal team. After two days of discussion and argument and gentle pressure, the Chambers attorneys finally agreed that the marketing division could trumpet the film's new logo: *Based on true events.*

Throughout this entire period, Lawrence Abbott had continued to sow poisonous rumors wherever possible.

Rand Bethany's first big assist was to bypass Lawrence entirely and go straight to the company's sales team. The ad execs did backflips over the news that they actually had a product to fill the Valentine's Day primetime vacuum, then again when they heard about the true-events logo. Audience preferences were cyclical, and just then true-to-life was a big selling point. According to Rand, Lawrence actually punched a hole in his side wall when he heard the news.

The following Monday, Megan and Lane Pritchard arrived at CBC's headquarters. Rand had arranged a meeting with the heads of ad sales and program marketing. They presented a rough edit of what could potentially become the film's first trailer. The sixty-second spot included two brief glimpses of Emma's performance at the Soho Club. Her music formed the background for the entire piece. Alex supplied the spoken overview. The final climactic shot was of Jennie's unscripted departure from the restaurant, arm over Emma's shoulders.

As Lane put it afterward, they'd succeeded in creating the first-ever silent thermonuclear explosion.

Megan left the Chambers executive building with Rand Bethany. They crossed Wilshire and walked up Beverly Drive, passing some of the most expensive shops on earth, and entered a bistro-style restaurant called simply The Farm. Rand was well known there, which meant they snagged one of the six outside tables.

As they were seated, Megan's phone rang. She checked the readout and said, "It's our bookkeeper, Emma's mother."

"No problem."

"I won't be long." Megan touched the screen. "Hi, Robin."

"Two men just left my home. They're private investigators from Los Angeles."

Rand saw the change to Megan's features and demanded, "What's wrong?"

Megan held up one finger. She said into the phone, "Please tell me you got their names and badge numbers."

"Of course."

"Wait, I need pad and pen." She reached for her purse, but Rand was faster. "Okay, go ahead."

Robin read them off. "They're with Blackwater and Associates. I called after they left and confirmed that. Do you need their office address?"

"No." Megan felt her pulse accelerate. Three types of PIs worked the greater Los Angeles area. The largest segment by far was the bottom-feeders, low-rent private detectives who trolled for the salacious and the rotten. Next up the ladder were former police officers and their associates. Megan's former firm had kept two of these on retainer. The third group was by far the smallest, an elite order of six high-end firms that specialized in intelligence gathering, corporate espionage, and guarding the rich and famous. Blackwater was a boutique company that focused exclusively on servicing the Hollywood studios.

She did not have any idea what this meant, nor did it really matter. She could sense her prey coming into view. Almost. "What did they want?"

"They told me I should be extremely worried, letting Danny Byrd anywhere near my daughter."

Megan's heart rate sped up faster still. "Give it to me word for word."

"They said they were building a case of fraud and financial misconduct against Danny, and in the process they had uncovered evidence so troubling their client ordered them to warn me."

"Did they say who their client was?"

"No. I asked them four times. They refused point-blank."

"Okay. Go on."

"They asked where Emma was at that very moment. They made it sound like she was in immediate danger. They asked if I could be absolutely certain she was being properly supervised, and how I could be so sure she was safe. They even suggested I was a bad mother, leaving her on set."

Megan's note taking became so jerky she could not fit the words into the lines of Rand's notebook. "Which one accused you?"

"Both. They were a tag team. They didn't say anything outright."

"I understand."

"And they sounded rehearsed. Like they had practiced their lines before they showed up."

Megan set down the pen and closed her eyes. Running through the elements. Looking for the unseen. It was how she prepared for a case. Allowing the puzzle to take shape in the dark recesses beyond conscious thought. When she was ready, she opened her eyes again. She liked how Rand watched her, the purple streak and the overly styled clothes masking a bright and determined young woman. She liked how Robin waited in silence, granting her time to move through the high grass. Hunting. She liked how she could claim her concern was simply in service of a client.

Even when she knew it was not true, for the moment she could place her turbulent emotions and her painful yearnings to one side. Almost.

When she was ready, Megan asked Robin, "Anything else?"

"As they were leaving, they made a casual reference to the case they were building against Danny. Like it was an offhand comment."

"They were avoiding any hint of libel," Megan explained. "What did they say?"

"That you got Danny off on a technicality. They said it worked in a criminal case. But their client was going to bring civil charges and make them stick."

"I wish they'd try," Megan said. "I'd have them for lunch."

"Danny is lucky to have you in his corner."

"I don't need to tell you all this is bogus, do I?"

"Of course not," Robin said. "What's going on?"

"Motive. We need to know why this is happening."

"What can I do to help?"

Megan hesitated, then said, "My gut is telling me it's tied to the hotel."

Robin went quiet. "I am specifically ordered not to talk about that."

"Which is why I need you to call Sol Feinnes. Tell him exactly what you told me. Tell him I think all this is somehow connected and it's time to reveal everything he knows."

After Robin cut the connection, Megan shut her eyes and compressed the phone between her hands. She felt as though the day was whispering secrets, but they remained just beyond her ability to hear and understand. She heard Rand order them coffees, the voices coming from a far distance.

The confidentiality surrounding the ownership of Thrashers Ridge, Danny's trial, the film project that almost didn't happen, the involvement of Legend Partners, and now this—a scripted warning passed to Robin, one that was clearly nothing but a lie.

All of it connected by threads Megan could not identify. Yet. But she knew the links existed. She was certain of it. Danny's only hope of safety lay in her identifying . . .

Danny.

Megan opened her eyes.

Rand waited until the waitress returned with their coffees to ask, "Will you tell me what just happened?"

"Yes," Megan said. The setting was not ideal, but the time had come. "But first I need to bring in Lane."

Rand looked worried. "I could move to another table."

"No. I want you both to hear this together." When Lane's assistant answered, Megan said, "This is Megan Pierce. I have a problem. Can I please take a few minutes of—"

"Certainly, Ms. Pierce. Lane said to put you right through."

The young man's response was enough to have Rand looking for her escape button. "Really, it's no—"

"Rand. Stay. It's time."

That was all Megan had time to say, because Lane came on and demanded, "What's up?"

Megan laid the phone on the table and gestured for Rand to lean in close. When she hesitated, Megan reached across the table and drew her forward until their heads almost touched. She said to the phone, "I'm here with Rand Bethany from CBC. I want to lay something out. Give you both a chance to draw your own conclusions."

"Shoot."

When Megan finished relating the conversation with Robin, all Lane said was, "Fascinating."

Rand pushed her untouched latte to one side, totally into the conversation now. "I have to ask you about Danny Byrd."

Hearing his name like that should not have hurt Megan like it did. "Danny is squeaky clean."

"It's a valid concern," Lane said. "You're absolutely sure about that?"

"I checked. Extensively." Megan related the search she had done for Pei-Lun Zhang. "Danny Byrd is one of a kind."

Rand said, "Sounds like a guy on the rise."

"He should be," Megan replied. "If he can catch a break."

Rand nodded slowly. This close, the banked-up fatigue and tension that formed the LA imprint was evident. "You think Legend is involved? That's why you asked me to check?"

"I have no real evidence," Megan replied. "But my gut says yes."

Rand continued to nod. "Larry found out I was asking questions."

Lane said, "Larry Abbott?"

"He called me in. Demanded to know why I was asking about Legend. I said the name had come up in relation to the project I was handling. He threatened me with firing. Said nothing would save me, not Danny and his team, not Lane Pritchard, nothing."

Megan said, "I'm so sorry. I should never have asked—"

Rand waved it away. "I'm tired of being afraid of Larry."

Lane said, "All right. Where are you now?"

"The Farm on Beverly."

"Stay there. Don't move. Have a meal. This could take a while."

When Lane cut the connection, Rand asked, "What just happened?"

For the first time that day, Megan had a sense of absolute rightness. "Things just got kicked up to a new level."

43

MONDAY AFTERNOON Danny walked the path around the lake. He was accompanied by seven others, all the crew who were not laying the groundwork for that evening's shoot. Toward sunset they were filming a crucial location scene. Annie walked alongside Greg, their heads together as Annie shaped the next scene in the air between them. The story had solidified now. She was coming up with two new scenes each day, sometimes three. Her writing was now approaching the climactic third act. During rehearsals and meals, sometimes in breaks between takes, she and Greg gathered so he could do the initial read-through and supply comments, like now. Annie was in her element, her face perpetually wreathed with an adrenaline glow so strong her feet scarcely touched the path.

Every now and then, Emma smiled at Danny. Seeking the reassurance he had been offering on a fairly constant basis. What he had not told anyone was how brutally raw these days had become. The more Emma opened up and trusted him, the more affection he saw in her gaze, the more he missed Megan.

Her absence was a wound that sometimes made it hard to breathe. He no longer tried to tell himself that she had only done what he had intended, that he should be grateful, that it was for the best. His burdens were too heavy. He could not be bothered to carry lies as well.

The idea hit him where the path started up the slope. He motioned Emma on ahead, waited for the others to pass by, then scrolled down his contacts and dialed the number. He did not hesitate because he didn't want to give himself time to think up all the reasons why this was a terrible idea.

When Megan's mother answered the phone, Danny started with an apology. "I'm really sorry for bothering you—"

"Oh, don't be silly. I can't count the number of times I've lifted the phone and started to call you myself."

Danny found the swirl of confusion already begin to settle. "Really?"

"Yes, Danny. Do I sound like I'd make something like that up?"

"No, it's just, Megan and I . . ."

"Oh, I know all that. And the reason I wanted to call you was to say you're still welcome here." A voice rasped from the background. Sarah paused long enough to say, "Danny is the one who phoned me, Richard. I'm not meddling. I'm being a friend."

When the voice didn't respond, at least so Danny could hear, Sarah went on, "Danny, can you come for dinner? Megan's just called from LA. She's been held up, some unexpected meeting. She'll probably stay the night down there."

"We're shooting a sunset scene. I could maybe stop by after."

"Come whenever you like. I'll have a plate ready."

———————— // ————————

When they arrived at the sea captain's grave, Danny held back, wanting to gauge Emma's reaction. He had been up here four times early on, discussing how the place could be used in the story and setting up the basic structure. The grave was to play a crucial role, and what Emma did today was vital for the story's emotional tapestry.

Greg quietly discussed how he wanted to block the first scene they would shoot with Rick. For many young directors, blocking scenes was where they failed. It remained for many a terrifying component of their job, especially if they had difficulty putting their vision into language the actors could follow. Greg was different. He began the blocking process while he read the script for the first time. He entered into every new setting with the blocking process foremost in his mind. The result was that he blocked scenes faster than any director Danny had ever met. In television and on low-budget films, such speed was essential for success.

To begin the blocking process, the director needed to determine where the actors would be stationed. This was known as setting their marks. Once this was established, the cameras were positioned, then the lights. Only then could the actors be brought in and their moves worked out in relation to the cameras. This required a choreography as tightly arranged as a ballet. Actors, extras, equipment, lights, cameras—all had to move in perfect harmony.

Danny stood beside Emma, looking at the grave and ignoring the activity behind them. He was close enough to feel her tension and her heat. He waited for her to speak, giving her time.

Finally she said, "I've been up here so many times. Ten, maybe. And I never can toss the stone."

The captain's grave occupied the ridgeline's highest point, a rocky knob rising above the surrounding woodlands. The tomb's ceremonial fence was coated in candle wax. In some places the wax was half a foot thick. Hundreds and hundreds of candles, burned through countless nights, had added to the mystery of the grave itself. The entire area, tomb and earth, was blanketed by pebbles. Thousands of rocks, so many they formed a second burial mound.

To the west, beyond the grave site, the hills were burnished by the late afternoon sun. The ridge formed a meandering line that snaked off to their left. Birds flittered among the trees, quick flashes of jewel-like brilliance, then gone.

Emma took her cue from Danny and ignored the bustling activity. She pointed to a ranch house that probably dated from the same era as the hotel. "That's where the captain's love made her home. With the other man. Rinaldo. The one she married."

When Danny didn't respond, she led him around to where he could read the headstone. There was neither name nor date. The stone marker was the only component of the grave not touched by candle wax. The seaman's epitaph was five lines long:

> Cast aside all regrets
> So that ye might live,
> Toss away the bitterness that binds,
> Throw aside all anger ere the sun descends,
> Lest you join me here before your time.

Standing there beside Emma drew the words into razor-sharp focus. Danny felt they might as well have been written just for him. Carved into granite. Waiting a century for him to arrive.

Emma stepped away and returned bearing two stones. She placed one in Danny's hand. Then she tossed the other onto the grave. It landed with a soft click.

Danny looked down at her. He did not need to glance over to know Greg and Rick and Annie were watching them now. "That's exactly the sentiment we're after today. There will be two visits. We're going to shoot both today if the light holds. The first time, you and your mother will stand apart. Neither of you can let go of the rocks you hold. And the inability is a wedge that burns between you. The two of you have arrived up here, separated and apart. And then you leave apart. The tension between you needs to be evident without you saying a word."

Emma nodded. "The second time, we hold hands and toss the stones together. I like that."

"Do you?"

"Yes, Danny. I like it a lot."

He pretended not to notice her unshed tears. "What say we go make some magic."

As Greg phoned for Jennie, Danny slipped the stone into his pocket.

44

HALF AN HOUR AFTER Megan and Rand finished an early dinner, Lane's assistant called and told them to meet her in Harvey Chambers's office. They walked back down Beverly, crossed Wilshire, and reentered the CBC executive office building. From the instant they passed through the doors, everything seemed different. The glances cast their way, the immediate response from the guard/receptionist, the way all the CBC executives tracked their every step. Megan felt as though the air held a faint electric charge. Rand must have felt it as well, for when the elevators closed she released a tight hiss, like a kettle giving off steam.

Harvey Chambers ran his empire from a penthouse suite that occupied more than half the building's top floor. A vast outer office contained secretaries, senior staffers, and a waiting area that was clearly intended to host informal gatherings. The room's hexagonal shape was rimmed by interior glass, so Megan could observe a clutch of visiting producers pitch a story in one conference room while Harvey and two senior executives argued with a trio of architects standing before a series of electronic images of a vast campus.

Lane was on the phone when they entered. She waved them to chairs and continued her conversation.

Rand looked around and whispered, "I've never been here before."

Megan watched Rand do a little-girl scope of the elegant decor and the scurrying assistants and the busy world up above the clouds. It touched her heart. "You deserve better than you've gotten. So far."

The brittle exterior that had been baked into place fell away, and Rand looked at her. Really looked. "Thanks, Megan. That means a lot." Then a shadow passed over her features. "I better go check in. You know. With the guy running my life."

"Larry," Megan said.

"It's either that or pack my bags as soon as I descend back to earth." She tasted a smile. "If I'm lucky, he's off making somebody else's life miserable."

After Rand left, Megan stepped over to the windows facing Wilshire and gazed at the LA afternoon scene. From this angle, the fierce street-level world was invisible. All she could see were the tops of imperial palms and sunlit clouds and other penthouses. The air was fragrant with the scent of hundreds of fresh-cut flowers. Vases adorned every flat surface. All the ceiling lights were crystal chandeliers. All the carpets silk Persian. All the women lovely. All the speech musical.

She found herself thinking back to her first days in Hollywood, when she assumed doors to this level were all about to open. The day she had signed her contract with K&K, she had celebrated by purchasing a go bag. Of course, there had been the party and the fine dinner and the smiling faces of friends. Naturally there had been a man, handsome and claiming to care for her.

Megan stood there and watched another production team rush past, ready to pitch the idea that CBC had been waiting desperately to receive. She wished she could remember the handsome man's name. But the only thing that came to mind was the go bag.

Italian leather. Nine hundred and seventeen dollars. For an overnight suitcase. Megan had returned from her party and spent hours selecting items that went into her bag. Each article of clothing was intended to be perfect for the moment the call came through. The one that ordered her to drop everything and fly off immediately and seal the multimillion-dollar deal. The bag would rest in the credenza in her corner office. The room with the view over all of Hollywood. Her city. Her industry. Her time. It was coming. The go bag was an investment in the future that was hers to claim.

As she stood in Harvey Chambers's executive suite, Megan suspected she had already realized in those first heady days that her LA life would require an escape option. To pick up and leave her job, her life, and her relationships at a moment's notice. That mind-set would go a long way to explaining why her LA life had been held to such a superficial level.

Megan saw Rand step out of the elevator and resume her place at the corner sofa set. The young woman carried a whiff of scorched earth and clearly wanted a private moment to recover. Megan turned back to watching the electric rush of power that surrounded her. So many people trying desperately to dance to Hollywood's music. It was all they knew, the only thing they wanted. So they danced even when no one cared.

She could almost see Danny standing behind the camera, willing all the components to come together and make a film for CBC. He totally ignored the fact that some of their senior executives willed him to fail. Danny used what he had, playing from the hand he was dealt, doing the best he possibly could. If she were forced to name one trait that defined Danny Byrd, it would be his determined ability to make the best of what little he'd been given.

If only he could open up and let her help him.

Megan's yearning to join her life to his burned like a branding iron upon her heart.

Which was why the receptionist appeared rimmed by liquid crystal when she stepped in front of Lane and said, "Harvey will see you now."

———————————//———————————

Harvey Chambers was chubby and on the small side, a couple of inches shorter than Megan's five nine. He looked like a child's drawing of an ideal grandfather, with his gentle smile and feather-white hair and plumpish red cheeks. All except for the eyes. They shone with a piercing intelligence and all the warmth of two grey blades. His voice was smooth, cultured, and accustomed to holding power. "Lane, always a pleasure."

He ushered them to a corner suite of suede and silver. A secretary served coffee and tea in bone china so thin Megan could see her trembling fingers through the porcelain. Harvey and Lane exchanged a few pleasantries, then Lane said, "Megan, why don't you share with Harvey what you told me."

Harvey remained silent and unblinking through her recap. He kept his steel-grey gaze on Megan as he said, "You're making a big ask here, Lane."

"That was why I requested this meeting," she replied calmly. "So we could discuss precisely what is going on."

"To assist with this requires me to declare my position," Harvey said. "The issue involved is a crucial one. Up to now I've avoided coming down on one side or another."

"The clock is ticking," Lane said. "And some very good people's futures are in the balance."

"It's never been just about the Valentine's Day project."

"We have suspected that from day one."

"Not to mention how I'll be required to dismiss claims made repeatedly by one of my senior executives."

"Lawrence Abbott is a bad smell and you know it."

"Put that aside for a moment. You also want me to accept

that a growing number of accusations against Daniel Byrd, as both a producer and a human being, are bogus."

"They are," Megan said. "They're utterly without merit."

He turned from Lane to her. "I'm listening."

Megan started with the meeting where she met Zhang. She then took Chambers through a number of her subsequent experiences. The day-by-day summary was far more painful than she could ever have anticipated. By the time she made her last point, about the film crew's universal willingness to work with Danny again, Megan thought she sounded partly strangled.

To his credit, Harvey remained silently intent throughout. When she went quiet, Rand handed her a refilled cup of tea.

Harvey rose and walked to the window overlooking Wilshire. He said to the glass, "My senior team is split right down the middle. Gun to my head, I'd say Abbott's allies hold a slight majority."

Lane said, "They want CBC to buy its way into the big league."

He glanced over. "What have you heard?"

"Nothing, Harvey. Not a peep. But the signs are there for anyone to read. They are impatient for your ratings to climb. They think their only chance to swiftly raise audience viewing is to spend on talent. Buy the big names. Pay what they ask, put it down as a loss leader. Aim for a return to profit on future projects."

Harvey pondered the scene beyond his window. "They may be right."

"They may also have their own personal careers in mind. They could well be saying this for themselves and not CBC," Lane countered. "They need to show a dramatic climb in the ratings before they can jump to one of the bigger networks."

He nodded. "There is that."

"I've been in this business for a long time, Harvey. I've seen too many other big spenders come and go. You know the old adage. The most certain way to have ten million dollars is to invest a hundred million in Hollywood."

Harvey walked back and sighed his way into his seat. "Now you know why I'm not sleeping well."

Lane caught Megan's eye and gave a fractional nod. Megan took a breath and said, "You have an opportunity to build a strong partnership with Danny and his team. They will know you've backed them because I'll tell them. Loyalty breeds loyalty, Mr. Chambers."

Harvey studied her. "You make an interesting point, Ms. Pierce."

"It's Megan, and here's another. Let's say for the sake of argument that all the accusations against Danny Byrd have originated from the group that wants you to write the big checks."

Harvey remained silent and still as a poker star.

"The question you need to ask is why. What makes Danny so important that they would go after him like this? There can only be one answer. They see Danny as a genuine threat. It's not just that he has every chance of succeeding in delivering a solid product on time and under budget. It's more than this. Far more."

"I'm listening."

It was Megan's turn to rise and stalk the silk carpet. "Given half a chance, Danny would sign on for the long haul. Produce good films for budgets that permit the buyer to make a solid return. Build a loyal base and elevate the entire channel as a result. And if Danny is successful, it means CBC maintains an in-house lock on theme. Your company can develop a set of core concepts based on audience response. Not what some big-name producer or director tells you they're going to do. What *you* want. What your *audience* expects you to deliver."

He smiled at Lane. "My, my."

"The pretty head holds a far prettier mind," Lane said.

"Megan, are you interested in a job?"

"Thanks, but I'm happy where I am."

"Well, be sure to look me up if you change your mind." He rose and offered her his hand. "You'll have my answer tomorrow."

45

IT WAS AFTER NINE when Danny parked in front of Sarah and Richard's home, and the end of a very long day. He had not enjoyed a decent night's sleep in over a week. His back and neck throbbed. None of it mattered. The two scenes they had just completed were nothing short of solid. The entire crew knew it. The grips were still hauling gear off the ridge after an eighteen-hour day. Danny could almost hear their distant laughter as he rose from the car.

Sarah met him at the door with a swift embrace and led him to the rear porch. Richard shifted over and settled at the table while Sarah served Danny. She explained how Richard needed everything steamed or boiled or pressure-cooked to a near-mash consistency. Anything firmer risked him choking. Tonight it was a beef brisket so tender it flaked off Danny's fork. He ate three portions.

"This is great."

Sarah smiled as he added another spoonful of her homemade horseradish sauce. "Megan says I should use that stuff to peel varnish off the porch floor."

"She's a great lawyer," Danny said, trying to hide the impact of hearing her name. "She can be excused for having no taste in food."

Finally he had no choice but to lean back, set down his utensils, and admit defeat. "Wow."

Sarah refilled his glass, set his plate on the sideboard, and said, "You're welcome."

"Would you mind if I talked work?"

"Can you talk work." Sarah humphed. "You ate three helpings of my brisket and you pretended to like my horseradish."

"I didn't pretend anything."

"You can talk about anything you want, Danny. We want you to consider this your second home. Don't we, Richard."

"Friends," he said. "Regardless of what happens with Megan."

"Of course we want you two to work things out. But even if you don't, you're our new neighbor, and we like you for who you are." Sarah covered his hand with hers. "So talk work."

Danny told them about JR's phone call.

When he was done, Richard asked, "How long have you carried this by yourself, son?"

The man's final word almost cost Danny his control. "A week."

"You need to tell Megan," Sarah said.

He was about to object, say how their relationship was defined by the current project and nothing more. How he had not spoken with her directly since their conversation in the front drive. How . . .

Richard adjusted the plastic pipe connected to his nose. "Some burdens just can't be carried alone."

Sarah let the silence hold for a moment, then asked, "Has the thief called back?"

"Four or five times a day. I gave JR his own ringtone so I know to cut it off. 'Ride of the Valkyries.'"

Sarah shook her head. "Tell Megan, Danny. Tell her tonight."

"I thought, you know . . . I'd finish the film and then handle JR."

"You don't *handle* anything," Richard replied. "You *distance* yourself."

"Danny, I'm going to speak to you like you're my own son," Sarah said. "You're being an idiot. And I mean that in the most motherly fashion. A complete nincompoop."

"You're falling back on what worked before," Richard said. "This is different."

"You've spent your entire life carrying things alone. If you needed help, JR was there. You trusted him. He landed you in jail. Now he's back. And you want to *handle* the situation? *Alone?*" Sarah huffed softly. "Please."

Richard asked, "What do you want from this?"

Danny nodded slowly. It was the question that had plagued his nights. The answer was, he had no idea.

———————— // ————————

Danny returned to the hotel after midnight. He parked by the fence and started toward his cabin. Midway down the path, however, he stopped. The night was utterly silent, the air still. The lake's surface reflected a moon only a fraction off full. The surrounding hills shone pewter. Danny could hear Sarah's parting words as clearly as if she stood beside him.

You can't do this alone. The need for partnership is now.

Danny took the path leading up the hill. He turned on his phone's light, then decided he didn't need it after all. The moonlight was that strong. Four times he stopped and picked up pebbles as he hiked the empty path. Each time he named the stone. The first was for JR, the second for all the wrong people inserted into his early years, the third for all the wrong moves he had made with other ladies. The fourth . . . Danny was not certain why he felt it was important to carry one more rock. Future mistakes, perhaps.

The grave shone like an imperfect crown set upon a rocky skull. Danny stood at the perimeter for a while. It felt good just to be there, alone with all his regrets, and hope that it might actually be possible to turn away from the past. The old candle wax glistened in the light, rimming the grave with a history of ancient tears. He felt close to all those who had stood here before him and wished them well. One by one he tossed his stones, listening to them click and bounce before coming to rest with all the others.

46

AFTER THE MEETING, Megan saw Rand off to Solvang. She had to remain in LA in order to be ready if Harvey Chambers wanted to deliver his decision in person.

Megan turned off Wilshire and headed toward her condo, wishing she was driving to Solvang so she could sit down face-to-face with Danny. Talk with him heart to heart.

She ached to hold him.

She stopped by a favorite Korean restaurant on Melrose and ordered takeout, then called Robin, who had not yet managed to speak with Sol Feinnes about the hotel's ownership. Megan asked her to call back whenever she knew something, no matter the hour.

At her condo, Megan unpacked her solitary meal and watched the news for a while, but the words washed over her and left her untouched. She cleaned up her meal, took a long bath, then went to bed. She felt tired in her bones, like she often had in the middle of a long trial. Weary in a way that no single night's sleep could remove. She lay there for a time, wishing her condo was not such a lonely place. Her last thought before sleep was of Danny.

The phone woke her a little after midnight. Megan glanced at the screen, saw it was her parents' number, and in that one instant felt her heart rate go from languid to redline. She touched the connection and demanded, "What's wrong?"

"Nothing, except I've probably woken you up." Her mother sounded breathless. "I wanted to wait and call tomorrow. But your father insisted."

The words jangled around the electric pulse in her brain. "Mom, you're not making sense. Dad is okay?"

"I just said that." Her voice shifted. "I told you we should have waited, Richard. We woke her up."

Megan heard her father's hoarse response. "She'll want to be woken up when she hears."

Megan demanded, "Hears what?"

"Danny just left."

Whatever came next, Megan needed to be on her feet to hear it. She turned on the light and rose from her bed, taking her time now. "Danny was with you?"

"He came for a late dinner. We talked for hours."

"About what?"

"Honey, that man is so in love with you it brought tears to my eyes."

"Mom, we don't, we never . . ."

"Danny is trying his hardest to work through all the lifetime reasons to be alone. Your father and I just wanted you to know that there's hope."

Megan squeezed the space over her heart, trying to make sure it didn't break free of its cage and go flying off. "Should I call him?"

"Give it at least until tomorrow. That's what we think. See if he'll make the first step. If not, then yes. Tell him we spoke. You need to hear about JR."

Megan heard her father protest in the background. "Wait. John Rexford contacted Danny?"

"Yes, but that's not . . . All right, Richard. I heard you the first time. Megan, if he hasn't phoned you by lunch, call and say I insisted you needed to hear about JR. That's all, Richard, I'm not saying a single thing more."

Megan wished them a good night and stared down at her feet. She felt so weightless she needed to be certain she still managed to remain bound to the earth.

47

THE CALL WOKE DANNY from his first decent sleep in over a week. He fumbled the phone off the side table, dropped it on the floor, then bumped his head reaching for it. He checked the readout, saw it was not JR again, and answered with, "Ow. What."

"Is this Daniel Byrd?"

"Depends."

"This is Chief Wright of the Solvang Police. Are you Daniel Byrd?"

Danny swiveled his feet to the floor. "Speaking."

"We have taken Alex Cross into custody. He asked that we use his one phone call to alert you."

Danny was already up and fumbling for his clothes before the chief stopped talking. "What has he done?"

The chief had a rough-and-tumble voice and a sense of humor to match. "Your boy was arrested for wedging his fancy car between a park bench and a fire hydrant. What he ingested before that point is anybody's guess. From the state he's in, I'd say your boy has enough in his system to fell a rhino."

On a couple of shoots in which Danny had been involved, visits to the local police station had been almost commonplace. This time, Danny had to say, "Sorry, I don't know where you're located."

"Which is one reason why I'm happy to make this call," Chief Wright said. "You know the old Solvang Hotel on Main?"

"Sure."

"Take that left. Station is two blocks down on your right. Park in the gated lot."

———————— // ————————

The pre-dawn light filtered grey and feeble off to the east. As he started for his car, an idea struck. Danny stood thinking at the point where the gravel forecourt met the path leading to his cabin. The longer he studied the concept, the more he liked it. Finally he turned and started toward the hotel.

He climbed the stairs and knocked on four doors, one after the other. First Greg, then Annie, Rick, and finally the sound-man. When he faced all four sleep-tousled faces, he related what he had heard. Even before he started on his idea, Rick and the soundman were already back inside their rooms. While he and Greg and Annie discussed possibilities, the main door leading to Jennie's suite opened and Evelyn asked what was going on. Midway through his explanation, Evelyn interrupted to say that Jennie most definitely needed to hear this for herself.

That was the moment Danny decided that his idea might actually work.

He pulled out his phone and hit the speed dial. When Emma's mother answered, Danny gave her the bare bones. Even so, Robin was clearly wide awake by the time he finished.

She said, "You want to shoot it."

"If Alex is in as bad a shape as the chief said, it might wake him up."

"Kevin Wright is a good man and an excellent police officer," Robin said. "Did you tell him about your idea?"

"Not yet."

"Let me call him."

"Thanks, Robin. Could you also find out if Alex has been formally charged?"

"If Kevin didn't mention it, my guess is he's hoping to make this go away quietly."

"Bringing a film crew into his station couldn't be anybody's idea of quiet."

"You know what I mean." Robin thought a moment. "Do you want Emma there?"

"It could be a total waste of time."

"That's not what I asked."

"Then yes. If Emma could come, there's a chance, a very small one, that we could get something we could use."

From behind Evelyn, Jennie asked, "You want me too?"

"The time-wasting issue goes double for you," Danny replied.

"Won't be the first. By a long shot."

Greg said, "No makeup."

"Oh, please. Like this is my first time on location."

Annie smiled. "Yeah, Greg. Get real."

Robin said, "I'll wake Emma, then call Kevin."

Danny thanked her and cut the connection. "We leave in ten minutes."

Annie said, "Go make yourself useful, why don't you. Put on a pot of coffee."

48

CHIEF KEVIN WRIGHT was a large man in his late forties who held himself with a hunter's stillness. He made no move as three vehicles pulled into his fenced lot and parked. Robin stood on the station's third step, which brought her almost in line with the chief's head. She rested a hand on his arm. Emma stood just inside the station's entrance, watching the new arrivals over her mother's shoulder.

Danny took a moment to inspect Alex's ride. The Maserati was missing its front right headlight. The bumper was crumpled downward, as though the car frowned over its owner's behavior. A deep gash ran down the fender and passenger door.

Kevin's voice matched his build, deep and resonant. "I've been standing here making a mental list of all the regs we're about to break."

"You're a good man," Robin said. "And you're doing this for the right reasons."

Kevin shook Danny's hand, nodded in response to his thanks, then inspected each of the others as Danny introduced them. If he was impressed by Jennie French's appearance, he did not show it. "Robin tells me the guy inside isn't holding up his corner of the tent."

Greg replied, "So far, Alex is present in body only."

"He reads his lines like he's never seen them before," Annie agreed. "I wonder sometimes if he even knows where he's at or what he's acting in."

"Unlike Emma and Jennie, who are doing stellar work," Greg added.

Emma blushed.

"Alex Cross is a highly gifted pro," Jennie said. "Some of his earlier work was incredible."

Kevin asked, "So you're hoping this might just wake the boy up?"

"We want to try," Danny said. "This wouldn't be a single still photograph of Alex having a bad hair day. This footage could wreck his career."

"Not that we'd ever release it," Annie said. "Right, guys?"

Kevin studied them each in turn. "So how do you want this to go down?"

———————————— // ————————————

Alex's role as Annie had written it was ambivalent. He tried to stay sober. He wanted to do the right thing. Or rather, he claimed that was his desire. But when it came time to turn from his former ways, his excuses rang hollow. He mouthed them. Nobody on the set believed him because he was not putting anything into the lines. Even so, Alex suited the role they had designed, and the result was some very powerful scenes. But only because Annie had written the guy as he was. The character was a film version of Alex living on the edge.

Growing up, Danny had known a lot of guys who wanted to do good, and failed. But giving up on the rage or the hurt or the drug of choice was too big a step. They could be just as addicted to anger as they were to their high. It had come to define them.

Danny thought this was the case with Alex. He had tried to reach for the next rung on the Hollywood ladder. He had wanted to become a writer-director as well as a star. A few had accomplished this—Orson Welles, Clint Eastwood—but most failed. Alex could not handle the failure. He fell apart. And now he was stuck in a drug-induced idleness.

The station's front room served as both the reception area and a bull pen. Seven desks were arrayed behind the counter, only one of which was occupied. When they entered, a middle-aged deputy with a pie-shaped face, a solid paunch, and a widening bald spot looked up from his computer and said, "Jennie French. As I live and breathe."

Danny asked, "Is this where I post bail?"

Kevin replied, "We're a small town, Mr. Byrd."

"Danny."

He nodded. "We do what we can to make newcomers feel welcome. Especially when they're doing right by the locals and trying to make a home for themselves. If we can make this mess vanish, it'd be fine by me."

"Thanks, Chief. That means a lot."

Kevin gestured to his deputy. "Ken Crowder here is my second in command. Ken, you checked on our guest?"

"Ten minutes ago. He's awake enough to be holding his head and groaning."

"All the other cells are empty, which is the main reason I'm even considering what you have in mind," Kevin said. "Ken, you okay showing these folks down to the tank?"

The deputy rose from his chair. "My wife is just going to die."

Kevin took a step back and said to Danny, "It's all yours."

Greg stepped forward. "Jennie."

"Here."

"Your first mark is there in front of the deputy. Rick, you follow her."

Jennie asked, "What about Emma?"

Greg looked uncertainly at Robin. "You're sure you're okay with this?"

"We're fine. Right, honey?"

"Mom never lets me stay out this late," Emma replied. "I'm breaking all the rules."

"Don't get any ideas," Robin said.

"Okay, Emma, you step up alongside Jennie and follow her moves." Greg motioned to the soundman. "Wire them all up."

While the soundman fitted them with mikes and battery packs, Greg and Rick followed the chief back into the cells. When they returned, Greg's eyes sparked and Rick was grinning.

"Ready?" Greg asked.

The soundman said, "Sound check."

Jennie turned to Emma. "Pay attention and follow my lead."

"You sound like my mom."

The soundman said, "We're in the green."

"Okay, let's do this," Greg said.

49

THEY SHOT JENNIE'S ENTRY TWICE. The first time, Rick stood over by the doors leading into the rear cells. Jennie's face was set hard as concrete. She marched in, moving so fast she dragged Emma and kept her off balance. Danny knew that was her way of wiping away the girl's smirk. Jennie rushed up to the counter and demanded to know where he was, not even naming him. Just like a local might do, since her brother-in-law was well known for going off the rails.

The second time, the cameraman waited just inside the door and followed Jennie and Emma. Greg disliked the deputy's nervousness and the way it edged his words with a false formality. So between takes he told Ken to stay quiet and move like he had weights sewn into his uniform. The result was solid.

The deputy buzzed them into the bull pen, then hesitated on cue before opening the rear door. He asked Jennie, "You sure you want her with us?"

Emma replied, "I want to be here."

Jennie gave a weary shrug. "She's seen him like this before."

The deputy keyed the electronic lock and pulled open the steel door. The smell billowed out and was evident on both women's faces. Jennie had to pull on Emma's hand to get her moving. Perfect.

The deputy entered the rear hallway first, followed by Jennie and Emma. Rick sidled over to the left, his back against the cell bars, shooting with a shoulder-mounted camera. He used a single light attached to the rig, like a journalist team doing a quick on-site interview. It flattened the vista, erasing all depth of vision and etching the people in starkly unattractive lines. The soundman trailed behind Rick and held a boom above their heads. This external mike was crucial for balancing any ambient sounds.

Rick framed their progress with the cell bars as background. Emma kept holding back slightly, her eyes round as she studied the empty cells. Jennie appeared both impatient and angry as she kept tugging Emma forward. Her gestures said it all. *You wanted to see, now see.*

The deputy reached the steel door at the end of the corridor. He opened the sally port, checked inside, then said, "Your boy's not a pretty sight."

Jennie released Emma's hand and stepped forward. Emma hesitated, then followed her.

Jennie said, "Open the door."

It was only when the deputy fit the key in the lock that Danny realized he was sweating. Up to then, it had all been about Alex and the shoot. But the sound of clanking locks and the bars and the echoes resonating down the concrete hall took him straight back. His heart pounded and his skin turned clammy. He had never known the meaning of claustrophobia until that moment.

The door clanged as the deputy pulled it open. To Danny it sounded like a nightmare he only now recalled. He stood to the left of Rick and the soundman, with Greg in front and Annie behind him. They watched as Jennie released Emma's hand and stepped into the tank.

The disinfectant odor wafted back, causing both women to squint. Jennie played it like the pro she was. The normal reaction would have been to stop in the doorway, blocking the way. But Jennie stepped to the right, pulling Emma through the portal and over beside her. Rick slipped past, his movements swift and practiced and silent. He positioned himself by the left-hand wall. Only when the camera's light was stable and shining brightly through the door did Jennie step forward. Her features were tight, strained, and very tired. She wore a shapeless thigh-length beige sweater, so old it looked like a bathrobe. Below were drawstring khakis and rope-soled canvas slip-ons. The result was a weary woman looking down at a situation that almost broke her heart. Again.

Emma stepped forward and wrapped her arms around Jennie. Jennie responded by settling one arm around Emma's shoulders. The two of them finding comfort in each other.

Greg pointed at the floor by the deputy's shoes, silently ordering the police officer to remain precisely where he was. The deputy leaned against the door frame and crossed his arms.

The tank was a windowless cement cube. The floor, walls, and ceiling were all painted a dismal greyish green. The floor angled slightly toward two central drains, and six steel benches lined the walls. A steel toilet and sink were embedded in the left corner, near where Rick stood with the camera.

Alex was a mess. He sat on the rear bench, his head leaning against the wall. His hair was spiked on one side, mashed flat on the other. His shirt was buttoned to his neck, but a rip ran from his right shoulder to his rib cage.

Jennie's voice was flat and harsh as the light. "You promised me you were going straight."

Alex slowly lifted one hand, as though the effort required all the strength his body had left. He shielded his eyes and groaned. "Turn it off."

"You *promised* me." Jennie pointed to Emma. "You promised *her*."

Only then did Danny realize Alex was weeping. "Please. Don't."

The emotion was too real, the pain etched into Alex's features too raw, to be faked. The reality caused Jennie to hesitate.

Emma released her and slipped forward. Jennie reached out to her, almost drawing her back, but stopped before she touched Emma's shoulder.

The girl walked over and settled onto the bench beside Alex. "It's okay."

"It's not." Alex jammed the heels of both hands into his eyes. "I'm so sorry."

"Promise her you'll stop."

"No more lies." Alex heaved an awful breath and dropped his hands. His face was wrenched by an ancient's agony. "I don't know if I can."

Emma was the calm one now. The one who defied her years. "What if we helped you?"

Alex huffed. Then again. "You'd do that?"

"We both will. We *want* to."

He looked at her. Or tried to. "Why?"

"Because." Emma touched the tattered fabric over Alex's heart. "There's a good man in there. Trying to come out."

Alex stared at her.

"It's what Daddy would have told you," Emma said.

Alex wiped his face, struggling for control.

"Ready?" she asked.

He nodded.

Emma rose to her feet. "Let's go home."

50

MEGAN PULLED INTO the Chambers basement lot at a quarter to eight. Harvey's secretary had called her forty-five minutes earlier and given her an assigned space. She was fairly certain it was the same space where her boss had always parked. Her Suzuki looked out of place among the Aston Martins and Mercedes. She shared the sidewalk with four execs, all of whom gave her the sort of tense inspection that suggested they knew why she was there.

The building's ground floor contained a boutique coffee shop. This time of day, virtually all the clients were Chambers employees. Which made the fact that Harvey Chambers was there waiting for her all the sweeter. He asked what she would have, then sent an intern scurrying for her cappuccino and muffin.

When they were seated in the coveted corner table, he said, "Thanks for joining me."

"Harvey, as far as I'm concerned, this beats champagne and caviar at the Polo Lounge."

"I wouldn't go that far."

"You're meeting me here so the world will know you've made up your mind. And you're coming down on our side." She smiled as the intern deposited her breakfast. "I suppose it would be out of line to hug you."

He used his cup to indicate the tall man scowling in the service line. "Certainly as far as Larry is concerned."

"What can you tell me about Legend?"

"Right to the point. I like that." He toyed with his cup. "They have offered us a five-picture deal."

"But only if you start with the Valentine project."

"In a nutshell," he confirmed. "If we do business with you, there's no deal."

"Does that make sense to you?"

"No, Megan. It doesn't. And not even your nemesis there can offer me a decent explanation. That's what finally brought me to this meeting."

"They want something," Megan said. "And it has nothing to do with the films."

"Legend claims to have an almost completed project, one that would fit perfectly on Valentine's with a minimum amount of editing." He pushed his coffee aside. "They also claim to want to use us as an entry point into television work."

"Do you believe them?"

"That's an interesting question. I would like to work with Legend. But only if they're genuinely interested in working with me."

"Did you ask them why K&K brought you their initial offer?"

"I would if I could have direct contact with their key executives. Aaron Seibel claims they're busy with a reorganization of their top ranks." He smiled. "You remember Aaron."

"All too well."

"Aaron would like to become my new best buddy, which is another curiosity. I've met him a number of times in the past. Before this deal arose, he treated me as, well . . ."

"The head of a television start-up who isn't within shouting distance of his minimum revenue requirements."

"You were smart to quit that group, Megan."

She changed the subject. "What is the proposed budget for the Legend projects?"

Harvey nodded. "Another interesting question. They've come down to what you are costing. Three and change."

"So five of these projects will total less than half of one of their studio projects. They do four films a year, contracted in advance to Paramount. Where is the logic in this offer they've made CBC?"

"I asked Larry the very same question."

"How did he respond?"

"He said he'd have to get back to me on that." Harvey checked his watch and rose from the table. If he noticed how every eye in the room tracked him, he gave no indication. "You understand, Megan, nothing can be formalized until we've viewed your team's first cut. But if your Mr. Byrd and his group deliver as promised, I hope we can come to some sort of long-term understanding."

Megan wished there was some way to take the man's words, distill them, and fashion a bond that would make Danny truly hers. "Could you possibly elaborate?"

"Not until the project wraps. Until then, it's to remain our little secret."

Megan waited until he had departed to reply, "Not so little, not by any stretch of the imagination."

51

MEGAN DROVE STRAIGHT from LA to Thrashers Ridge. She had hoped desperately to see Danny, and feared the contact in equal measure. But when she arrived, Thrashers Ridge was quiet. The cook showed Megan a note from Danny saying they were on location and asking for dinner to be ready at six. Megan left a terse note of her own, saying simply that they needed to talk.

Just as she was pulling into the law firm's parking lot, her phone rang. The readout said it was a blocked number. Megan feared another confrontation with Aaron and was tempted not to answer. The day was already too full. "This is Megan Pierce."

A distinctly feminine and heavily accented voice spoke loudly over static. "My name is Mei-Li. I call for our mutual friend."

As Megan listened to what the woman had to say, she wondered if perhaps it had been good not to speak with Danny after all.

When Sol Feinnes entered his office at a quarter to four, Megan rose from her chair, crossed the central space, and followed him. Something in her expression silenced Sol's secretary before she could protest.

Megan did not march and she did not storm. Sol was not someone who would respond well to histrionics. But he was going to tell her what she needed to know.

Sol set his briefcase on the desk and said, "Can this wait?"

"No, Sol. It can't."

Though she spoke calmly, something clearly alerted him to the change. "Megan, I'm due at a conference with my client's board of directors in ninety minutes. We need to prepare a settlement offer. Tonight."

"We can do this here, we can do this in your car, we can do this in their waiting room. But it is going to happen today. The information you have withheld from me is no longer about Thrashers Ridge. This has become a beast, Sol. If we don't handle it now, it could grow fangs and devour us all."

He shook his head. "Save the poetry for your next jury."

"Today, Sol."

"Explain." He opened his briefcase and began setting files in it. "I can give you five minutes."

"I'll do it in three."

Sol's movements slowed as she spoke. Megan sat down and walked him through her findings, summarizing her conversations in thirty-second bites. When she finished with her breakfast meeting that morning, Sol had gone completely still.

Finally he said, "I have no contact with Legend Partners. Not now, not ever."

When Megan did not respond, Sol walked to his open door and called for someone named Gerald. A fresh-faced young man bounded down the hall. Sol said, "I need you to prepare the financial documents for our meeting."

The guy could not have been more than four years younger than Megan. Even so, his high-pitched eagerness made Megan feel ancient. "No problem, Mr. Feinnes!"

Sol watched the young man depart, then told Megan, "If he fouls things up, you and I are going to have words."

He left to make a call from his secretary's desk, returned to his office, and told Megan, "Permission granted. Reluctantly."

"By whom?"

Sol sank into the sofa across from her. "Eleven years ago the new director of Thrashers Ridge approached me. His name was Daniel Byrd."

"Wait . . . what?"

"Danny's grandfather married into the family who has owned Thrashers Ridge for generations. He and his wife were both in their sixties when they met and fell in love. Daniel Sr. then invested all his own assets into turning the place around. It was not enough. He and his wife watched helplessly as the hotel steadily lost all their money. I arranged subsequent bank loans. Three of them. Finally last year the bank demanded all their money must be repaid, without any further delay. Nine months ago Daniel made yet another appointment, I assumed to enter chapter 11. But when he came into my office and sat where you are now, he announced that he had been approached by a buyer. At first I couldn't understand why he wouldn't accept a cash offer for an outright sale. But he was my client, and he insisted. Forty-nine percent or nothing. The negotiations dragged on."

Sol stopped talking. Glanced at his watch. Sighed.

"Tell me!"

"He died. Stroke. His widow insisted that we hold to her late husband's terms. She said she'd burn the place to the ground, leave it to a charity, deed it to the county on the understanding they'd never sell it to . . ." Sol shook his head. "The lady was alone, bereft, and in bad physical shape. I'd assumed she would actually be the one to go first."

"So the buyer agreed."

"The firm representing them did. I made them understand it was this or nothing. They relented, but only when they retained an absolute right to acquire the rest at fair market value if the property ever came up for sale."

"Who was the buyer?"

"I have no idea. Everything was handled by an LA law firm that told me in no uncertain terms that their client was to remain anonymous."

"Not K&K."

"None other."

The news pushed her back in her seat. Megan stared at the space above Sol's head. Watching all the pieces fall into place. "Legend. It has to be."

"Given what you've told me, I assume that's the case." Sol started to check his watch again but resisted the urge. "Apparently Daniel Sr. knew his health was failing and tried to find his son. No luck there."

"They found his grandson Danny instead."

Sol nodded. "This is where things get confusing."

Megan shook her head. Actually, things were finally becoming clear. "The sale of half the hotel's ownership to Legend went through. Mrs. Byrd continues to honor her husband's last wishes. She ordered you to help Danny when JR skipped town and landed Danny in jail. You reported back to her what you learned about Danny through me. Because of her ill health, she deeded Danny the remaining half of the hotel. But her late husband made no decision about contacting Danny directly, so she has ordered you to keep quiet. How am I doing so far?"

Sol just stared at her.

"One last question. When did K&K discover Danny's involvement?"

Sol studied her. "Not until Danny was released from jail. Why?"

"I'm not sure. But I think it might be important."

"The widow's name is Louisa Dellacourt. After Danny's day in court, I informed K&K that Louisa had passed on her share of the hotel to her husband's named heir."

"Who was the attorney of record?"

"Aaron Seibel."

Megan stood. "I have what I need. Go negotiate your settlement."

Sol rose slowly. Still staring. "What are you going to do?"

For once, the answer was crystal clear. "I'm going to protect my client."

52

DANNY DROVE to Robin and Emma's home that night with Megan's note burning a hole in his pocket. He felt as though the world just would not let him go. The weight of everything he needed to get done, all the things he wished he had done better, Megan's absence, his own flawed life. All of it bundled together at the end of this invisible chain.

As he started to enter the home, his phone rang.

Kate, Jennie's bodyguard, said without preamble, "You've had visitors."

"Excuse me?"

"Three nights running. Two couples, or so they appear at first. They pull into the lot about midnight and pretend to be heading up the ridge. Then they slip away into the brush."

"Does this mean you're not really a lone bodyguard?"

"Jennie decided she wanted regular patrols, the hotel is so isolated."

"Why wasn't I informed?" Danny read Kate's silence and added, "Never mind. Go on."

"We assumed they were fans at first. Then I heard sloshing."

There was no reason that last word should send his heart into overdrive. "What was it?"

"They were carrying containers of gas, rags, and a timer."

"What?"

"Good thing Jennie had me add some extra staff, huh."

"Where are they?"

"That's a question you shouldn't be asking." Kate's voice showed a new and sharper edge. "Let's just say they won't be coming back anytime soon."

Danny was still digesting that information as he entered the home and accepted Emma's welcoming hug. He sighed his way onto the sofa, wishing he could curl up in the corner and sleep for a week. Then his phone rang a second time.

Emma watched him check the screen and send the call to voice mail. "Aren't you going to answer that?"

"No. Definitely not."

"What if it's, you know, important?"

He slipped the phone back in his pocket. "It's JR. Again."

Robin stepped out into the hall leading to their kitchen. "Your partner? The guy who landed you in jail?"

"Yes. Is it okay if we don't talk about JR tonight?"

"Aw." Emma slid onto the floor. "Really?"

Danny realized she was kidding. "How do you have energy left for jokes?"

Robin called from the kitchen, "She's fourteen."

"Fifteen, almost." Emma lay on her back, her hair fanned out like a copper sheath. "Today was fun."

"Maybe for you."

They had done a series of quick location shots, all possible because Robin and Emma had escorted the crew through their world. Solvang lived from the constant stream of tourists, which made the locals insular. They were friendly enough, but only to a point. The things that mattered, the elements that could make or break their film project, were kept hidden away.

Robin had arranged for them to meet with five regional support groups. Grief groups, Emma had called them. Sob moms.

Dreary dads. Robin had told her daughter to be quiet, but Danny could tell she partly agreed with Emma.

Danny had repeatedly taken his place in five circles of chairs and told the groups what their project was all about. When he ran out of air, Emma and Robin chimed in. Describing the characters and the story and the impact it was having on them. Emma's words proved the most powerful of all. How she had started coming back to a normal life all because of Danny's voice. That was how she said it—returning to a normal life. None of the gathering had needed to ask what she was talking about.

Afterward each group had allowed Jennie to come in, along with the entire film crew. They listened as Jennie spoke her lines, two and sometimes three times. When the crew departed, Danny personally made the final request. In reply, each group had agreed to serve as extras when they shot the final series of scenes.

Danny looked down at the young woman sprawled on the carpet. "Thank you for today. A lot."

She smiled up at him. There was a freshness to her features that he had not noticed before. A light to her eyes. "You can call today payback."

"What are you talking about?"

"You know. Your lessons."

"Oh. That."

Every day he had started her scene with another question. Making the shift from Emma the fourteen-year-old actress to the role she was playing. Today he had returned to the very first thing he had asked her. To think of a secret she had never told anyone, then think of one her character held close.

Emma went on, "The secret I came up with today? The one you said I never told anybody? Mom thinks you're a hottie."

There was the sound of crashing pots in the kitchen. "*Emma Sturgis!*"

Emma might as well not have heard a thing, she was so calm. "I heard her say it."

"I said no such thing!"

"She was talking with her friend on the phone. Consuela."

"The bartender," Danny recalled.

Robin remained hidden inside the kitchen. "Young lady, that is *enough!*"

"Mom said you probably weren't house-trained. Yet. Whatever Consuela said made her laugh." Emma did a teenager thing, rising from the floor like she was a liquid pretzel. "Would you like to hear a song I'm working on?"

"Sure."

Robin did not appear until Emma had left the room. Then she stepped into the doorway, showing Danny a scarlet face. "There's probably something I should say at this point. But I have no idea what it is."

"It's fine. Really."

"Can we pretend my darling daughter didn't actually say what she just did?"

"Sorry, I don't know what you're talking about."

"Maybe I was wrong about the house-trained part." She licked the wooden spoon she held and inspected him thoughtfully. "Do I need to say something about how you're safe in this house?"

"No, Robin. You don't."

"I mean, everybody knows about you and Megan."

Danny said softly, "It's all my fault."

"Of course it is. You're a guy. Admitting it is a very good start."

"What, men are to blame for every wrong move?"

Robin smiled as she returned to the kitchen.

Emma came back carrying the tenor sax and her tablet. She plugged the latter into the living room's sound system, wet her reed, hit Play, and launched straight in. With the first strands emanating from the wall speakers, Danny instantly recognized the song.

Emma did not attempt to match Jesse Cook's flaming speed. Instead, she played backup, melding her sounds into the riffs played by Cook's violinist, Chris Church. Danny felt himself becoming lost in the music, a sure sign of true talent.

When she was done, Danny found himself reluctant to return to the here and now.

Robin said, "That was lovely, dear."

Emma asked Danny, "You liked it?"

He nodded. "Very much."

Robin said, "Go put your instrument away, honey. Dinner's ready."

Emma seemed to find what she was looking for in Danny's subdued response, for she kissed his cheek before bouncing away. Robin remained in the doorway, watching him.

Finally Danny said, "What?"

"You don't know, you can't imagine, what an impact you've had on that child's life," Robin said. "And mine."

Danny had no idea how to respond. So he remained silent.

"Now you can help me set the table. Consider it your next lesson in becoming house-trained."

———————

After dinner, as Danny drove back to the hotel, he could still feel the hugs that Robin and Emma had given to seal his departure. Now that he was alone, their gift felt like it marked a turning.

He parked in front of the hotel and stood there a long moment, drinking in the sight of the starlit building and all the mysteries it represented. The dark path that skirted the barn and corral was familiar enough that he felt no need for a light. The closer he came to his cabin, the wearier he became. As he skirted the lake, his fatigue whispered a lullaby as strong as any he had ever known.

But none of that mattered, because seated on his cabin's top step was Megan.

53

MEGAN HAD LEFT SAN LUIS OBISPO with one goal in mind. She could not think further than parking in the hotel lot and looking Danny in the eye. Every time she started to wonder what she would say, her mind deflected.

Facing a jury for that first opening statement was always like taking a cliff dive at midnight. She prepped as best as she possibly could. She had all the available data on the people seated before her. The sort of deep-background investigation seen in movies was not possible on smaller trials, which was where she had always operated. So Megan had treated her first words as a joining. She and the jury were about to enter a mystery together.

Megan liked to make her opening remarks in the space between the defense table and the judge. Under California law, this was the only time when the lawyers were allowed to step in front of their tables and approach the jury box. As a result, LA attorneys called this space the proving ground, and for good reason. Megan never used a lectern or prepared notes. It was just her, standing there exposed and vulnerable, revealing herself to the people who would decide her client's fate. She had never lost a case that had gone all the way to a jury trial.

She recognized Danny's silhouette the moment he appeared

around the hotel. Her first reaction was to do what she always did. She wanted to build a defense, do her best to take control. Starting with an explanation as to why she was sitting on Danny's top step in the dark. Waiting and hoping. Desperately.

Just then, though, all she could manage were a few tight breaths.

Danny stood in front of her for a time, not moving. His silhouette was made luminescent by the moon, the lake, and a single light shining through the kitchen windows.

Finally he said, "You're stronger than I am."

Megan tasted several responses. But the air just wasn't there to shape them.

Danny went on, "I've wanted to do what you're doing. Meet you. Call you. Something. But every time I started, my mind was such a jumble. And everything I wanted to say sounded so wrong."

Megan forced herself to say, "I'm here. What do you want to say?"

"That you were right. I'm fighting shadows. I've been doing that since forever. Every relationship I've ever been in, the littlest thing has set me off. And then I've blamed anything within reach just so I don't have to face the truth. That it's me, and it always has been."

Danny stepped forward and lowered himself onto the step beside her. Megan felt his warmth, strong as heat off the sun. She wanted to melt into him. But she resisted. He wasn't done. And she needed to hear him out. Drink in every word.

"When it's over and the air is filled with the stench of arguments I started, I blame my past. But I know that's just been another convenient lie. I think maybe I've always known. How can it be the fault of something years ago? The past is over. The problem is what I've insisted on carrying."

"You have to let it go, Danny."

He nodded slowly, then surprised her by saying, "Emma has

302

been showing me the exact same thing. How the only way to move forward was to do what you just said."

She wrapped her arms around him and said the words a second time. "Let go."

"Walk away from the chains I've had holding me down since forever." He sighed. "It's so hard."

"Yes. It is."

"I don't know how."

"One step at a time," Megan said.

Danny puffed several hard breaths. "Will you help me?"

"There's nothing on this earth I want to do more," Megan replied. "Except . . ."

"What?"

She turned and cradled his face in her hands. "This."

Her kiss held such a yearning hunger, it felt like she had carried the need for years. She stopped, pulled back, and loved how he sat with his eyes still closed. As if he too was captivated by the dreamlike moment.

She kissed him again.

54

THEY MOVED OVER to the kitchen and made a pot of coffee. They were still talking when the cook arrived at five. Danny had never known a situation like this. Tired as he was, he marveled at how it felt. Here he was, holding hands with a woman who exasperated him with the way she took control of every situation he presented to her. And yet with the way she talked, he could tell she held his best interests at the forefront of her mind and heart. Of course, there had been others who had put him first, at least for a while. The Marine who had taken him and JR in and reshaped them into the men they had become, for one. But this was different. Megan's eyes shone with a dark, molten love. Now and then she paused in their discussion and took time out for a kiss, an embrace, a soft word of how much she had missed him. How glad she was they were here together. Waiting for the dawn of another very busy day.

Even the fatigue they shared was okay. They accepted the cook's offer of breakfast burritos, thanked her for the freshly re-filled mugs, and continued with their planning. The day would be long and stressful and full of monumental events. But that was okay too.

For the first time in his life, Danny Byrd was learning what it meant to give up control. Willingly. For all the right reasons.

He knew this was one cause behind the wreckage of his partnership with JR. At some level Danny had probably always known. He entered into most situations with the unspoken assumption that he could do things better than anybody else. But Megan proved him wrong. She was smarter. She knew things he had never even considered. She talked in a way that crystallized things.

It threatened him.

Several times he came face-to-face with a new truth. Turning away from the past was only the first step. This was what came after. Walking into a new definition of life.

The more they worked through what needed to happen next, the more Danny became certain he could not have done this himself. At least, not successfully. Several of the issues Megan raised were precisely the sort of things he would have tried to avoid. Starting with JR.

Danny said, "I don't want to talk with him."

"You won't."

"I don't want to see him."

Megan didn't push. She simply waited. Her silence was a dagger that carved away at all his arguments.

"The guy landed me in jail."

"He did more than that. He broke a lifetime trust. He hurt you. Of course you want to avoid him." She reached across the table and took his hand. "But it probably will be necessary to meet him once. The people on the other side of this mystery may insist on it."

That was the moment Annie and Greg and Rick crowded through the kitchen door and saw them seated there.

Annie said, "Well, all right."

Greg said, "Now my day is complete."

"Where's the coffee," Rick asked, "and can I have mine through an IV?"

Megan did not give any indication she heard a thing. She held

Danny tight with her gaze. "Sooner or later you're going to run into him. And then what? Right now you're the one in control."

Danny nodded slowly. "And I won't have to do it alone."

"That's right. I will handle JR. Your job is to get through the meeting. You don't need to say a word. In some respects, it'd be best if you kept silent the whole time."

"Fine by me."

"You may change your mind when you see him," she warned.

"Doubtful."

"If you do, you just . . ."

Megan stopped because Emma came through the door with her mother, saw how they were seated, and said, "Finally."

Megan smiled at the two women. "Good morning to you too."

Emma gave Danny a quick hug. "Hey there, hottie."

"Emma, please, just stop." This from a very red-faced Robin.

Megan asked, "What's that all about?"

Emma accepted a burrito and a hug from the cook and headed for the back door, singing, "Hottie, hottie, hottie."

Robin said, "All the guns around here are loaded with blanks, right?"

Evelyn entered, smiled at the two of them holding hands, scooped up a tray the cook had prepared holding a thermos, mugs, and burritos, and asked Greg, "When is she due on set?"

"Forty-five minutes."

As Evelyn departed, one of the grips entered the kitchen and said, "There's a guy out front saying he needs to talk with Danny about a soundtrack."

And so their day began.

55

EMMA HAD NEVER LOOKED more like a young teen than now, skipping down the stairs behind Danny, almost singing the words, "You and lawyer lady? Really?"

"Her name is Megan."

"And don't you forget it."

"Pay attention. This is important."

"When did it start? Last night? Who's she on the phone with now, her bestie? Telling her all the deets?"

Danny stopped when his feet touched the gravel and turned back. He wished Rick could appear like magic, capture the smile and the light in Emma's eyes. "Megan is talking with JR."

"The guy who landed you in jail?"

"None other."

"What's she saying—hands off, he's mine?"

There was no reason why he should tell her anything. Even so . . . "Megan is arranging a conference for this afternoon."

"With JR? Ewww. Why?"

"She thinks we should tie up loose ends. And get answers to some questions that have been bugging me."

For some reason, Danny's words caused Emma to shiver. "That lady is totally *ice*."

"I'm glad you approve. Now can we get down to business?"

"I thought you said I wasn't filming today."

"You're not. Matter of fact, what are you doing here anyway?"

"Jennie said she'd give me some pointers between takes."

The news doubled the sun's warmth. "I want you to have time with her, but it may need to wait for another day." He walked her over to the man standing beside the eighties-vintage Mercedes convertible. "Emma, say hello to Myron Riles."

"Hi."

Danny had never met the gentleman, but the photographs did not come close to capturing Myron's courtier charm or the mischievous gleam to his gaze. Though in his early eighties, Myron held himself impossibly erect. He was also blade-slender and dressed in a double-breasted suit, highly polished shoes, a striped shirt with white dress collar, and a foulard matched by his silk pocket handkerchief. His features were movie-star clean, his eyes crystal grey, his smile a thing of brilliance.

Myron gave a fractional bow and said, "A genuine honor, Ms. Sturgis. May I say, after viewing your first cut several times, I detect a star on the rise."

Danny could tell Emma had no idea how to respond. He said, "I grew up loving your soundtracks, sir."

"If you noticed my hand on the tiller, young man, I failed in my duty to the film." His smile carried a grandfatherly warmth. "Nonetheless, I am eternally grateful for your lifting me from a premature grave."

Emma said, "What did you mean about not noticing?"

Myron showed the good sense not to talk down to her. "A soundtrack should never enter the spotlight, Ms. Sturgis."

"Emma."

He played the courtier once more. "An honor, I'm sure. And I am Myron. My job is to heighten the emotions that the audience feels, yet remain always in the background."

"But Danny is putting my music front and center."

"And well he should, from what I've witnessed. But that is different. You see, *your* music is part of the story. *My* job, if Mr. Byrd here decides to let me remain on set, is to weave a series of subtle melodies that will come and go *between* your solo acts. I am here merely to help dress the background. The correct term for that process is 'setting a thematic structure.' If I'm successful, I'll deliver the audience, ready and eager, to your next time on stage."

Danny could see Emma was taken with the gentleman. "I'd like Emma to play several of her favorite pieces for you. We're not tied to any of them, but it would be great if you could use songs she already is comfortable with in forming the central themes."

"I agree."

"Greg is thinking we'd like to have her play four times through the film. Once at the Soho Club, twice by herself, and then in the finale. We need you two to work those out."

Myron did the right thing by asking, "Does that seem acceptable, young lady?"

"Sure. I guess."

Danny went on, "Greg has been thinking ahead. In case this is as big as we hope."

Myron did not need to have things spelled out. "You are considering a possible album."

Danny ignored Emma's round eyes. "We'd have to keep costs to a minimum. Find musicians who would work for studio scale and a cut of the profits."

Myron kept his crinkly eyed gaze upon Emma. "How would you feel about my putting together renditions of a few top-ten melodies and adding voices? Small albums do a great deal better if singers are included."

Emma turned to Danny. "Is that okay?"

"Only if you like the idea. Understand, we wouldn't move forward until we see the audience's initial reaction to the film.

But if it generates enough heat, we'd bring you into the studio and use an album as the next step in launching your career."

Myron said, "All the people you'd be working with would be trained studio musicians. But you will remain in control throughout, both of the melodies and of the people who accompany you. Mr. Byrd and I would see to that."

Danny could see her digesting that immense word. *Career.* All she said was, "Wow."

56

DANNY TOOK TIME to shower and change, then he and Megan drove in both cars to her parents' house. She hopped out and showed him five splayed fingers, meaning she would be quick. Danny nodded like her swiftness was of any great concern. He leaned against the car and felt the sunlight warm his bones. Then he felt the first wave of fatigue strike. He had endured other sleepless nights while on set. He knew he could still go all day and well into the next night if he had to. The weariness was a measurable factor, like a familiar component of the life he had chosen for himself.

The front door opened and Sarah stepped out. She walked over, bearing a steaming go-cup. "Something for the road."

"This is great. Thanks."

Sarah waited until he had fit it between the seats. When he straightened, she gave him a strong, warm hug. "It's good to see you both together."

"Your daughter is amazing."

"She is." Sarah smiled. "Megan is also a handful and a half."

Danny wasn't sure what to say to that.

Sarah seemed to approve of his silence. "Richard and I both think she's finally met her match."

Megan stepped through the front door, hurried down the walk, and demanded, "Is she bothering you?"

"Absolutely."

"Mom, stop." She hurried around the car. "Let's go, Danny. We don't want to be late."

Sarah smiled at Danny and asked, "Where are you headed?"

"Los Angeles," Megan replied. "Off to kill a few giants."

———————— // ————————

Given what lay ahead, Danny found himself comforted by Megan's professionalism. He waited until they became caught in the first highway snarl, where the Pacific Coast Highway joined the freeway at Rincon and traffic slowed to a crawl. It gave him the chance to turn from the wheel, look her square in the eyes, and say, "Thank you for being here with me."

"It's what I've always wanted," she said softly.

"Always?"

She nodded slowly. "Since long before we ever met."

The traffic opened up just north of Long Beach, and they made good time until Danny started the climb up past the Getty. Driving in Los Angeles most days meant getting caught somewhere in a metallic sludge. If Megan even noticed the snarl, she gave no sign. She held a yellow legal pad in her lap and made designs of words and exclamation points and daggers and nuclear explosions. She went through the points she expected to emphasize in the day's conference, giving Danny a glimpse into her interior world. This was how she prepared for trial work, she explained. Going over and over the visible until the unseen became clear.

Whenever they reached a pause, Megan returned to the day's core issues. She repeated her very first questions, giving Danny yet another chance to change his mind. No, he wanted nothing whatsoever to do with his former partner beyond this meeting. But he also had no real interest in seeing JR go to jail. Yes, he understood that this could well be his only opportunity for payback. But there was nothing to be gained from making JR go through what Danny had endured. All Danny wanted was a clean break.

As far as he was concerned, the entire day had shaped into a realization. This was it. The turning.

Danny Byrd was going it alone no longer.

57

THE PARKING GARAGE BELOW K&K's offices was blocked by a Full sign, so Danny entered the lot across the street. He drove to the top level, from which he could look across Santa Monica Boulevard at the shimmering glass cube. He turned to Megan and waited. Their meeting was scheduled to start in twenty-five minutes. He had no interest in moving until she gave him the green light. Studying her was a pleasure in itself.

She was dressed in the navy-grey suit whose weave contained some silk because of how it caught the light. She had done something new with her hair, a carefully controlled French twist that was severe and alluring at the same time. Danny thought she looked incredibly beautiful and told her so.

For one brief instant, the other Megan shone in her face and her eyes. The heat, the affection, the love, all of it. Then she said, "This isn't the time."

"Or the place," he agreed.

Even so, she held her open-hearted gaze in place for a moment longer. She reached over and took his hand. "Promise me something."

"Okay. I promise."

She smiled. Danny thought she looked almost as tired as he felt. "When this is over, we will have some us time."

"Us time. I love it."

"When this is over," she repeated. "It has to wait until then. You understand, don't you?"

"Totally. And Megan?"

"Yes?"

"Thank you. So much."

"You're welcome, Danny. I'm glad to be here for you."

And just like that, the moment passed. Megan flipped down the visor, inspected herself, and fit her game face into place. Danny regretted the transition but was glad at the same time. This was who she was.

Danny said, "All the new information you gave me last night . . ."

She nodded. "It's a lot to take in."

"Will you run it by me once more?"

She glanced at her watch, nodded once, then said, "For years, Sol's firm has represented the family who until recently owned Thrashers Ridge."

"A guy who claims to be my grandfather," Danny said. "A guy I've never met."

"He doesn't claim anything. He is. Sol is certain the man's evidence is solid, and I think you need to accept this." When he didn't respond, she continued, "Your grandfather married into the family. Together with his wife, they ran Thrashers Ridge for almost two decades. He tracked you down. The details of that search can wait. But it happened, and it's part of why we're here today."

He nodded acceptance. "A big part."

"After your grandfather died, his widow followed her beloved's final wish and deeded you fifty-one percent of the hotel. But as Sol's group was preparing to contact you, the family's investigators reported that you had been arrested. Your grandfather's widow instructed Sol to represent you. Because Sol had never tried a case in the Los Angeles court system or had anything to do with the entertainment industry, he sought me out."

Danny stared across the parking deck to the sunlit vista. When Megan went silent, he continued the conversation in his head. How because of the arrest, Danny had met Megan. The love of his life. Which meant they were together because of JR. The same JR who had robbed him of everything and was now back in LA as a K&K client. Waiting for him next door.

Megan brought him back with, "You know what to do, yes?"

"From this point on, keep my trap shut."

"You can speak to JR if you must. Only, please signal me in advance."

Danny shook his head. "I have no interest in talking to that guy ever again."

58

DANNY AND MEGAN were kept waiting for over half an hour. He didn't mind in the least. Among the lower LA film dwellers, the K&K lobby was a mythical place, one that might as well have a neon sign posted where the elevators opened: "Abandon All Hope, Ye Who Earn Less Than Ten Mil per Year."

The lobby's central waterfall was exactly as a young director had described it to Danny. The stream rushed down curved plates of what might have been polished tungsten steel. Or maybe sterling silver. The lobby's only source of light came from the spotlights that flickered through the flow. Danny had heard the waterfall cost a cool two million dollars.

The resulting effect was a little eerie. Three different groups occupied the forty-by-forty cube, clustered on the backless sofa stools that dotted the shadowy space. The waterfall smothered all other sounds. The groups looked like semi-frozen set pieces, part of a shifting artwork combining stress, hunger, ambition, and film.

Danny stared at the sparkling waterfall and the liquid rush of mysteries. His lack of understanding was not all that important, even though a lot of what Megan had told him the previous night had been hard to take in. What he had heard most clearly was how she had worked through the weeks, putting together a puzzle the attorneys inside this high-rise legal palace assumed remained concealed.

Danny watched Megan pace and text, then grip her phone in both hands and frown at the water. And he decided that just then, he really didn't need to understand. He didn't need to take control. He didn't need to figure things out. Because he had Megan to do this for him.

———————— // ————————

When Brandon Lee came through the portal leading back into the offices, Megan knew how it was going down.

Or so the power guys inside K&K assumed.

They expected her to respond just as she had in Lawrence Abbott's office—become so involved in her simmering ire against Brandon, her former nemesis, that she would miss the big picture. While the real players, the real power, the real issue, all remained hidden.

Not today.

Brandon smirked his way toward her, with three junior associates in line behind him. Megan halted him with, "Don't even think about handling this meeting."

Brandon laughed. "Megan, please. You're not calling the shots—"

"Aaron Seibel. Here. Now. Or I walk. Now get out."

———————— // ————————

Fifteen minutes passed. Megan paced and planned. She liked how Danny did not press her with questions she could not answer. Every time she glanced over, he met her with a calm gaze. For once, the latent rage that had defined Danny was not present. But she didn't need to be thinking about such things just now. For the moment, Danny Byrd was her client.

Aaron barreled through the door minus his suit jacket. He

had the sleeves of his tailored seven-hundred-dollar Turnbull & Asser shirt rolled up. His tie was down a careful inch and a half. His suspenders glinted in the uneven light. When he appeared, the cube's atmosphere instantly shifted. The water cascaded with an electric hiss. The other people waiting their turn in the inner sanctum rose slowly to their feet. The gazes of Brandon and the younger minions flickered about, nervous, fearful.

Aaron snarled, "Where do you get off, giving my people orders!"

Megan didn't respond.

He misread her silence as uncertainty. "You got some nerve. I'm in the middle of a major deal. You think I got nothing better to do than play nickel and dime with the likes of you?"

"This won't take long."

"It's already taken more than you deserve." He chopped the air. "I should have fired you—"

"Shut up, Aaron. Just be quiet. Your histrionics aren't working. Nobody is impressed. Either you behave or we walk, and you have to tell the people hiding in your office that the deal they want isn't happening." Megan resisted the urge to smile at Aaron's need to clamp down on his customary rage. "Now go tell the Legend execs they need to join us."

"I have no idea what you're talking about."

"You're wasting my time, Aaron. And theirs. It's the only way this meeting is happening. With Legend seated at the table."

59

DANNY FOUND HIMSELF PULLED in two opposite directions, entering the boardroom and finding JR seated across from him. The guy was dressed like he belonged, a Canali suit over a black silk T-shirt, sporting the little reddish-blond goatee he'd started growing about a year ago. JR was as fresh-faced as ever, a fashion-conscious pixie with his bad-boy grin. He stood a hair under five ten and never gained an ounce of fat no matter how bad his diet, which was pretty appalling. His idea of exercise was walking the four blocks from his Valley condo to the nearest gourmet coffeehouse. Usually he drove.

JR grinned at Danny's arrival. Actually grinned. Like it was all just part of the huge joke they had been telling each other for years. Underneath the Hollywood exterior was still the same old JR. Johnny Rocket. The guy Danny had always assumed would be with him to the end.

And JR knew it. The gaze locked on his held the same electric mirth, the challenge Danny could never resist.

Until now.

The other part of Danny, the one forged in the fires of the Beverly Hills jail, did not have room for sorrow over what might have been. The world had turned, the new day started.

Danny seated himself across from his former partner and

gave himself a mental shove backwards. Off to the thousand-yard line.

Megan slipped into the chair opposite Aaron Seibel and said, "Let's get down to business."

———————//———————

All Megan's suppositions locked into crystal clarity the moment Carl Legend entered the room. The man himself. Green-light king at Legend Partners. He was compact in the manner of a tight fist. He wore his greying hair in a modest bowl cut. His suit was good, but he wore it carelessly.

Major studios might have a hundred execs burnishing their vice-president brass plates. But only one person within each group held the real power, the ability to make the crucial go/no-go decision on a new project. Carl was the eldest of three brothers and the one whose voice mattered most. He looked furious to be caught out. Which Megan regretted, at least a little. Carl Legend was one of the LA powers she had admired.

"I wasn't kidding you," JR said to Danny. "This new gig is the real deal."

Megan touched Danny's wrist, a one-finger restraint. But she had not made the gesture to silence Danny. She was showing the opposition who controlled their side of the boardroom table.

Aaron had a bruiser's ability to turn everything he said into an invitation to do battle. As soon as Carl Legend took the seat next to his, Aaron said, "So we're here. Now what?"

Megan held to her bland courtroom voice. The best impact she had found for both judge and jury was when she wove a story that carried its own emotional impact. She spoke directly to Carl Legend. "Thank you so much for joining us."

Both Aaron and Carl grimaced like they had bitten down on something putrid. Hating how she was declaring herself their equal. For now.

There were nine people rimming the table's opposite side.

JR, Brandon, Aaron, Carl, and five minions. She assumed at least one of the minions was a Legend in-house attorney. But none of them mattered except the green-light king.

Megan said, "With your permission, I'll try to save us time by bringing us up-to-date."

Aaron laughed, a tight bark that Megan knew preceded his bite. But whatever he was about to say was stifled by a single look from Carl.

Megan went on, "You've been looking for a unique property somewhere within chopper distance. A weekend residence that would become your secret retreat. Thrashers Ridge is perfect. The site is protected on three sides by a ridgeline that is actually part of the property. Not to mention a lake in case of another drought. A Victorian hotel you could turn into a palace. Outbuildings for guests and servants. But Sol Feinnes, the lawyer handling the estate, convinced you an outright purchase was not going to happen. Your research told you all the chips were on your side of the table. Even though Danny's grandfather died with the deal still not done, his widow's health was failing. The hotel was approaching bankruptcy. Your contract gave you purchase rights. It was only a matter of time."

She gave that a long beat, then finished with, "Until Danny Byrd entered the picture."

Everyone's gaze shifted over. Danny had a thousand-yard stare, his attention locked on the LA sky beyond his former partner's head.

Megan said, "Danny proved a harder target than you imagined. Not jail, not your attempts to pull the Chambers project, not even the lucrative offers to people JR had stiffed in Danny's name." Megan felt the heat build inside her chest and mind. "Or the way you tried to damage his reputation with your Blackwater detectives. Nothing worked. Did it?"

Carl Legend revealed a rough-edged voice as if he had shouted for years, yelled and pushed and bellowed until softer words came out as unnatural. "My brothers and I, we built our company from nothing. Eleven years of penny-and-dime horror flicks, scraping together the money and the contacts. Moving into mid-budget action features, the sort of stuff studios won't touch. But the theaters, they know. There's a market for them. It fills a few seats. As long as budgets are kept tight, everybody wins a little. And we made it. Twenty-one grueling years it took. From the trenches to the penthouse."

Megan had the feeling Carl had rehearsed the words a million times, at least in his head. "You're a winner," she offered. "In a tough town."

He jerked like he was scoffing silently. "Lady, you got no idea how tough."

Danny spoke for the first time. "I know."

Carl inspected him across the table. The exchange was tight. Hard.

When neither man budged, Megan said to Carl, "Here's how we're going to resolve the current situation. First and foremost, Legend Partners will honor its commitment to John Rexford, pay off his outstanding debts, and finance his current project."

JR jerked as though electrocuted. "Legend has offered us a three-picture deal."

Megan looked at him for the first time. "Point of order. There is no 'us.'"

"That's crazy. Danny and me, we're—"

Megan cut him off by turning back to Carl and continuing, "What Legend does after that initial film is entirely up to you."

JR started in once more. "No, hang on . . ."

One swift glance from Carl stifled JR. He then switched his attention back to Megan. "In exchange for what?"

Aaron said, "Matter of fact, it's time she remembers that deal was contingent on Byrd dropping the Chambers project."

"Aaron," Carl said, "shut up."

Megan breathed out once. A silent hum of pure pleasure.

Carl said, "Go on."

Megan turned to Aaron, ignoring the crimson burn from the internal rage he was forced to swallow. "In exchange, Mr. Rexford will formally agree to never seek contact with my client. We'll want that in writing."

JR said, "Wait, no. Danny, tell them—"

Carl turned to him. "Get out."

No one spoke or met JR's gaze as he rose slowly, shot a pleading look Danny's way, then departed.

When the door clicked shut, Danny released a long sigh. Megan resisted the urge to reach for his hand.

"Next?" Carl said.

"You now have a choice," Megan said. "Before I give you the alternatives, you first need to accept that you are not acquiring Thrashers Ridge for your personal use."

Carl sneered at Danny. "You think one television spot will pull that loser out of the fire?"

Danny had resumed his thousand-yard stare. If he even heard the question, he gave no sign.

Megan asked, "May I continue?"

Carl clearly disliked it. But he was curious. Drawn in. "Go on."

"You can sell your share back to Danny and his new partner. They will pay you in cash."

"What new partner?"

"It's a bluff." Aaron sounded like he had gargled with gravel. "She doesn't—"

Carl stifled his attorney with a look.

"I'll come to the new investor in a second," Megan replied.

"The alternative?" Carl said.

"You form a partnership with Danny. The Byrd-Legend Project. Thrashers Ridge becomes a haven for low-budget indie filmmakers. Similar in structure and function to what George Lucas and the Skywalker Ranch became for the early computer animators."

Aaron laughed. "You don't have the clout. Skywalker Ranch worked because they had the cash to make the projects move forward! You peons are hanging on by your fingernails."

"Which brings us to our new partner," Megan replied. "Danny Byrd has now been named head of a nine-million-dollar film investment fund."

She gave that news the long beat it deserved. Then she gestured at her silent companion. "Meet LA's newest green-light guy."

––––––––––––––––––– // –––––––––––––––––––

It all came down to the bombshell of a phone call from Zhang's associate. After Mei-Li had introduced herself, she had passed Zhang the phone. Zhang spoke briefly, just long enough for Megan to know it really was him. Then he handed the phone back, and the woman said, "I am Dr. Zhang's niece."

"Doctor?"

"He is a professor at Shanghai University. International accounting and bookkeeping standards." She had some difficulty with the word "international," but she managed. "Everybody trust him."

"I believe you."

"Yes. That is why he traveled to your country." The man spoke in the background, and Mei-Li translated, "Before he received your email, my uncle called your firm."

"Former firm."

"Yes. They refuse to say where you are. His emails were not answered. Dr. Zhang was very worried about you. He was most glad to receive news of your new partnership."

"I'm actually just an associate."

"Please?"

"It doesn't matter. I am fine. Better than fine."

"Dr. Zhang says, are you still in contact with the gentleman you and he discussed?"

"I serve as his attorney."

"This is very good. Because my uncle, he and his friends still wish to buy the product, you understand?"

Megan hesitated, then said, "I think so."

"Yes. He says, the first price you discussed, it was too high. He thinks nine dollars is a better price."

Megan pondered that for a time, then repeated, "Nine dollars."

"Yes. The original price you discussed, one hundred, it is not possible." The woman placed a heavy emphasis on each word.

Megan nodded to the sunlight shimmering off the concrete. "I think I understand."

"Perhaps in the future, you and Dr. Zhang can discuss a higher price. For future purchases. But right now he must stay with nine."

She had to assume the woman was speaking for all the invisible ears and tried to respond in kind. "But when we met, Dr. Zhang said even nine was impossible. There was an issue with transport."

"Yes. Exactly. One moment, please." There was a rapid exchange of Chinese. "Dr. Zhang says, the nine is now possible. Within one week, he thinks."

"That's wonderful."

"Yes. He says, can you please establish a bank account to receive his . . ."

"First payment," Megan said. "For the initial purchase."

"Yes, exactly. Email those details and he will send you confirmation when he is ready to make the first purchase."

"And details," Megan said. "About how to handle the first product shipment."

The woman did not laugh or sing. But it sounded to Megan as though she wanted to do both. "So nice to know you are exactly as my uncle has said."

Megan did not relate any details about the new investment funds or the people behind it. First of all, it was none of their business. Secondly, it would have reduced Aaron's burn, which she hoped Danny was enjoying as well.

"She's bluffing," Aaron said.

Megan slipped a single sheet of paper from her purse and slid it across the table. "An escrow account has been established with the San Luis Obispo branch of Wells Fargo. As you can see, Daniel Byrd and I are cosignatories."

The page represented a great deal of work on Megan's part, much of it done without any guidance whatsoever. The money was theirs. No restrictions. Which meant she had nine million dollars in an escrow account under the name of a film group that did not yet exist. By four that afternoon, Thrashers Ridge Films would become a going concern. And a wealthy one.

Carl shoved the paper back. His eyes glinted with bitter resignation. "So I've lost."

"With respect, sir, I would suggest the exact opposite is true."

His jaw muscles clenched and relaxed. Again. "Say I'm interested."

"Three things. First, you transfer your partial ownership of the hotel to Thrashers Ridge Films. We'll value that at four million, which is twenty percent above current market value. Second, you invest five million dollars more in the escrow account. Third, you agree to consider marketing and distributing the films developed by Thrashers Ridge."

"In return?"

"Thirty percent of the company."

"I want what I've got now. Forty-nine."

"Thirty for you," Megan repeated. "Thirty for our other investor."

He did not need to ask where the other forty percent went. "I green-light all projects."

Megan started to deny him when Danny spoke up. "Legend

works because there's only one green-light guy. That's how it has to be, and you know it."

Carl studied him intently. But to his credit, he did not argue.

Danny said, "We'll meet as often as you want. Discuss all projects under consideration. Go through the roster under development. I'll take all the input you want to give. But the green-light decision stays mine."

Carl's jaw muscles worked for a time. "Once a month. Maybe more often if you're going into production."

Danny rose to his feet and offered his hand across the table. "A pleasure, Mr. Legend."

He rose and took Danny's hand. "Carl."

Danny said to Megan, "I'm done here." He left the room without acknowledging Aaron or his minions.

Megan waited until the door clicked shut and all eyes returned to her. Then she rose, the movement almost sinuous with pleasure. She smiled at Aaron and said, "Why don't you go draw up the papers regarding John Rexford's future."

60

LOUISA DELLACOURT was a small porcelain figure with hair of spun silver-white glass. Her features held a Victorian perfection, a balance of refinement and strength. Her gaze was a pale golden brown, like autumn leaves seen in early dawn light. Danny liked her immensely even before she invited him to sit down.

When Megan started to take a chair by the parlor's west-facing windows, Louisa asked, "Are you the young lawyer who arranged for Danny to be released from jail?"

"Sol Feinnes did all the heavy lifting," Megan replied.

"That's not what the gentleman told me." She waved one arthritic hand. "Come join us. Unless of course the young man objects."

"The young man most definitely does not mind in the slightest," Danny replied, carrying over Megan's chair.

"So it's like that, is it." Louisa smiled. "How nice."

Her assisted-living facility was one block off the ocean in a residential neighborhood. Through the open window Danny tasted salt and heard the sound of children playing in the park to the south. "This place is nice."

Louisa inspected him closely. "Looking at you is like seeing my Daniel in his prime."

Danny worked through several responses and settled on, "I'm sorry I didn't know him."

"Are you really, young man? If anyone has reasons to resist the lure of family, it would be you."

Danny liked her directness. The sense of knowing she had no time for wasted words. "I'm learning to set down the past."

Louisa turned and gazed at Megan. "That's your doing, I assume."

"I'm trying to help. Danny's the strong one."

"Another trait he's inherited from my late husband." She touched the edges of her mouth. "My Daniel was born in the wrong season. Do you ever feel that way, young man?"

"Not really."

"Daniel used to say that living in this century left him feeling like he was wearing someone else's clothes. He yearned for the gold-rush era. He would not have been a miner. He had no interest in hunting wealth in the muck. Gambler, casino owner, hotel operator. I think he and Mark Twain would have been the best of friends."

Danny didn't know how to respond.

Megan filled the silence. "You and Thrashers Ridge gave him rest."

"We gave him a home, most certainly. The first my Daniel ever knew. Oh, he had houses before then. And a family, of course. Daniel never spoke of his first wife with anything but remorse. They were only married a year. Then he took a job working the offshore oil rigs, first in Alaska and then in the gulf and finally off Long Beach. It was a dozen years later that he learned he had a son. He had the occasional nightmare about the boy right up to the end."

Danny struggled with the surge of conflicting emotions. It must have shown, for Megan reached over and took his hand. She asked, "What did your late husband learn about his son?"

"Very little, and almost none of it good. His name was Daniel also, ironically. You are a third, young man, if that means anything." She sighed and stared at the afternoon light glinting off the glass. "Your father was not a good man, by all accounts. He did not marry your mother. He—"

"I don't want to know anything more about him," Danny said softly.

"That may be best." She turned back and inspected him once more, her gaze as gentle as her voice. "The detective my Daniel employed was very thorough. I know far more about you and your early years than is polite, young man. Have you managed to heal?"

"I'm trying."

"And I am glad to hear it. I have seen far too many wounded people lay down in the grave before their time and never get up again. Your grandfather had an upbringing similar to yours, orphaned early and handed from one family to another. He struggled with his wounds for most of his life."

"Until he met you," Danny finished.

She shrugged. "I gave him a reason to move on, perhaps."

"A home. A place that fit him as well as anything in this era might."

She shrugged a second time. "I like to think that is the truth."

Danny felt the warmth and the strength in Megan's hand. He turned to her and found the molten heat strong enough to ease his own aching heart. His gaze still on Megan, he said, "You can come back and live with us if you like. At Thrashers Ridge."

Megan added, "We can arrange for home care."

"Thank you both. I am touched by the offer. Truly. But my Daniel's absence would be too keen there, do you see? He loved Thrashers Ridge, something I never did. Until he entered my life, the place was just an albatross, tied to my existence by too many years and obligations. He turned the old place from a wreck into our home."

"If you ever change your mind, the offer stands." When she didn't respond, Danny asked, "Can I come see you again?"

"I would count that a rare treat." She stared at him, but her gaze was unfocused now. Looking through him to the man who was no longer present, at least in human form. "I have become a citizen of two worlds. It would be incorrect to say that I look forward to the passage ahead. But I do not especially regret its coming. The tie of a love like ours is not severed by one's demise."

Megan swallowed and said, "A part of you left with him."

"Indeed." Louisa's gaze refocused. "Do be sure to bring your young lady when you return."

Danny rose and thanked her and started for the door. Then he turned back and said, "Would you be willing to come to Thrashers Ridge just once? Next week we're going to have a party."

61

THE FOLLOWING WEEK, Louisa rose slowly from Megan's car. She took her time inspecting the hotel property, the ridgeline, the crew hustling to set up lights framing the entrance. As Megan unfolded the wheelchair and helped Louisa settle, Danny emerged from the hotel. Louisa smiled and said, "Good afternoon, young man."

"Thank you for coming, Louisa."

"I wasn't sure I should. Twice yesterday I started to call and say I wouldn't be able to make it. But I'm glad I did." She allowed Megan to settle her into the wheelchair and said to her, "Be so good as to show your young man the photograph."

Danny felt an electric shock when Megan turned the framed picture around. "Wow."

"Yes." Louisa traced an arthritic finger down the edge of the frame. "This is my Daniel."

Daniel Sr. resembled a pre-war film star. He was dressed in a three-piece suit, either black or dark grey. His tie was fastened with a diamond stickpin. A matching silk kerchief was tucked discreetly into the jacket pocket. He smiled into the camera as he stood with both hands resting upon the shoulders of his lovely bride.

A magnetic power reached from the frame and gripped Danny. Like the man came as close as he could to shaking Danny's hand.

"He's a stunner," Megan said.

"Take a good look, my dear. I suspect your Danny will age well."

Megan asked, "Shall we go inside?"

At a gesture from Danny, two muscled grips hefted Louisa's chair and carried her across the gravel forecourt and up the front stairs. Danny handed Megan his grandfather's photograph and personally pushed Louisa inside. "Welcome back."

The hotel's interior had not looked so good in decades. Louisa said as much, and Danny thought the compliment sounded real. Rick's crew had lit it to hide none of the flaws. Their aim was to create a softened reality. The threadbare carpet, the peeling varnish, the split planks—all of it remained visible and yet gentled in the manner of an Impressionist painting.

Greg had brought back the two Santa Cruz film crews for this day's shoot. The locals who had agreed to participate had signed release forms that also required them to stay as long as they were needed. But the emotions would only stay fresh and real for so long. Greg's team needed to get as much as possible in the can during the first few takes.

As the guests arrived, Rand and Annie and Megan prepped them just outside the camera's reach. The families had all brought photographs of their beloveds, the ones who would not be joining them that day. The hotel's interior was filled with Valentine's Day decorations that sparkled in the candlelight. One by one the families found a place for the pictures they had brought. As the main chamber gradually filled, the walls and side benches became encircled with smiling faces, only some of which rested in picture frames.

The cook had truly outdone herself, creating a buffet feast of Central and South American delicacies. There was *pargo vera-cruzana* from Mexico, *casado* from Costa Rica, *pupusa* from El Salvador. They dined on *sudado de pollo* from Colombia and Argentina's *puchero* and Brazil's *fiejoada*. Soon enough the guests grew accustomed to the roving cameras and chattered and visited and ate.

Danny was the one member of the film crew with almost nothing to do. Myron Riles, the film's newly hired director of soundtrack, had asked if he might prep Emma alone that day. Because the shoot was focusing on her music, Danny agreed. He filled one plate for Louisa and another for himself and seated himself next to her wheelchair.

Louisa complimented the food, ate almost nothing, and asked him, "You know the story of Captain Wainwright?"

"Some of it."

"Your grandfather considered him a close personal friend. He went up to the grave site every few days. They talked, or so my Daniel claimed. One buccaneer to another." When Danny didn't respond, she changed subjects. "I like your lady friend. Very much."

"Megan is more than I deserve," Danny said. "Or ever hoped for."

"If my Daniel were still here, he'd tell you to mind that your scars don't become hers as well."

Danny set down his fork. "Ouch."

She patted his hand. "I'm so glad you and I understand one another."

When the time came, the crew collected the plates while Greg arranged the families and Rick adjusted the lights. When Danny explained what they intended, Louisa asked, "Might I hold my Daniel?"

Danny thought it over, then went and asked Greg. The director was rushing from one mini crisis to another, trying to frame a shot with seventy-odd extras. Even so, Danny's words halted him. "That's your grandmother?"

"Sort of."

Annie had slipped up unnoticed. "Can I meet her?"

"Of course."

As Annie drifted over, Greg asked, "Which is your grandfather?"

Danny pointed to the black-and-white shot by the central staircase's landing.

Greg picked it up, studied it intently, and said, "The guy could be Clark Gable's better-looking brother." He carried it over to Louisa, spoke words Danny did not need to hear, then clapped his hands and said loudly, "Okay, folks. It's time."

62

UP TO THIS POINT, the locals had formed a disjointed gathering. The kids played and ran around or ate with their parents. The elderly sat with people they knew and were led around to meet others from different groups. They totaled somewhere over a hundred, a good number for the size of this room. The noise was massive, and the sense of excitement was heightened by how Jennie kept moving from group to group. She spoke a few words, she signed slips of paper, she treated each person she met as important. These might be California natives who had been around the film world all their lives. But Jennie French was a true Hollywood icon at the top of her game.

It was a strange way for a star to spend her last day on set. Jennie was leaving that evening. The contract stated she would be there through the next afternoon, but Greg was releasing her half a day early. Even with the final crucial scene to shoot, Greg was confident now. Even Alex was turning in solid performances. The news that a director was not trying to fill every last remaining hour on a star's contract had silenced Lane Pritchard.

Now Greg stood on the central staircase's landing and lifted his voice, silencing even the kids. As he began outlining what was about to happen and what he wanted from the extras, Danny watched as the group dissolved and re-formed. The kids became isolated, subdued. Even the youngest ones slipped over to where their mothers or fathers waited with outstretched arms. The families clustered together, one incomplete unit after another. The smaller kids reached out and gripped the chairs holding their photographs. The sight brought tears to Danny's eyes.

He missed Jennie's approach until she said, "Doesn't that just break your heart."

Danny was too full of the moment to deflect. "Brings up a lot of memories."

She reached over and took his hand. "You're a good man, Danny Byrd."

They stood like that and observed Greg set the lights and direct the camera crews. Then Jennie said, "You'll thank everyone for me?"

"Of course."

"I won't leave without saying goodbye to Greg."

"And Annie. And Emma."

"Of course. But if I can, I want to slip away without everyone else noticing." She squeezed his hand. "Sorry I won't be able to make the wrap party."

"You'll be missed."

She glanced over to where Alex stood by the reception desk, frozen in place while the cosmetician finished with his makeup. "He's done well since that night."

"Thanks to you."

"And Emma. She's a keeper."

"I think so too."

"So are you. When the young lady grows into a star, I hope she remembers the role you played."

Danny had no idea what to say to that.

Jennie nodded as though she had somehow managed to hear the unspoken. "When you're done with the first edits, call Evelyn. I want to have you over for dinner."

"Wow, Jennie. Thank you. Can I bring a date?"

"As long as it's the lawyer, sure thing."

Then Greg motioned to Jennie and the moment was gone. She slipped her hand free and started away. Then she turned back and said, "At the start of week two, I told Lane I thought we were making magic in a bottle. She asked if I had seen the dailies, and I told her Greg offered and I refused. I said I was too caught up in the beauty of what we were creating to worry about details." Jennie smiled with the brittle brightness that had snared a hundred million hearts. "It'll be nice to tell Lane, 'I told you so.'"

63

EMMA STEPPED THROUGH the kitchen door holding her alto sax. Rick had lined the path she would follow with little crystal cups holding candles. She wore a fawn-colored full-length dress with a bolero jacket that tied across the front. The sleeves and collar were laced with silver thread that caught the flickering light. Alex followed behind her, carrying a photograph of Emma's own father. Greg did not need to motion for quiet. Even the smallest children were caught by the moment and held to utter silence.

When Emma passed where Jennie sat with Robin, her film mother and her real mother holding hands, she paused long enough to hug them both. It might not make sense the first time the audience viewed the scene, but Danny was glad Greg did not object to Jennie's request. If they had a hit, this would form a component of the film's lore.

From his position beside the sound tech, Myron started the playback so that the music preceded Emma's arrival at the low stage. She climbed up and swayed slightly to the music, waiting while Alex positioned the photo on a chair to her right. As he stepped down and moved into the shadows, Emma took a long look at her father's picture, wet her reed, and launched straight in.

347

Myron had decided to go with three ballads from David Sanborn. He had discussed it with Emma and Greg and Danny, but really the decision had been all his. The aim had been simple enough. Go with one emotive flow. One core structure. That way if Emma slipped up at any point, they could segue easily into another song and capture the same emotion throughout.

There was another element, one Danny only knew about because Myron had told Emma and she had shared it with him. As a child, David Sanborn had suffered from polio for eight hard years. He had started playing the sax at the suggestion of his doctor and continued it as a salve for his loneliness. Besides earning Grammys for several of his solo works, Sanborn had also played backup for a number of singers, including Cat Stevens, Stevie Wonder, Paul Simon, Michael Franks, and David Bowie on the hit "Young Americans." Emma had related the story with a mixture of awe and shared sorrow. Danny knew she had found someone whose career she wanted to emulate. Which of course was why Myron had told her in the first place.

Myron had decided it would be easier to maintain a tight hold on the extras, especially the kids, if they did not stop between songs. So he had melded three together, and that was how Emma played them. Shifting smoothly between melodies, creating one long sweeping ballad. She brought a number of the audience members to quiet tears in the process.

When she was done, the crowd went crazy. Jennie rushed forward, followed by Rick and a shoulder-held rig. She hugged Emma and said words Danny knew had been rehearsed half a dozen times, but even so the smile that bloomed on Emma's face held a sharing of real emotions. As the two of them turned and looked down at the photo of Emma's dad, the kids applauded and then filled the central area, dancing their excitement of being part of something they could not name. Nor did they need to.

Danny surveyed the rim of professionals, the people responsible for melding this into a single climactic scene, and found smiles everywhere. From her spot beside Robin, Megan gave him a thumbs-up. He smiled in reply, wondering how it was possible to hold this much good in one heart.

When Greg called a ten-minute break, Megan slipped over and said, "So what did you talk about with Jennie French?"

"How you're incredibly special," Danny replied. "And I should hold you for the rest of my life and never let you go."

"She did not."

"No." He drew her into a fierce embrace. "But that was what she meant."

64

AS GREG RETURNED EMMA to the stage and began settling the extras in for the next take, everything changed.

When Danny thought back to the moment, he had the sense that everybody knew except him. There was surprise on many faces, but not what he might have expected.

Randy Willis entered the room. He was followed by the same two pros who had joined him at the Soho Club.

As the three crews filmed the crowd applauding and some of the extras rose so Randy could give them quick hugs, Greg drifted over to where Danny stood with Megan. "This day just keeps getting better."

Danny asked, "You knew?"

"I might've heard something somewhere," Megan said.

Greg explained, "Myron knew Randy from somewhere. They went over and talked with Michelle. She said she would ask."

Megan said, "Randy only got back from location this morning."

"Thanks for the heads-up," Danny said.

She hugged him. "Surprise."

"I hate surprises."

"Liar." She hugged him again.

Randy waited while his crew settled in with their instruments, then he said softly, "Here we go."

They launched into an instrumental version of Sting's "They Dance Alone." The artist had written it after watching women dance the *cueca*, the national dance, in the streets of a Chile torn apart by the Pinoche regime. The women became known as *arpilleristas*, the symbols of silent protest.

Danny said, "This is one of my absolute favorites."

Megan hugged him once more. "Shush now."

Then it happened.

As Emma soared far above the melody, a young girl with two blonde pigtails stepped away from her mother's arms. She could not have been more than five or six years old. She picked up a photograph stationed on the chair next to her mother and carried it into the empty central floor.

And began to dance.

Within half a minute, perhaps less, there were a dozen half-couples. Then twenty, thirty. The dancing photographs smiled on the people and the times that were no more. The faces shone with tears and too many lonely hours. But there were smiles as well.

Danny watched the families and saw people determined to find small joys in the vacuum. He decided they were some of the bravest people on earth.

Greg stepped onto a chair at the back of the room and rolled his hands, signaling to Randy and Emma that they should play it again. Randy drew them together and started afresh. If the crowd noticed, they gave no sign.

Megan buried her face in Danny's chest and wept.

65

THE PRIMETIME EMMYS took place in mid-September at the Microsoft Theater in downtown LA, an enormous concrete monolith with a seating capacity of over seven thousand. Early in his career, Danny had secretly joined the screaming throngs clustered to either side of the red carpet. He had come in order to take aim.

And now he was here. A contender.

Upon its release, *A Ballad for Valentine* had gained the highest audience rating ever for Chambers Broadcasting. Since then CBC had aired the film six additional times. Three of those times, it topped the ratings for all cable channels, an unheard-of event for a rerun. Tonight Danny's film was up for seven awards, including Outstanding Television Movie.

Danny had signed a multiple-film contract with CBC. His team remained the same. Lane negotiated the deal. Megan supervised the contract.

The signing bonus took his breath away.

The previous evening, Danny, Megan, Greg, and Annie had met and dined with Lane, Emma, and Robin at the Beverly Hills Hotel main dining room. It had been filled with industry heavies and the world's press. Afterward Danny had asked the limo driver to take the four of them to the Microsoft Theater.

No one had asked why or objected to his adding this trip onto the end of a long day.

The crew had been busy prepping for the event, rolling out the red carpet and draping it in protective plastic sheeting, positioning the lights, building the camera stations. The four of them had stood and watched a sickle moon rise over the LA skyline. It hung there, huge and sharp-edged and luminous.

Danny found it strangely calming to be there with Megan and his two dear friends. He had become caught between all that had come before and what might now be unfolding. In the midst of their frantic and high-pressure days, Danny liked standing there and listening to the whisper of . . .

Something more.

That was what he had found in the moonrise. A gentle reminder of why he had become involved in this crazy business. So he could join with people he trusted and fill an electronic canvas with images strong as the night sky. And create his own brand of luminosity.

------------------ // ------------------

The line of limos crawled forward. Danny shared his ride with Emma and Robin. Greg and his wife and Annie and her fiancé followed in another stretch limo, from which Annie toasted LA through the sunroof. Alex came next, accompanied by his flame of the hour. Every time he met Danny, Alex claimed he was holding to the straight and narrow.

Lane and Jennie were in the car directly behind Alex. Bringing up the rear was Myron Riles accompanied by his daughter, and Rick Stanton with his wife.

Up ahead of Danny, Megan rode with her parents and the president of Chambers Broadcasting.

Robin pointed through the side window and exclaimed, "There's another billboard about your next project."

Emma covered her eyes. "I can't look. I'll faint."

"I told you those shoes were too tight."

"Shoes don't make you faint." Emma lifted one leg. "Besides, these are Ferragamos. If I do faint, I'll look fabulous."

Robin ran one hand down Emma's shoulder. The dress was by Vera Wang, a sheath of blue silk with a high collar and a froth of hand-sewn crystals down the sleeves and both legs. "What ever happened to my little girl?"

"She's still in there," Emma said. "I saw her in the mirror. If only I can remember her name."

Danny caught sight of the weaving spotlights that fronted the red carpet just as the first faint screams pierced the limo's soundproofing. "Last chance," he said. "Robin can escort you."

"No Robin can't," her mother replied.

"I want you there holding my arm," Emma said. "It's important."

Then it was their turn. The door was opened by a red-jacketed valet, and Emma accepted his hand. As she leaned forward, the crowd shrieked with one voice, "*Emma!*"

Robin kissed Danny's cheek as he started out and said, "I will remember this moment for the rest of my life."

———————————//———————————

They were given half a row, six from the front. Their breathless escort explained this was easier for everybody since *Ballad* was up for so many awards, and they should be ready to shift seats so whoever was up at that moment would be positioned on the outside. That became impossible at one point, because both Jennie and Emma had been nominated for Outstanding Lead Actor in a Limited Series or Movie.

Jennie won.

Her acceptance speech would be played by the entertainment shows around the globe. She stood at the podium for a long moment, her eyes filled with tears she refused to wipe away. "Greg. Annie. Danny. Emma. Lane. If only all of life could be filled with people like you." Then a wave of the award and she was gone.

Then it was Emma's turn.

The lights dimmed, music swelled from the orchestra pit, and Emma walked on stage. Robin's grip on Danny's hand was so tight he figured it would be the middle of next week before circulation was fully restored. Not that he minded.

Screens descended from the ceiling, and as the spotlight focused upon the lovely young woman center stage, she began playing Sting's song, now up for the Outstanding Main Title Theme Music. Images from the final gathering flickered upon the screens that surrounded her. And as she played, the children danced, the mothers and fathers with them now, then alone, then all together, the music joining them in shades of both sorrow and joy.

Myron's acceptance speech was the shortest of the night. He lifted the statue high over his head and said, "I dedicate this to all the people out there who assumed I was dead and buried."

Then it was Danny's turn.

It had been a long night by that point. Danny had half assumed his capacity for another adrenaline high was long gone. But as soon as they shifted him over so that he sat on the aisle, his heart threatened to punch out of his chest and run screaming out the rear exit.

The competition was intense. All the other names were well established, and the bookies had given Danny a slim-to-none chance of winning. He prepared his face for the inevitable smile of graciously losing and freed his hand from Megan's so he could applaud the winner's parade.

Jennie had asked to present this award. She opened the envelope, covered her mouth, and swallowed hard. Then she leaned toward the microphone and said, "The award for Outstanding Television Movie goes to . . ."

Davis Bunn (www.davisbunn.com) is the award-winning author of numerous national bestsellers with sales totaling more than eight million copies worldwide. His work has been published in twenty-four languages, and his critical acclaim includes four Christy Awards for excellence in fiction. Bunn is a writer-in-residence at Regent's Park College, Oxford University.

His work within the world of film began ten years ago, when he completed the graduate course in screenwriting at the British Film Institute. Since then he has completed a number of scripts, including *Unlimited*, starring Fred Thompson and Robert Amayo and released by Pureflix in 2015.

In the spring of 2019, Starlings Entertainment acquired Bunn's screenplay *Island of Time* and is currently developing it as a major feature film.

Sign up for
DAVIS'S NEWSLETTER!

Keep up-to-date with Davis's news, book releases, and events by signing up at

davisbunn.com

LET'S TALK ABOUT BOOKS

- Share or mention the book on your social media platforms. Use the hashtag **#UnscriptedBook**.

- Write a book review on your blog or on a retailer site.

- Pick up a copy for friends, family, or anyone who you think would enjoy and be challenged by its message!

- Share this message on Twitter **@DavisBunn** or Facebook **@DavisBunnAuthor**: I loved **#UnscriptedBook //@RevellBooks**

- Recommend this book for your church, workplace, book club, or small group.

- Follow Revell on social media and tell us what you like.

 RevellBooks

 RevellBooks

 RevellBooks